Marriage
Most
Scandalous

Also by Johanna Lindsey
in Large Print:

A Loving Scoundrel
A Man to Call My Own
Prisoner of My Desire
Captive Bride
Hearts Aflame
Keeper of the Heart
The Magic of You
A Pirate's Love
Say You Love Me
Until Forever
Warrior's Woman

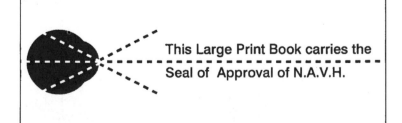

This Large Print Book carries the
Seal of Approval of N.A.V.H.

JOHANNA LINDSEY

Marriage Most Scandalous

Thorndike Press • Waterville, Maine

Published in 2005 by arrangement with Pocket Books, a division of Simon & Schuster, Inc.

Thorndike Press® Large Print Core.

The tree indicium is a trademark of Thorndike Press.

The text of this Large Print edition is unabridged. Other aspects of the book may vary from the original edition.

Set in 16 pt. Plantin by Elena Picard.

Printed in the United States on permanent paper.

Library of Congress Cataloging-in-Publication Data

Lindsey, Johanna.
    Marriage most scandalous / by Johanna Lindsey.
       p. cm. — (Thorndike Press large print core)
    ISBN 0-7862-7698-3 (lg. print : hc : alk. paper)
    1. Large type books. I. Title. II. Thorndike Press large print core series.
    PS3562.I5123M36 2005
    813'.54—dc22   2005010543

To Larry and Jennifer,
You found love,
may you always cherish it.

As the Founder/CEO of NAVH, the only national health agency solely devoted to those who, although not totally blind, have an eye disease which could lead to serious visual impairment, I am pleased to recognize Thorndike Press* as one of the leading publishers in the large print field.

Founded in 1954 in San Francisco to prepare large print textbooks for partially seeing children, NAVH became the pioneer and standard setting agency in the preparation of large type.

Today, those publishers who meet our standards carry the prestigious "Seal of Approval" indicating high quality large print. We are delighted that Thorndike Press is one of the publishers whose titles meet these standards. We are also pleased to recognize the significant contribution Thorndike Press is making in this important and growing field.

Lorraine H. Marchi, L.H.D.
Founder/CEO
NAVH

* Thorndike Press encompasses the following imprints: Thorndike, Wheeler, Walker and Large Print Press.

Prologue

1808, England

They met at dawn. It was a narrow opening in the trees, just off the forest path, but a well-known spot nonetheless. An old rock there, partially hidden in the brush, nearly two feet round, was reputed to mark the site of some ancient battle. It was now known as The Dueling Rock.

At least seven duels were verified to have taken place there over the years, many more were mere rumors. There were other places in the south of England, of course, for men to settle their differences, but none quite so renowned as The Dueling Rock. Men even came from as far away as London to satisfy their honor at this site in Kent.

Sebastian Townshend and his best friend Giles had explored the area as children, fascinated, as boys will be, by tales of honor and bloodshed. They were neighbors and had grown up together as their estates bordered each other. The Dueling Rock was located in the forest north of their homes.

It was the natural place for Giles to name for them to meet, just after Sebastian had said to him, "My God, you married a whore?"

Giles had socked him, and rightly so. Sebastian shouldn't have been so blunt. His only excuse was that he'd been in shock. But then he'd just found out he'd unwittingly slept with Giles's new wife.

How the devil was he to have known? The woman shouldn't have been at that soirée in London — alone. She shouldn't have given the impression that she was available, introducing herself by only her first name, Juliette. But she had done more than that. She'd flirted outrageously with him and hinted they should meet to get better acquainted. Sebastian had been delighted. She was lovely, a new face, a sophisticated woman who knew what she wanted and obviously went after it. He was pleased to oblige her. Not once, by her actions, did he guess that she was married.

That quick marriage had been a rash move on Giles's part. So unlike him. He had a fiancée at the time, a lovely English heiress, Eleanor Landor. So he'd been hesitant to break the news to his father, was keeping his new bride in London until he could figure out a way to explain her. She shouldn't have been at that soirée, alone, without her husband.

Giles had come to Sebastian's home to make his accusation. His new wife, in her apparent guilt over the matter, had tearfully confessed everything to him. She'd put the blame entirely on Sebastian, even swore that he'd seduced her, when that hadn't been the case at all. And Giles, in his fury, wouldn't listen to Sebastian's account of it.

"The Dueling Rock, at dawn," Giles said before he stormed out of the house.

The accusations had been delivered in the entry hall of Edgewood, the Townshend ancestral home, the moment Sebastian came downstairs. Unfortunately, Sebastian's father, Douglas, had been drawn from his study by the shouts and had heard most of it. He wasn't angry. His disappointment in his oldest son and heir was apparent, though, and that cut Sebastian deep. He couldn't recall a single time in his life that he'd ever given his father a reason to be ashamed of him — until now.

Douglas Townshend, eighth earl of Edgewood, had settled into marriage at an early age and was now only forty-three. Tall, with black hair and amber eyes, he was a handsome man who frustrated the local matchmakers because he had refused to remarry after his wife died.

He'd bequeathed his handsome visage and impressive height to his two sons, Sebastian and Denton. A year apart in age, with Sebastian being the older at twenty-two, the brothers should have got along splendidly, but that wasn't the case. Sebastian was much closer to his friend Giles Wemyss than he'd ever been to Denton. Not that he didn't love his brother. But Denton had a jealous nature that he'd long since given up trying to conceal. It had grown over the years, until now he was a bitter young man driven to excesses in drink due to his resentment that he'd never wear a title other than lord, simply because he was a second son. Unlike Sebastian, Denton had often gained their father's disapproval.

Douglas sighed now. "I will assume you didn't know this woman was Giles's wife."

"Good God, no one knew he'd married while he and Denton were touring France. Denton didn't know, or he was sworn to secrecy, because he said nothing about it when I went to London to welcome them home. And Giles didn't tell me, hasn't even told his family yet. He's obviously kept her secretly in London since he returned to England, probably to give him time to break off with his fiancée before she hears of it. I didn't know the woman was married, Father, to anyone, least of all to my best friend."

"But you did make love to her?"

Sebastian flushed, wished to hell he could deny it, but couldn't. "Yes."

"Then go after him, explain your part in this, make amends however you must. But you will not meet him in the morning. I forbid it. He's not some passing acquaintance. You two have been inseparable since you were children, just as Cecil and I have been. And he's Cecil's only son."

Sebastian had every intention of doing just that, and not just because he loved Giles like a brother. His father said it aptly just before he left to find Giles.

"I know you, Sebastian. You wouldn't be able to live with yourself if you harmed him."

Unfortunately, the harm had already been done. There was nothing that could undo it or explain it away. Sebastian realized that clearly as the day wore on and he agonized over how to make amends to his friend. His explanations did nothing but enrage Giles more. He was in no state of mind to listen.

Whether he believed Sebastian or not, it still came down to the simple fact that however unintentionally, Sebastian had slept with his wife.

Dawn barely lightened the sky the following morning. The rain had started several hours earlier and continued, with no sign of letting up. Sebastian's second, Theodore Pulley, was hopeful the duel would be canceled because of it. He was only an impartial acquaintance, but he was behaving as if he'd melt if the rain didn't stop soon. Actually, it was the accompanying thunder that made him so jumpy.

Sebastian said nothing in response to the man's nervous chatter. He was numb. Over the long, sleepless hours of the night, he'd decided what he had to do, the only thing he could do to redeem himself. It wouldn't be the first time a man had gone to a duel with the intention of dying.

Giles was late. Theodore was suggesting they leave when Giles and his second arrived. Sebastian didn't recognize the fourth man, who was acting as Giles's second.

"Couldn't find the bloody path in the rain," Giles explained.

Theodore still wanted to get out of the rain sooner rather than later and put the suggestion to the late comers. "Ought to cancel this, don't you think? Wait for a clear morning?"

"At this time of year?" the other second countered with a slight indistinguishable accent. "When is there ever a clear morning?"

"We duel now or I murder him," was Giles's clipped response.

So much for hoping a night's sleep might have dredged up some forgiveness, or at least the realization that Sebastian hadn't wronged him intentionally. But Giles appeared to be just as angry as he had been the day before.

Theodore coughed and said, "Quite right. We'll keep it sporting, then."

Giles's pistols were brought to Sebastian for inspection. He waved the man away. His own pistols were taken to Giles for the same. His friend seemed interested only in making sure the chambers were loaded. Sebastian was aware that Giles knew he didn't want to kill him.

"Prepare yourselves, gentlemen."

They stood back-to-back, shouldn't have spoken, but Sebastian's remorse was torn from him with the simple words, "I'm sorry."

Giles said nothing, giving no indication that he'd heard him. Instructions were given, the count begun. The rain hadn't let up, nor had the thunder, which boomed every few minutes, but the sun had risen enough to spread a gray gloom through the trees. It was enough light to see by, enough light to kill by.

They paced off the required steps, each man holding his chosen pistol in his hand, pointed at the ground. The count was continued, then the call to turn, take aim . . .

Sebastian stood with his gun pointed toward the sky, intending to fire the obligatory shot anywhere but at Giles. But Giles fired the very second it was called to do so, nicking Sebastian under his arm just as he was pulling his own trigger. Giles was a good shot; he should have done better than this at such close range. The wound he delivered was minor, but it brought Sebastian's arm down in an involuntary reaction. His bullet fired, the sound echoing through the trees along with another crack of thunder. It should have been wildly off the mark, but instead it landed at the dead center of Giles's chest.

Sebastian watched as his friend dropped to the ground. The look of surprise on Giles's face as he crumbled would forever haunt Sebastian. Shock kept him rooted to the spot while Giles's second bent down to examine him, then looked toward Sebastian

14

and shook his head.

"I will inform his father," he said. "I assume you will inform yours."

Beside him, Theodore said, "You weren't going to fire at him, were you? What changed your mind?" He paused, seeing the blood under Sebastian's arm. "Ah, so that's why. What bloody rotten luck, eh? Or rather phenomenal luck, depending how you look at it."

Sebastian didn't answer, hadn't really heard him. It was impossible to describe what he felt in that moment of realization that he'd killed his best friend. Grief, horror, rage — it was all there choking him. And guilt, so strong it took root in his heart and would never let go. And he still had to tell his father that he'd defied him, that his plan to exonerate himself with his own death had backfired.

Sebastian should have died there at The Dueling Rock that cold, gloomy morning. As far as he was concerned, he did.

Chapter 1

Like many towns and villages throughout Austria, Felburg had its share of Baroque architecture in its churches and its plaza, its fountains and charming squares. Where Vienna overwhelmed, Felburg offered peace and quiet, which was why Sebastian Townshend decided to spend the night there as he passed through the Alpine hills.

The job he had just finished had been frustrating, taking him from France to Italy, back to France, then to Hungary, and finally to Vienna. His mission had been to retrieve stolen books, very rare books that a wife had absconded with. His current employer didn't want his wife back, just the books. Sebastian had them in his possession now. The wife hadn't been cooperative, though. He'd had to steal them from her.

It had been a distasteful task but not as abhorrent as some of the jobs he'd taken over the years since he'd left home. For quite a few years he hadn't discriminated. He simply had little reason to care about anything. Disowned by his father, all ties to his family broken, and carrying a bitterness deep inside himself that he refused to acknowledge, Sebastian wasn't a man to trifle with. You had to have a reason to live in order to value life. He didn't particularly value his.

He used to. Wealth, title, good friends, and family had all been his. His life had seemed almost charmed. He had a tall, strapping body, exceptional good looks, and enjoyed splendid health. He'd had it all. But that was before he'd killed his best friend in a duel and had been told by his father never to darken England's shores again.

He hadn't gone back, had sworn he never would. England, once his home, held only painful memories for him. He'd been adrift now for eleven of his thirty-three years and saw no end to it.

Europe could be called his home if he had to name a place, but there was no place in particular that he favored. He'd been to every country on the Continent and a few beyond, spoke all of the major languages and a few of the less well-known ones, three acquired by necessity, six in all. He could afford a nice property to settle on. He'd left home penniless, but the jobs he took were lucrative, and with nothing to spend his money on, he was quite rich. But the idea of "home" reminded him too much of his real one, so he'd avoided establishing one. And he was rarely in one place for long. He lived in inns and hotels, and frequently when he was on a job, on a pallet on the ground.

He did buy one property in the north of France, though, only because he found it occasionally useful. The crumbling ruins of an old keep could hardly be called a home. The only thing intact in it had been the dungeon, but even that consisted of bare doorless cells that he'd never bothered to refurbish. He'd bought the ruins mainly to have a place where those looking to hire him could readily find him, or leave word with the caretaker he kept there. And because it suited his fancy to own a ruins, so similar to his life.

He didn't travel alone. Oddly enough, his valet had elected to go into exile with him. An adventurous sort John Richards had turned out to be, he actually enjoyed his new role. He still acted as Sebastian's valet, but he was also his source of information. As soon as they arrived in a new town or city, John would make himself scarce, then return with all pertinent information about the area and the important people who lived there. John could make himself understood in two more languages than Sebastian, though none of them fluently. He had become invaluable for Sebastian's line of work. He'd also become a friend, though neither of them would ever admit it, and John prided himself on adhering to his role of servant, albeit a superior one.

There was one other in their entourage now, a spunky ten-year-old lad who called himself Timothy Charles. He was English, though he'd been orphaned in Paris, which was where they'd met him last year when Timothy had been unsuccessful in picking Sebastian's pocket. John had taken pity on the lad because he reminded him of home and he was homeless in a foreign city. Somehow or other it was decided that they'd keep him, at least until they could find him a good home. They really ought to get around to doing that one of these days.

"Raven I believe you are called?"

Sebastian had been enjoying a glass of Austrian wine in the dining room of the inn where they were spending the night. The well-dressed man who had approached his table looked official. Tall, middle-aged, impeccably dressed. The two men who stood behind him looked like guards, not by their

19

dress, which was plain, and not by their stature, which was on the short side. It was their alertness, the way they kept their eyes not just on Sebastian but also on the entire room.

Sebastian merely raised a black brow and said indifferently to the tall fellow, "I'm called many things. That's one of them."

He had a reputation, unwanted, certainly not intentional, but it had developed nonetheless, no doubt partially at John's instigation, of being a mercenary for hire, capable of accomplishing the impossible. He wasn't sure how he got the name Raven, possibly because there was a certain sinister look to him with his black hair and golden cat's eyes, though he wouldn't be surprised if the name was John's doing as well. And John never failed to let his contacts know that The Raven was in town, which frequently produced jobs that he wouldn't have otherwise heard about.

"You are for hire, yes?"

"Usually — if my fee is met."

The man nodded and assured him, "A man of your caliber would be expensive. This is understood and will not be an issue. My employer is generous and will more than meet your price. Do you accept?"

"Accept what? I don't hire on blindly."

"No, no, of course not. But the job is a very simple one, will require only time and a little effort."

"Then you don't need me. Good day."

The man looked shocked at being dismissed. Sebastian stood up and finished his wine. He didn't like dealing with lackeys, no matter how official or important they were. And he certainly wasn't interested in a simple job that anyone could do. But frequently he encountered rich men who could afford him, who wanted to hire him just so they could brag to their friends that they had employed the notorious Raven.

He started to walk away from the table. The two guards suddenly moved to block his way. He didn't laugh. Humor wasn't part of his character anymore. That deep bitterness that he refused to acknowledge left no room for humor. He was annoyed, though, that he was going to be forced to expend effort just to say no.

Before any violence could erupt, the official said, "I must insist that you reconsider. The duke expects you to be hired. He cannot be disappointed."

Sebastian still didn't laugh, though this time he actually had a small urge to do so. He took a moment to deal with the two fellows who thought to detain him, grasping

21

each of them by their heads, which he smashed together. They crumpled at his feet while he glanced back at the official.

"You had a point to make?"

The man was staring at his guards on the floor. He looked disgusted. Sebastian couldn't blame him. Good guards were hard to come by.

The official sighed before he faced Sebastian again. "You've certainly made your point, sir. And allow me to apologize. I understated the matter, which on the surface seems simple enough but is far from it. Others have been sent to perform the task, and all have failed. Five years of failures. Have I intrigued you yet?"

"No, but you've gained a few more minutes of my time," Sebastian said and sat down again at the table. With a hand he indicated the man could make use of the other chair there. "Keep it brief, but be precise this time."

The fellow sat down, cleared his throat. "I work for Leopold Baum. This is his town, in case you were not aware of it. As you might guess, men of the duke's stature make enemies rather easily. It's unavoidable. One in particular happened to be his wife."

"She was his enemy when he married her?"

"No, but it didn't take her long to become one."

Sebastian raised a brow. "He's that difficult to get along with?"

"No, no, certainly not," the fellow insisted in defense of his employer. "But she possibly thought so. But to the facts. Five years ago she was kidnapped, at least it seemed so. A ransom was demanded and delivered, but the duchess wasn't returned. It was assumed she was killed. The duke was furious, of course. An extensive search ensued, but there were no clues to follow."

"Let me guess," Sebastian said dryly. "She perpetrated the kidnapping plot to extract some wealth before she went on her merry way?"

The fellow flushed. "So it would seem. Several months after the ransom was paid, she was seen traveling, quite in style, across Europe. Men were sent after her. A few more clues were found, but she never was."

"So what exactly does the duke want? His wife, his money, or both?"

"The money isn't important."

"If that's the case, why wasn't more expended in finding her? It sounds like he didn't really want her back."

"Frankly, sir, I must agree with you," the fellow confided. "I would have devoted more effort myself if she were my wife and I'd yet to produce an heir."

Sebastian sat back, somewhat surprised, though his expression remained inscrutable. He waited for the man to clarify his statement. He did appear slightly nervous now, after saying it.

"That is not to say that a great deal of effort has not already been made in the search. But the duke is a busy man. He has not spent every moment of these last years actively pursuing the matter. Now, however, he has become obsessed with finding her so he can divorce her and remarry."

"Ah, finally to the heart of the matter."

The fellow flushed, and his nod was so slight it was almost imperceptible. His nervousness was understandable now. He was saying things his employer wouldn't like him to reveal.

"When he heard you were in town, his hopes soared. Your reputation of success, no matter how difficult the job, has preceded you. He has every confidence that you will find his wife and bring her home."

"If I take the job."

"But you must!" the fellow began, then amended, "Or does it seem too difficult a task, even for you?"

Sebastian didn't take the bait. "I don't

particularly like jobs that deal with women. I also haven't finished my last job, am on my way to France now to do that."

"But that is not a problem," the fellow assured him with some relief. "This job will take you in that direction. A brief detour would be quite permissible."

"That's where the duke's wife was last seen, in France?"

"The trail led there, and beyond. The duke's arm is far-reaching. Putting a great distance between herself and Austria appears to have been her priority during her escape."

"Did she head to the Americas?"

"No — at least we pray not. And a woman of her description took ship to Portsmouth at the time. The last report we had was that she took ship again, but only farther up the coast of England. Another ship was available, to North America, but since she didn't take that one, we concluded she decided to settle in England under an assumed name. There were no further reports. Every other man who was sent there to find her has never returned." And then the fellow whispered, "It's my guess they were afraid to return to the duke with only failure to report."

Having heard enough, Sebastian stood up

to leave. "I am afraid I will have to decline after all," he said, a coldness having entered his tone. "England is one place I will never go. Good day."

He expected the man to try and stop him again. He didn't, probably because he realized it wouldn't do any good. Just as well. Jobs that dealt with women had an extra level of difficulty. On every single one he'd taken, the female involved had tried to seduce him.

John found it amusing, hilariously so, claiming that Sebastian was too handsome to be a mercenary. Sebastian disagreed. It was his reputation, the sinister persona of The Raven, and his indifference to the women that created the problem. He believed in putting the job before pleasure. But the women felt differently. Intrigued by him, they saw no reason to wait until the job was finished to become intimately acquainted with him. Which is where the added difficulty came in.

He had an ingrained sense of duty, which was probably why he excelled at his chosen occupation. Anything that deviated from getting the job done was to be avoided. Anything that distracted him was to be avoided as well. And a woman trying to seduce him was a definite distraction. He

might not call himself an Englishman anymore, but he was still a man. So it really was
just as well that he couldn't accept the
duke's job.

Chapter 2

His head hurt. That was the first thing Sebastian noticed as he woke. The second, and more disturbing, was his surroundings, not the cozy room at the inn where he'd gone to sleep last night, but a dark, musty dungeon. He was in a cell. Torchlight passed through the small barred window on the wooden door, revealing a hard-packed dirt floor, a clean chamber pot in the corner, and bugs crawling in and out of cracks in the stone walls.

It was an airless, medieval room but it was in better condition than his own dungeon, which indicated it was frequently used. He'd been in prisons before, but modern ones, never an actual, authentic dungeon. He'd seen the old fortress on the hill overlooking Felburg, so he knew exactly where he was.

"Bloody hell."

He'd mumbled, but in the absolute silence of the place, it had sounded more like a shout, and he got an immediate response. "Is that you, sir?" John called out, from which direction Sebastian couldn't guess.

Sebastian moved to the door, but before he could answer, Timothy's frightened voice came from his far left. "Raven, I don't like it here. Really I don't. Can we leave now?"

The boy, too? That was going too far. He knew why he was there. It wasn't the first time someone had tried to force him to work for him. The last time he'd been inside a cell had been for the same reason. Bastards thought alike.

"Did they hurt you, Timothy?"

"No, not much," the lad answered, trying to sound brave now. "They stuffed something in my mouth and tied me up to carry me here. I've been awake all night."

"What about you, John?" Sebastian asked.

"A small lump on my head, sir," John said, his voice coming from the right. "It's nothing."

It wasn't nothing. Injury to himself he could stomach, but when his people were hurt in order to get to him . . .

Sebastian didn't get angry often, but this was one of those times. He stood back, lifted his foot, and kicked at the door in front of him. It didn't budge, not even a little, though he'd certainly knocked the dust off of it. It probably wasn't as old as the stone it was attached to.

He inspected the room more closely. There was a stand with a tin water pitcher and bowl, a towel folded on its single shelf. The water was fresh. The bedding was clean on the narrow cot, fine linen, actually. The plate of food that had been slid under the door had probably been appetizing before the bugs found it: eggs, sausage, bread with butter, melted now, and several pastries.

Apparently the intent wasn't to deprive him, merely to keep him from leaving. A forced guest, as it were. But for how long? Until he agreed to find the missing duchess? As if he wouldn't disappear the moment he was out of this dungeon, no matter an agreement or not?

The fellow who brought their next meals was mute or pretended to be. He wouldn't say a word or answer a single question. The day wore on, long and boring. Sebastian spent his time exercising and imagining his hands around Leopold Baum's neck. John and Timothy played word games. On opposite sides of the dungeon, they were soon hoarse.

The evening meal arrived and still there

was no communication from their host. Dumplings and fried veal cutlets with a creamy cheese sauce was the tempting fare, very filling, very typical of Austrian cuisine. There was some type of cake and a bottle of fine wine. He left the dessert for the bugs and took the wine to bed with him.

The next day was the same, and the next. So he was to have a taste first of what it would be like if he didn't agree to the duke's terms? Did the man really think he could be coerced into working for him?

Leopold Baum arrived early on the fifth morning of their confinement. He didn't take chances. Four big, strapping guards preceded him, entering the cell with their pistols drawn. One of them tied Sebastian's hands behind his back while the other three kept their guns pointed at him. It was a tight fit in the small cell with the guards filling the corners.

The duke offered few surprises other than his age. Sebastian, who had expected a younger man, could see that the duke was close to the half-century mark. Dark blond hair trimmed short in the fashion of the day. Sebastian wore his hair long and usually clubbed back, only because John made a lousy barber, and they traveled too much to visit a good one with any frequency. The duke had a superb barber.

Sharp blue eyes, keenly intelligent, or so they appeared. Tall, though not quite six feet. His frame was stocky, leaning toward fat. His jowls were starting to sag, though it wasn't that noticeable under the full, short blond beard. He still held himself regally, a man of extreme consequence and privilege.

Sebastian guessed that he had either just been riding, or he still had it on the morning agenda, as he wore a jade green coat and buff-colored riding breeches, and held a crop in hand, which he tapped against his well-polished black knee-high boots.

His expression was actually congenial, as if Sebastian wasn't sitting in a cell with four pistols pointed at him but was instead a real guest. "Are your accommodations satisfactory?"

Sebastian didn't bat an eye. "The floor could stand a few boards, but otherwise, I've enjoyed the vacation."

Leopold smiled. "Excellent. It's too bad we couldn't come to terms sooner, but I assume you are ready to get back to work now?"

"You shouldn't assume."

Leopold's smile didn't falter. He was obviously certain he held the upper hand.

Sebastian couldn't quite figure out how. Keeping him imprisoned wasn't going to get the job done. Letting him go wasn't going to get it done either.

He pointed out, "Detaining me here because I refuse to work for you is illegal."

"But that's not why you are here," Leopold said jovially. "I can think of any number of crimes you have committed. Execution is possible, though I suspect even that won't sway you. But come now, let's not be melodramatic. You've been my guest —"

"Prisoner," Sebastian cut in.

"Guest," Leopold insisted. "If you were a prisoner, these accommodations wouldn't be nearly so pleasant, I do assure you. But perhaps I've visited too soon. Shall I return next week, to find out if you tire of this 'vacation'?"

Sebastian finally raised a brow. "And then the week after that, and the one after that? This doesn't get your wife found, does it?"

Leopold seemed surprised. "You would be so stubborn? Why?"

"As I told your man, I can't take this job because of where it leads. I swore an oath I'd never return to England. I'm not going to break that oath for monetary gain."

"Why did you make that oath?"

"That, sir, is none of your business."

"I see," Leopold said thoughtfully. "Then I suppose I must appeal to your sympathy."

"Don't bother," Sebastian replied. "A man in my occupation can have none."

Leopold laughed. "Of course not — on the surface. But hear me out, then we shall see."

The duke began to pace as he gathered his thoughts. With such limited space, and four burly guards filling up most of it, he soon gave up and stood still again. Sebastian wondered if what he was going to hear would be the truth, or a fabrication to stir his so-called sympathies.

"I married my wife in good faith. It was an unhappy match, though, as we both soon found out. She could have had a divorce. She need only have asked for it. Instead she chose to run off, pretending to have been kidnapped so she would have the means to live comfortably."

"I know all this —"

"You know nothing!" Leopold interrupted, a bit more sharply than he probably intended.

In that brief moment, the real man was revealed, a hot-tempered autocrat. A man who assumed he had unlimited power, true or not, was very dangerous. Sebastian might have to rethink his situation.

"Why didn't you appeal to the English government to assist you in finding her? They have branches that are quite good at that sort of thing. That would still be your best course of action."

"I am an Austrian duke," Leopold said, a degree of annoyance mixed into his condescending tone. "I cannot put myself in a position where I would owe favors to another government. I've sent men, a countless number. That should have been sufficient."

Sebastian held back a snort. "When did you send the last one?"

Leopold frowned, his eyes moving about as if he were searching for an answer, and in fact he was. He really couldn't remember.

"Last year — no, the year before that," he finally said.

Sebastian shook his head, couldn't keep the disgust out of his eyes. "What am I doing here? It's obvious you don't really want her back."

Leopold stiffened, said in his own defense, "I had given up! I was going to have her declared dead. But my darling Maria won't marry me without proof of death or divorce. She's fearful of giving me heirs that could be declared bastards if my first wife should ever return."

Smart girl, Sebastian thought to himself, then abruptly amended, not smart at all if she was willing to marry this fellow. Of course, the duke might be a completely different man when dealing with his "love."

Leopold continued, "If I had known there were men like you, I would have seen this matter resolved long ago. Your arrival in my town has given me new hope. It is said you have never failed to complete a job successfully. A sterling record like that demands a challenge like this, don't you agree? Or have you based your career on simple jobs that any fool could accomplish?"

"Save your breath," Sebastian said. "I am impervious to insults. My answer stands, for the reasons given. Whether I would like to help you or not is moot. Your wife's location is the deciding factor."

"Then let me offer a new deciding factor," Leopold said coldly and glanced at the guard closest to the door. "Go kill the other man — no, wait. He might be useful to The Raven's work. Kill the boy."

Sebastian stiffened, was incredulous. Unfortunately, he didn't doubt at all that Timothy would die in the next few minutes if he didn't buckle under to the duke's will. Killing and mayhem were nothing to a despot like this man, just part of doing business. If he hadn't met other men of this type to know that, he might have suspected a bluff and even called it. But not with this man.

Curbing his own emotions, Sebastian said tonelessly, "You made your point. Leave the boy alone."

Leopold nodded and called his guard back. He was smiling again, puffed up pleased with his victory. Did he really think Sebastian would honor a forced commitment?

"I'm curious," Leopold said, his tone jovial again now that he assumed he'd won The Raven's compliance. "The boy isn't related to you, at least I'm told he bears no resemblance. Why would you break your oath for him?"

"I've made myself responsible for him until we find him a good home. He's an orphan."

"Commendable," Leopold remarked. "Now that we've come to an amicable agreement, you might need this." He removed a miniature portrait from his pocket, dropped it on the cot next to Sebastian. "She has assumed a new name, but she can't change how she looks."

That was debatable, but Sebastian merely said, "I'll need better than that. What was she like?"

"Hot tempered —"

Sebastian cut in to clarify. "Not in relation to you, but to others."

"She was hot tempered no matter whom she dealt with," the man insisted. "Vain, greedy, condescending, spoiled. She came from a wealthy family."

"Why didn't she return to them, instead of running away?"

The duke flushed slightly as he admitted, "They forbade her to marry me. They cut her off completely when she did. They no longer acknowledge her as one of theirs."

That touched too close to home. If Sebastian's sympathies hadn't favored the wife before, they did now.

"My next question is pertinent," he said. "Do you think she had the men you sent to England killed, or were they just afraid to return to you empty-handed? Were threats made if they didn't succeed?"

The duke flushed with anger again but waved his hand dismissively in response. "There might have been, but that isn't important."

"I disagree. I need to know if I should be watching my back."

"A man in your profession would do so as a matter of course, would he not?"

Sebastian conceded the point. And he'd

asked enough questions for a job he had no intention of doing. "We'll be leaving in the morning," he told the duke.

"Very good," Leopold replied and glanced at his guards. "Escort The Raven and his man back to their inn." He turned back to Sebastian, adding as an afterthought, "The boy will stay here, of course."

Sebastian didn't move a muscle, then simply said, "No."

"Oh, yes. Not here in the dungeon. That isn't necessary. But I will most definitely keep him. You didn't really think I would let you go without — insurance? The boy will be returned to you when you bring my wife back to me. You'll have your fee then as well."

Bloody hell. Keeping the boy is what Sebastian would have done, but he'd hoped the duke wasn't that clever.

"You needn't worry about him," Leopold assured him. "I will turn him over to the palace women. They'll spoil him to his heart's content, so much so that he probably won't want to leave. I have no reason right now to hurt the boy. Don't give me one."

Leopold's meaning couldn't have been more clear. He even smiled one last time before he turned to leave the cell. But he paused in the doorway as one of the guards began untying Sebastian.

The duke glanced back to ask curiously, "Why the name Raven? Why not The Panther? Or The Tiger? You have the eyes of a cat, after all."

Sebastian looked directly at him, his tone expressionless as he replied, "I have the eyes of a killer." He paused, waiting for the last of his bonds to slip away. "You should have guessed that," he added as he shot across the room and locked one arm about Leopold's neck in a position that would require no more than a slight twist to break it.

The guards reacted quickly, drawing their pistols, but they appeared hesitant about firing in the direction of their employer. And it didn't take but a moment for Sebastian to position Leopold in front of him.

"Drop them," he said, looking at each guard in turn, "or I break his neck right now."

They hesitated, not wanting to give up their advantage.

The duke snarled, "Do it!"

The pistols fell on the hard dirt floor almost simultaneously. One discharged. The bullet ricocheted for several long moments, finally coming to rest in one of the guards' legs. The man screamed, probably more in surprise than pain, and fell to the floor. From the looks of it, the wound was minor. The bullet hadn't hit an artery. But another guard bent down to help him.

"Tie that wound off," Sebastian told the man kneeling by his friend. "Fetch the rope you used on me to do it. The rest of you start removing your shirts, and be quick about it. You're going to use them to tie each other up. I'll check the knots. If even one is loose, I'll shoot the lot of you, rather than leave you."

Ten minutes later, the last guard to be bound presented his wrists and one of the cut strips to Leopold, there being no one else left to do the honors. Sebastian loosened his hold on the duke slightly, so he could accommodate the fellow. There were several long moments while Leopold decided whether he should or not, but in the end, he did.

With that done, Sebastian told the tyrant, "You, I'll give a choice. I can smash your head against the wall to put you out for a while, tie you up with the rest, or I could just break your neck, to assure I've seen the last of you. Which shall it be?"

"You'll never get out of here alive," the duke spat back.

"Never mind, I'll choose." Sebastian moved closer to the wall.

"No!" the duke exclaimed.

Sebastian wasn't going to give the man a reason to come after him again. He merely dragged him over to the cot, forced him facedown on it, and wrapped up his wrists with the remnants of the cut-up shirt.

"There's a man like me in Vienna at the moment looking for work, a chap I've crossed paths with from time to time. Name of Colbridge. And that's the extent of my 'sympathy' help, more'n you deserve."

Sebastian checked all the bindings before he left the cell and locked it. He almost laughed when he found the last fellow, whom the duke had tied up, with loose bonds. A few minutes later, he was letting John and Timothy out of their cells.

"Did you kill him?" John asked as they hurried out of the dungeon. One guard at the top of the stone stairs had to be punched unconscious.

"No," Sebastian said, rubbing the fist he'd just used. "I probably should have, though, just to save a lot of people a lot of grief."

"You don't think he'll try to retrieve us, then?"

"No. I'm not the only one available for such work. He knows that now. In fact, I steered him to Colbridge, that incompetent fellow in Vienna who should have no trouble failing. Baum was determined to hire me merely because I was already here and could have started immediately — if I'd been willing to work for him. I actually hope his wife continues to elude him. I have the feeling he'd rather kill her than go through the bother of a divorce."

Chapter 3

A kitchen wasn't a bad place to live. It contained pleasant aromas — usually — and warmth to counter the chill of old stone. Deep in the heart of the keep's ruins, it was the only room that Sebastian had refurbished. The old armory, located on the eastern side of the ruins, had been paneled, furnished, and divided into three rooms that served as bedrooms.

They had been back in France for almost a week. Mme. LeCarré, the mother of the farmer who lived down the road, came each day to make their meals. They kept no servants other than old Maurice, the caretaker, who lived in the only intact guard tower that was still attached to the crumbling outer walls. They had tried hiring a maid a few years back to tidy up their rooms, but they couldn't get one to stay more than a week or two. The local women simply had an aversion to working in a pile of old stones.

John had been spending most of his time in the conservatory since their return. He'd built it himself. His flowers had gone to seed as usual while he was away. Maurice refused to tend the flowers while John was gone and had to be bribed to at least keep the braziers burning during winter so the flowers didn't all die. Many died anyway from neglect.

Since he had joined them, Timothy had taken over the task of caring for the horses, which were kept in the old great hall. A small portion of it still retained a bit of ceiling, enough to shelter the horses from rain and snow. Timothy didn't like the ruins and was always somewhat gloomy while they were in residence there. Today he was pouting, having failed, once again, to draw Sebastian's attention for more than a moment.

A threat to Timothy's life might have moved Sebastian to action in Austria, but ironically, the boy meant nothing to him. John had grown fond of him, but Sebastian barely noticed Timothy when he was around. Nonetheless, he'd chosen to be responsible for him, and he took responsibility seriously. Which meant the boy couldn't come to harm while he lived under his protection. What had happened in Austria he'd seen as a failure of his responsibility, which harkened back to the sense of familial duty that had been instilled in him in his youth.

John viewed his relationships from a simpler perspective. He came from a small family with no siblings, just him and his father. His father had been a butler for the Wemyss family for many years, had groomed him in the same line of service, though John preferred a more personal level of commitment. Actually, he simply didn't like the high responsibility and authority of the butler position.

The Wemyss family was very closely associated with the Townshends. The eldest sons of each family had been the best of friends, their fathers were the best of friends. And as servants will talk, John was one of the first to know when Sebastian lost his valet and he jumped at the opportunity to take his place. He never dreamed that choice would lead to such adventure, but he didn't regret it for a minute.

He had enjoyed working at the Townshend estate, had been there for a little more than a year when Sebastian left England. He wasn't asked to go into exile with him, he volunteered. He'd formed an attachment to the young lord, thought of him as family, and couldn't bear for him to go off with no one to care for him properly.

But truth be known, John thrived in his second line of work, derived immense satisfaction from it, and had fallen into it almost naturally. He simply had a way with people, of getting them to open up and reveal things that weren't common knowledge. He wished he'd put that talent to work in Felburg before they'd been incarcerated in that dungeon. But they hadn't planned to be there more than one night, so he'd taken the opportunity to rest instead. His mistake.

They'd done some hard, fast riding, escaping from that area. "I really don't think he'll send anyone after us, but I don't want to be tempted to go back to make sure of that," had been Sebastian's last words on the matter.

John was more pragmatic. "We could have just saved ourselves the trouble of making a new enemy and losing a country of opportunity — we won't be able to return to Austria now — by accepting the job. You probably could have gotten triple your normal fee from him."

"Go to England? No."

John had expected the curt reply. It had been worth a try. Not once, in all these years, had Sebastian been tempted to return to England, not even to find out how his fa-

47

ther and younger brother fared, if they were even still alive. When his family had disowned him, Sebastian had disowned them.

Timothy was late for luncheon today. The two men didn't wait for him.

"Shall we do a little refurbishing while we're in residence this time?" John asked as soon as Mme. LeCarré left to return to her home.

Sebastian raised a brow. "Why do you ask that every time we're here?"

"Well, sir, this is a large property, yet only the kitchen and bedrooms are up to scratch."

"Exactly. What more do we need than a place to sleep and eat while we're here? We don't stay here for very long."

"But this place has such potential!"

"It's a bloody ruins, John," Sebastian said dryly. "Let's leave it that way."

John sighed. He'd hoped to bring Sebastian out of the ennui he'd fallen into since leaving Austria by giving him something to do besides brood. Unfortunately, Sebastian fell into a dark mood whenever England came up in a conversation, which had occurred too frequently during their stay in Felburg. Word had been left with Maurice about three new job possibilities, but Sebastian had yet to inquire about them.

John went back to work in his conservatory behind the ruins. It was midafternoon when Sebastian wandered out, a glass of brandy in hand. A bad sign, that brandy. The brooding was getting worse.

"Tell me, John, is it luck that has followed me all these years, or merely coincidence?" Sebastian asked, his tone somewhat bored.

"In what regard, sir?"

"My career, of course. I can count on both hands the number of times I probably should have died, or at the very least been maimed for life, yet I've received no more than a nick or two, despite the numerous times weapons have been turned on me. And these jobs I take, no matter how bizarre or seemingly impossible, I always manage to accomplish, and usually with minimal effort. So your honest opinion, is it luck or amazing coincidence?"

"You've neglected to include skill in the choices," John pointed out.

Sebastian snorted. "I'm no more skilled than the next man. I wield a pistol well enough —"

"With exceptional aim," John added.

Sebastian waved that aside as inconsequential, continuing, "Hold my own in a fight —"

John cut in again. "Have you ever looked

at the unlucky man's face after your fist has been there?"

"These are not remarkable talents, John," Sebastian said with a tinge of annoyance. "And quite unrelated, as it happens."

John frowned thoughtfully before he asked, "What brought on this bout of introspection?"

"I risked four pistols being fired at me, at close range, no less, to get my hands on that blasted duke back in Austria. The odds were that at least one of those guards would have been quick enough to fire before I reached my target. My phenomenal luck has lasted eleven years. I'm beginning to feel uneasy about it. It's bound to turn soon, don't you think? A man can't go on being lucky indefinitely."

"Are you thinking of retiring?" John asked. "You certainly don't need to continue in this line of work. Time to start a family perhaps?"

"A family?" Sebastian scowled darkly. "No. I wouldn't wish myself on my worst enemy. But I was thinking of putting it to the test."

"What?"

"This extraordinary luck of mine."

Good God, the brooding had gone too far this time, John realized with alarm. He knew that a part of Sebastian had a death wish. He'd had it since they'd departed England. And nothing in all these years had occurred to alter his belief that he should have died instead of his friend Giles. Honor hadn't been satisfied that day at The Dueling Rock, it had failed miserably.

"How do you plan to test your luck?" John asked worriedly.

Before Sebastian could respond, Maurice showed up to announce, "You have a visitor, Monsieur. A lady. You want I should show her to the kitchen?"

It was said with a snicker. The caretaker thought it was hilarious that a man as rich and renowned as The Raven was living out of a kitchen.

Sebastian didn't even notice Maurice's tone, or he chose not to. "A lady?" he said. "Or one of those tavern wenches trying once again to win their bet? You called them ladies, too, as I recall."

Maurice flushed. John managed to hide a smile. The day the three tavern lovelies had shown up had been rather entertaining. They'd had a wager going, on which one of them could entice Sebastian to sample their wares. Sebastian would have been accommodating — all three were rather pretty — but none had won that day because they'd ended up fighting over him, literally.

Quite a few repairs had had to be made to the kitchen after they'd departed. And the wager was now as renowned as The Raven was, at least to the locals, since the women had continued their fight after they'd returned to the tavern. It wasn't just a three-way bet now. Half the town, or more by now, had placed wagers as well.

"This one, she dresses like a lady," Maurice assured. "And she is as English as you."

John groaned. Maurice could be wrong. The woman might not be English at all. But it didn't matter. Sebastian's former homeland had been mentioned and now his brooding would only get worse. He would send her away without even finding out why she was there.

Predictably, Sebastian snarled. "Tell her the kitchen is closed and will remain closed — to her."

Looking puzzled, Maurice turned to John. "Monsieur?"

Sebastian might not be the least bit curious about their visitor, but John certainly was. "Run along, Maurice. I'll take care of it."

Chapter 4

Margaret Landor stared at the pile of crumbling stones and wondered if she was wasting her time. Three times they had passed this ruins, having determined it simply couldn't be what they were looking for. But they'd found no other ruins in the immediate area, and finally, on the fourth pass, when they were heading back to town to get better directions, they'd seen the man in the ruins and stopped.

Incredibly, this was where The Raven lived, which was why Margaret was now having doubts. After all the glowing reports she'd heard of the man, and especially that his fees were extremely high, she simply couldn't fathom why he'd live in a place like this — unless everything she'd heard about him were lies.

That was a possibility, of course. Maybe the locals had been trying to amaze the English visitors with tales of the local hero.

But for a whole town to be involved in the lie? No, she couldn't credit it.

Besides, the town had been abuzz with his name merely because he was back in residence nearby. Apparently he wasn't often at home, his work taking him far and abroad. So if he hadn't been at home, she probably wouldn't have heard of him at all.

Margaret was traveling with her maid and footman. Edna and Oliver were a married couple who had been working for the Landors long before Margaret was born. Edna hailed from Cornwall and had been hired as nurse for the Landor children, first Eleanor, then Margaret. Brown hair, pretty blue eyes, she'd been working at White Oaks for only six months when she married Oliver.

Oliver, now, had grown up at White Oaks, the entailed manor of the earls of Millwright, which was currently in Margaret's possession. His father had been a footman there, his grandfather before him, and even his great-grandmother had served the second earl of Millwright. Tall and strapping, Oliver came in right handy when a bit of muscle was needed.

Both middle-aged now, they made fine chaperones for Margaret's shopping expedition. German lace, Italian silk, restocking her wine cellar, and new lilies for her garden had been on her European agenda, as well as a little touring, since she'd never been to the Continent before. But that wasn't why she'd really come to Europe. It had merely been the excuse she'd used. No, she'd come to find her former neighbor and drag him back home to investigate the suspicious occurrences happening there.

The Raven appeared around a corner of the ruins. He had to keep his eye on his step, since so many broken stones littered his courtyard. He looked friendly enough, though, was of medium height, with brown hair and eyes, and appeared to be forty years of age. She shouldn't be nervous. She just didn't like having doubts.

"Are you sure you want to go through with this, Maggie?" Edna leaned out of the coach to ask.

She found it interesting that her maid seemed to be having second thoughts as well, because she'd brought the man to Margaret's attention. "Absolutely," Margaret said with as much confidence as she could muster for Edna's sake. "You were right. I'd given up. We were going home. We had no last resort. Now we do. And what more could I have asked for than a man of his talents?"

"Well, go on, then," Edna urged her. "It's doubtful he'll be here long. The townspeople say he never stays here for very long."

Margaret sighed and approached the fellow. She hated last resorts, but she supposed they were better than none at all. She'd had no trouble hiring those chaps in London last year. Both of them had come highly recommended, too. And had failed to deliver. Such a waste of money. This fellow seemed more promising — if what was said about him was really true. And she'd failed herself, miserably. Four months she'd spent on the Continent, and she hadn't found a single clue as to the whereabouts of her missing neighbor.

"Good day," she said when she reached the fellow. "I've come to hire you."

He was smiling. Quite a warm smile for a Frenchman. It settled the matter in her mind. He'd take the job. They merely needed to work out the particulars.

"I'm not for hire."

That disconcerted her, but Margaret was quick to recover. "Hear me out, if you will."

"But I'm not the man you're looking for. My name is John Richards. I merely work for him."

"Oh?" She was slightly embarrassed. He

wasn't French, either. His accent as English as her own. "Sorry. I shouldn't have assumed. Be a good chap and take me to The Raven, will you?"

The smile was gone, and his tone seemed almost sad as he told her, "There would be no point in that, Madame. He won't work for you."

"Why not?"

"Because you're a woman."

She was disconcerted again, and quite annoyed, too. Her money was as good as any man's. "Preposterous. I'll have a better reason than that before I leave. Now show me to him. Never mind, I'll find him m'self."

She didn't wait for him to try to stop her. She didn't notice his grin, either. Nor could she have guessed she was doing exactly what he'd hoped she'd do.

The Raven's ruins had no door to bar entrance. After taking a few steps, Margaret was in what appeared to be the old great hall of a keep, or what was left of it. Not much, actually. A few short walls with large stones piled around them, a crumbling hearth, and in a corner, a little of what must have been a wood ceiling, which had probably been added a century or two after the keep had been built.

In that corner, she saw a boy and three horses. She had an eye for good horseflesh, and the black stallion that the boy was grooming was as fine a specimen as she'd ever seen. The boy was giving her a cheeky grin. When her eyes settled on him, he even winked at her.

It was so unexpected that Margaret burst out laughing. Impertinent little fellow. Blond, blue eyed, scruffy. He couldn't have been more than ten or eleven but was already taking on the mannerisms of an audacious rogue.

"Where might I find The Raven?" she asked, her annoyance somewhat relieved by the child.

"In the kitchen pro'bly."

"Eating? At this time of day?"

"No. It's where he lives."

That should have surprised her, but it didn't. The man lived in a ruins, after all. She did roll her eyes, however, but only because the boy was probably hoping for such a reaction from her, and he was. His grin grew wider.

"Point me to the kitchen?" He did. She smiled at him. "Thank you."

"My pleasure, miss."

"Lady," she corrected.

"Cor, really?"

He seemed so surprised, she guessed he'd never met a titled aristocrat before, or perhaps not one of the female gender. Which was more likely. The Raven wouldn't work for women, after all.

Her annoyance returned with that thought. She nodded and went the way he'd pointed.

After traversing a narrow stone passageway she came to a door. She opened it and was indeed in a kitchen, but not one of the medieval era. She was standing in a very large room that had been paneled in oak and contained a new-looking stove and other furniture one would expect to find in the kitchen of a fine manor house. She was surprised to see a dining table with six velvet upholstered chairs and a fireplace that was lit and crackling, with a window on each side of it that looked out on what appeared to be a conservatory behind the ruins. Indeed, The Raven's kitchen was rather cozy.

And he was in it.

Actually, after looking at him more closely, she hoped he wasn't the right man. Good God, he looked distinctly — menacing, she supposed, would aptly describe him. Taller than the other fellow, younger, dark, dangerous.

But that's a good thing, she tried to tell herself. He looked like a man who could get things done, which was what she needed. Her other option was to give up. She'd already hired other men. She'd already tried to accomplish her goal herself. She'd done all she could. This man came with a guarantee. He never failed. That's what people said about him, and it was the finest recommendation she could think of, particularly since she had so little information to offer about what needed to be accomplished.

Before she could change her mind, she marched across the room. He didn't glance up. He was so deep in thought, a glass of brandy in hand, she wasn't sure he even knew he had company.

She cleared her throat, but he either didn't hear her or was deliberately ignoring her, so she asked politely, "Could I have your attention for a moment, please?"

She got it, and wished she hadn't. His golden eyes were so bright they seemed to glow like those of a predatory animal — on the prowl. They were riveting . . . mesmerizing, in a face that was distinctly handsome. She hadn't noticed at first how handsome he was. The menacing aura about him had definitely taken precedence. And still, it took Margaret a few moments to notice anything other than those startling golden eyes.

Smooth cheeks, a firm jaw, narrow, hard lips pursed in annoyance. A long, straight nose, sharp cheekbones, black brows of medium thickness but with barely any curve to them. His hair was very short, blackest black, bangs divided toward each temple with a few strands loose across his brow, one long strand down his right cheek that she watched him push back automatically behind his ear, making her realize his hair wasn't short at all but clubbed back at his nape.

Those golden eyes were slowly perusing her. "I don't suppose you're one of the tavern wenches come to take on the bet?"

Margaret managed not to blush, even though she knew exactly what he was intimating. The locals had told Edna about the bet, and Edna had told her. Apparently, it was as renowned in this area of France as he was.

"Hardly," she said in her haughtiest voice.

He shrugged, his interest in her apparently gone. "That was my original assumption, so be a good girl and get out. You're trespassing."

It was the shrug, and the new angle of his face as he glanced away from her, that rendered Margaret incredulous. Not because he'd just dismissed her, but because she finally recognized him. She was too surprised to speak. She was so surprised that she started laughing.

Chapter 5

It had been twelve years since Margaret had last seen him. That had been at her sister's engagement party. She'd been only eleven at the time and not interested in the young men who'd been present — until he showed up. She'd always found him somewhat fascinating, the most eligible bachelor in the neighborhood, handsome and charming. Most females were fascinated by him, no matter their age. But her encounter with him that night had fixed him in her mind as a romantic hero to whom she'd unfortunately been comparing every man she'd met since. She wasn't surprised she hadn't recognized him immediately, though. Rude and menacing, this fellow was nothing like the charming young man who'd dazzled her all those years ago.

He was now staring at her as if she were daft. She couldn't blame him. Amazed and delighted, she explained what prompted her laughter. "I find this rather funny. I came here to ask you to find a man for me, and here you are, that very man."

"I beg your pardon?"

"So this is how you've been hiding yourself, Sebastian? By assuming this Raven identity?"

"Who the hell are you?"

"Margaret Landor. My father was George Landor, sixth earl of Millwright. You might remember him. My sister was —"

He cut her off. "Good God, you're little Maggie Landor?"

"Not so little anymore."

"No, I can see that."

His eyes were suddenly all over her. She blushed but said curtly, "None of that, now. I know what a ladies' man you were, before the tragedy."

His manner stiffened again now that he'd recovered from the surprise, and he was scowling at her. Because she'd mentioned the tragedy?

"You're here with your husband?" he asked.

"I don't have one yet."

"Your father, then?"

"He died six years ago. And before you come up with any more relatives you think should be accompanying me, let me clarify my situation for you. I currently live alone, since I am quite old enough to do so."

"What about your sister? Did she marry?"

"Oh, yes — and died. But I'll get to that."

She blamed Sebastian for Eleanor's death. She'd been hoping she could deal with him without that getting in the way, but she wasn't so sure now. He was definitely not the charming young man from her memories.

She continued, "I had a guardian. He suggested I have a come-out. I laughed at him. I suggested he should marry me. He laughed at me. We get on very well. I've come to consider him my friend rather than my guardian. And I'm twenty-three now, so he's no longer officially my guardian. But I lived in his home for four years after my father died. I still visit him from time to time, and occasionally act as his hostess when he finds it necessary to entertain. His daughter-in-law is useless in that regard."

"Is there a reason you're telling me about your guardian, or do you just like to hear yourself talk?"

"Not such a charmer anymore, eh?" she said dryly.

He just stared at her, waiting for his answer. She gave it to him. "My guardian was your father."

"Bloody hell," he swore. "Not another word about my family, d'you hear? Not one!"

She tsked, ignoring the ominous look that had come over him. "You'll be hearing more'n one, Sebastian. It's why I'm here. I'm quite fond of your father, you see, and I fear for his life. I suspect that your brother and his wife have gotten tired of waiting for their titles."

He reached across the corner of the table separating them, grasped the front of her jacket, and yanked her forward so her face was mere inches from his. "What part of 'not another word' didn't you understand?"

Margaret was actually intimidated. There wasn't much that could dent her dauntless nature, but he looked positively frightening with his golden eyes aglow. Still, she took a deep breath, reminding herself who he was and who she was. Calmly, at least she hoped she appeared calm, she pried his fingers off of her jacket.

"Don't do that again," she said simply.

"It's time for you to leave, Lady Margaret."

"No, it's time for you to listen. Good God, man, lives are at stake! Show some semblance of your former noblesse and —"

Margaret stopped, incredulous. He was

walking away from her! Intimidating her hadn't worked, so without a by your leave he was simply exiting the room. She supposed that was better than him tossing her out, but really, this was intolerable.

"Coward."

He stopped, his back to her, stiff as thick metal. She immediately regretted using that particular word. She amended, "That is to say —"

She didn't finish again. He turned, burning her with his eyes. She found herself holding her breath.

"The problem here," he said in a tone that was deceptively conversational, "is you've made the assumption that I give a damn about a family that disowned me, when I don't."

"Rubbish. Blood is blood, and you were very close to your father before —"

"That was then. It sure as hell has nothing to do with now."

"He overreacted. Did you ever consider that?"

"Did he tell you that?"

Margaret stifled a groan, forced to admit, "Well, no, he never mentioned you a'tall during my stay there."

He turned to leave again. His total lack of concern appalled her. Of course, she hadn't gotten to the heart of the problem yet.

She rushed on, determined to intrigue him before he got out the door. "I heard them fighting once when I lived there, your brother and his wife. I didn't hear all the words, only a few here and there. You were mentioned, and 'friend.' But I did hear Denton clearly say, 'didn't have to kill him.' I must say, I was aghast. But try as I might, I couldn't figure out who he was talking about. Now, I didn't assume they killed anyone. No indeed. What I heard was out of context, so it could have been anyone they were talking about, not themselves. However, it bothered me ever since. And I began to watch them after that."

It worked! He turned around to ask, "And what did you ascertain?"

"They really don't like each other. I can't imagine why they married."

"Who did Denton marry?"

"Giles's widow, Juliette. I thought I'd mentioned that."

"No, you did not!"

Margaret winced at his raised tone. For a brief moment, she saw just how livid he was. But he got his anger under control so quickly that she had to wonder if she'd imagined it.

"Why search for me now?" he asked, his

68

tone merely curt. "Why not sooner, when you first suspected something?"

"Because I had nothing really to point to, just feelings of unease. Until the accidents began."

"What accidents?"

"Your father's. But I did try to find you sooner. Last year I hired men to locate you. They cost me a lot of money and ended up telling me what I'd already suspected — that you'd left England for the Continent. So I tried to find you myself. I've been in Europe now for four months looking for you. I'd given up, though. I was on my way home when I heard of The Raven. Coming here was a last resort."

He shook his head. Not in amazement. Oh, no. She sensed he was about to tell her to leave again. It wasn't in his expression, which was utterly inscrutable. But she knew instinctively. The facts hadn't stirred him. Perhaps guilt would . . .

"I'll tell you up front, Sebastian. I don't like you. If you hadn't killed Giles, I think he would have come to his senses, divorced that French tart, and married my sister as he should have. It's your fault he's dead. It's your fault Eleanor ran off and married a poor farmer, then died in childbirth —"

"How in the bloody hell can you blame

69

that on me?" he snarled.

"You weren't there to see what Giles's death did to my sister. She loved Giles dearly, you know. She mourned him till the day she left. She was sad and angry by turns. Sad mostly. Angry every time she encountered Juliette. But she cried every single day from the day you killed Giles. My home became quite maudlin, I don't mind admitting. It was actually a relief when she took herself off. I'm guilty of having felt that way. I think my father felt the same way. We weren't happy that she was gone, but then we — were. Very uncomfortable feelings."

"Where did she go?"

"We didn't know for the longest time. She left a note, but it was so tear stained it was illegible. We worried ourselves sick over her whereabouts. I think that contributed to my father's decline. He died several years later."

"I suppose you blame his death on me, too?" he asked sarcastically.

She scowled at him. "I could. It's all related, after all. But I don't."

"I won't bear the guilt for your sister's death either," he insisted.

"I'm not surprised. You've obviously divorced yourself from all meaningful responsibilities," she said derisively. "But as I was saying, Eleanor finally got around to sending a letter, explaining that she just couldn't bear to live with us anymore, so close to Giles's home, visiting his grave every day. It was killing her, she said."

"Yes, but where did she go?"

"Not very far, actually, to live with a distant cousin on my mother's side who settled in Scotland. Harriet was her name and she was a bit of a wild card, if you know what I mean. She married down, which caused a scandal in her day and was why my father would have nothing more to do with her and made sure I had a guardian before he died. He greatly admired your father, you know. Anyway, Harriet was a bad influence on Eleanor, apparently, since my sister married down as well, then died in childbirth because there were no doctors nearby to deal with the complications of that birth."

"Which could have happened regardless of where she was or why she was there."

"Yes, but she was there because you killed the man she loved."

"A man who'd already married someone else," he reminded her. "Why the devil do I get the blame here instead of Giles?"

"Because he would have come to his senses."

"Supposition."

"Hardly," she replied dryly. "You made

Juliette an adulteress, if you'll recall. D'you really think he would have stayed married to her — if he'd survived that duel?"

She'd gone for blood and had succeeded in drawing it if his expression was a guide. The blasted man deserved it, though. Why was he being so stubborn about this? She couldn't have made it more clear that he was needed at home.

Even though she'd stabbed home her point, he still said, "You should have just laid your cards before the local constable."

"With what evidence?" Margaret countered. "Mere suspicions? Yet your father was nearly run over in London, and dangled from the bloody cliff for nearly an hour before someone found him, and, well, the list goes on, but even he thinks his accidents were just that, accidents."

"Which is probably all they were. You've overstayed your welcome, which you didn't have to begin with." And then he added coldly, "I'm done with my family. Why the bloody hell do you think I've stayed away from England all these years?"

"Must I hire you to discover if the accidents were truly accidents or something more sinister?"

"A hundred thousand pounds," he said.

Margaret gritted her teeth. He'd named

that outrageous figure just to prove he wasn't available to her. She knew it and wasn't going to let him get away with it.

"Done," she replied without inflection. "Shall we leave in the morning?"

"Wait just a minute. I wasn't serious."

"Too bad. I was. And if you renege now I will have you discredited. Word will spread immediately that The Raven isn't trustworthy."

"You're going to regret this," he said ominously.

"No, you will, if you do nothing after my warnings. Your brother and sister-in-law might despise each other, but I fear they are in agreement on having Edgewood to themselves. Someone has to put a stop to these accidents before someone actually dies, and I think you're the only one who can do it."

"I'd say they deserve whatever befalls them."

"Even if she instigated the duel that sent you packing?"

Chapter 6

Even if she instigated the duel that sent you packing?

Once the notion had taken hold, Sebastian couldn't shake it. Had he been set up? Was it even possible to manipulate a situation that far in advance? Carry out a seduction to cause a duel that will bury your husband? Inconceivable. Juliette had only just married Giles. Even if she wasn't happy with the arrangement, there were simpler ways to end it.

Sebastian paced the kitchen floor, a bottle of brandy in hand. John sat in a chair, quietly watching him. He'd offered Sebastian a glass at one point, though he should have known from experience that he would decline it. It didn't happen often, but anger tended to make Sebastian lose all semblance of nobility.

John waited, probably worried that Sebastian might do something rash in his current state. He'd seemed pleased when he'd entered the kitchen. Sebastian wouldn't be surprised if he'd listened at the door and so already knew they were going home. John had missed England as much as Sebastian had. He'd never said anything, but Sebastian knew he'd be glad to return. Sebastian wasn't.

There wasn't much that could disturb the iron control he'd mastered over the years, which was necessary in his line of work, but he'd really had to work at it today when faced with Lady Margaret's obstinacy. Blasted hard-nosed bluestocking. He'd bet she was an accomplished horsewoman, too. And wore those new masculine-looking riding habits. Probably an avid gambler. A good shot. Some women just had to compete with men. He couldn't imagine why, but they did, and he didn't doubt Margaret Landor was one of them.

And she reminded him of home. God, did she ever, which brought it all back so vividly, the last few days he'd spent there. If only he'd known that Juliette was Giles's new wife, or anyone's wife, for that matter. If only she hadn't been such a promiscuous whore. Giles wouldn't have married her if he'd known. Sebastian could have resisted her if he'd known. He didn't trifle with married women.

He'd actually considered himself lucky. There was the irony. Juliette was extremely lovely, vivacious, a bit too flamboyant for his usual tastes but so charming he'd been unable to resist her. He'd always enjoyed women, certainly didn't turn down such blatant offers like Juliette's. It wasn't the first time he'd left a party with a rendezvous arranged.

But it was the last time . . .

Even if she instigated the duel that sent you packing?

Good God, why? So she could marry him instead? Had that been her plan? She'd already seduced him, so she might have been confident that she could woo him to marriage as well — if Giles was out of the way. Maybe she thought he wouldn't marry a divorced woman. The upper crust were still sticklers about that. A widow was acceptable, though. But did she really think he'd marry his best friend's widow after he'd killed his best friend?

He wouldn't have, and that's why the notion that he could have been set up had never occurred to him. But Juliette might not have known that, or she could have been counting on her charms to sway him.

If that had been her plan, it had definitely

76

gone awry when his father disowned him because of the duel and he'd left England. So had she settled for Denton instead? And perhaps Denton was on to her? Margaret said they fought all the time. That could be why.

"Should I be packing, sir?"

John had to repeat the question before Sebastian finally heard it and joined John at the table. "So you were listening?"

"Of course." John grinned. "Part of my job, don't you know."

"Yes, we'll leave in the morning. And maybe I will refurbish this place when we get back. I'll need something to spend Lady Margaret's money on."

John started to laugh. "You're really going to charge her?"

Sebastian raised a brow. "When this job was forced down my throat, as it were? I see no bloody difference in what Margaret pulled off due to a slip of my tongue and what that tyrant in Austria tried to do. Neither job would I have accepted without their blasted machinations. So you're damned right I'm going to take every copper she's got."

"I wouldn't exactly call it a job, finding out what's happening at home."

"No, but if I don't treat it as one, then I

won't go. It's that simple," Sebastian said, then added, "I don't exactly give a bloody damn if she blackens my name across the breadth of Europe."

He said it without anger, but the anger was there. You just had to know him really well to detect it. And then he shrugged.

"It's my own fault for being sarcastic with her. She wasn't supposed to agree to that ridiculous price, but she did, so I'll live with it."

"I don't recall Lady Margaret as a child," John remarked offhandedly. "Turned out to be quite a handsome woman, though, didn't she?"

Sebastian grunted noncommittally. He remembered little Maggie Landor as a precocious, daring chit who'd been snooping on her sister's friends at Eleanor's engagement party and had interrupted him while he'd been kissing one of them — deliberately, he didn't doubt. She hadn't shown the promise of turning out this pretty. Her sandy brown hair wasn't remarkable, though her eyes were a striking dark brown, almost black. Rich sable came to mind. Her complexion wasn't quite ivory but a blend of snowy cream. She wouldn't tan well in the summer was his guess. She wore no makeup. Like many highbrows, she probably considered it too artificial. But then she needed none. Her dark lashes were naturally thick and long. Her dark brows were narrow, delicately arched. Her lips had their own rosy tint and a fullness that almost demanded a taste . . .

She was on the petite side, her head barely reached his shoulders. But she wasn't a narrow wisp of a chit. Some women starved themselves so they wouldn't have to fight with their corsets. Margaret didn't appear to be one of them. She wasn't plump by any means, but she was sturdy and curvaceous . . . very curvaceous. A man wouldn't have to fear she'd crumble in his hands.

She made quite the pretty package indeed, enough so that he'd actually found himself hoping during those few moments before she stated her business that she was one of the tavern wenches come to win the bet, because she would definitely have won it. It was too bad she had that stubborn chin, which had proved to be an accurate prediction of her nature.

He wondered why she hadn't married. She was a prime catch, after all, very pretty, an earl's daughter, and apparently rich, if she could frivolously squander one hundred thousand pounds. She hadn't even blinked at his price, blast it.

But he also wondered if her breasts were really as firm as they'd seemed, pushing against the velvet of her spencer jacket. Probably. He even had a feeling she'd fit very nicely beneath his sheets.

Bloody hell! The brandy must be getting to him at last. Margaret Landor infuriated him. She was the last woman he wanted to see beneath his sheets.

Chapter 7

Margaret waited inside her coach. It was toasty warm with a brazier burning and a thick lap robe, so cozy that Edna had fallen asleep on the seat across from her, the hour being so early. Oliver was driving them as usual. It was her father's coach, crested, and so comfortable she hadn't been able to bear the thought of traveling without it, so she'd had it shipped to the Continent with her.

It had cost her two extra days' wait in England for a ship that would agree to take on such a large piece of cargo without prior warning, but she'd been adamant and had waited. She hoped there wouldn't be another delay in shipping the coach back home, especially now that she'd be traveling the rest of the way with him.

Edna and Oliver had certainly been relieved to find out who The Raven actually was when she'd told them last night. Much better in their minds that she'd be traveling with the disgraced son of an earl who was at least known to them, rather than a deadly foreign mercenary who wasn't.

There was no light visible from inside the ruins, but then there probably wouldn't be even if the lamps were lit. The only windows in the livable rooms didn't face the front, after all. It was barely dawn. Margaret rarely rose so early, but she didn't want to be accused of being late and give him an excuse to beg off from their arrangement.

The road to the coast and the nearest harbor at Le Havre wound near Sebastian's ruins. They hadn't said where they would meet, so she'd taken it upon herself to start the journey and collect him on the way. She could just make out one of the horses inside the great hall, so she was sure she hadn't missed him. He was in there, and she hoped not still asleep. She'd give him twenty minutes more before she sent Oliver in to get him.

Twenty minutes later there was still no sign of anyone stirring within the old ruins. It had begun to occur to Margaret that her expectations could well be dashed. Sebastian had had time to sleep on it, after all. He'd probably changed his mind, the dratted man. He was going to come out and rudely tell her to leave again.

And then the boy came out, leading a placid mare. He waved toward the coach and flashed a grin so wide that Margaret couldn't help smiling. Such a likable young lad. She wondered what he was doing living with such a dour fellow as Sebastian Townshend. He was a bit young to have been hired as a stableboy, but she supposed he could be no more than that.

John Richards followed him, leading his horse as well. He stopped to adjust a few straps on the animal. There was no baggage of any sort that she could see. Surely they traveled with a few changes of clothes — or perhaps they weren't planning to come with her.

She wasn't going to be assured that Sebastian hadn't changed his mind until she actually spoke to him. She'd forced his hand, after all. He hadn't been the least bit serious about accepting the job, no matter the unheard-of price he'd arbitrarily tossed out as the deciding factor. And she'd been temporarily insane to accept that price. She didn't exactly have that kind of money lying around to pay him with. It could very well pauper her to come up with it.

She should have just accepted his refusal and gone home alone. She'd been gone for four months. For all she knew, there could have been another accident during that time. Douglas might already be dead. . . .

She paled at the thought. Good God, she hoped not. But the irony was there, that she could be paupering herself for naught. She didn't think Sebastian would have the decency to release her from the obligation if they did find out his father was already dead. He used to be a decent sort and a lot more. He used to be a charming young man, honorable, exemplary, quite the catch in his day, heir to an earldom, rich, exceptionally handsome, and well liked by his peers.

Of course, she knew none of that at the time, hadn't been interested in such things at the age she'd been before he left England. She'd heard it all after the fact, the bemoaning of certain ladies who missed him, the bemoaning of old dames who'd hoped to lure him into their families with one female relative or another.

But she had been fascinated by him, and she'd never been able to forget the night she'd spied on him in the garden behind her home. The terrace had been well lit, the garden just beyond it hadn't been, and he'd managed a rendezvous with one of Eleanor's friends there. She'd followed him only because she'd been surreptitiously watching him from the edges of the party since he'd arrived.

She hadn't expected to come around a hedge and almost collide with him and the lady. They were already kissing! That was so quick, he must have started it as soon as he'd found the lady there. And they were so involved in the kissing that they hadn't heard her approach. She'd jumped back behind the hedge, embarrassed at first, but then her curiosity got the better of her and she'd poked her head around to watch them.

Her eyes had adjusted by then to the moonlight filtering down through the treetop. They were in an alcove in the garden, with a tree at the center and a bench set below it, surrounded by flowers and hedges. She used to come there herself to read in the summer. She never went there again after that night, so potent was the memory of watching Sebastian in such a sensual embrace, the lady trapped in his arms and not minding a'tall. Or maybe the lady didn't notice when his hand caressed her derriere, or stopped briefly to feel her breast. She seemed too enthralled to be aware of anything other than his kiss, and yet, he was doing so much more than just kissing her. His hands were all over her, and his body, oh my, the way he used his body to such titillating effect . . .

Margaret always wondered what would have happened if she hadn't broken that twig when she'd lost her balance trying to get a better view of them. That twig had made a bloody loud noise. A slap had followed, then the lady ran back to the house. Maggie had watched her run off, then turned back to find Sebastian's golden eyes on her. He didn't appear upset. If anything, his raised brow indicated some amusement.

"Shouldn't you be in bed?" he'd asked her.

"Yes."

"Like breaking rules, do you?"

"Yes."

She could blame her frustration at being discovered for those silly answers, but he'd been amused enough to grin as he came to stand next to her.

"Why'd she slap you?" Maggie had asked curiously.

He'd shrugged, hadn't seemed the least bit annoyed about it. "Proper thing to do, I suppose," he'd said, "after she realized there were precocious eyes in the shadows." And then he'd tilted her chin up and winked at her. "Word of advice, moppet. Grow up a few years before you steal off for an innocent kiss or two at parties."

"With you?"

He'd laughed. "Doubt I can wait that long to settle down, but you never know." And then he'd strolled off, never realizing the profound effect he'd had on her.

He was no longer the heir to Edgewood. He was certainly no longer the charmer. And she didn't doubt that decency was now far beyond his capabilities. But he obviously knew how to get things done, or he wouldn't have such a glowing reputation as The Raven.

He finally came out — already mounted on his stallion! What a sinister picture the two of them made, black stallion, Sebastian in a black greatcoat, man and horse on the steps of those ruins, crumbling stones all around them, a cloud-laden dawn sky behind them. A shiver passed down Margaret's back. She must be mad to associate with him at all. He simply wasn't the man he used to be, wasn't the man she'd pictured when she set out to find him. What the devil was she getting herself into?

Sebastian walked his horse slowly to the coach, drew abreast of the window, which she opened. He had no luggage attached to his mount either. Maybe he was still going to order her to leave.

She held her breath, waiting for all her doubts to be abruptly realized. He raised a brow at her. Was her face turning blue? she wondered. She let her breath out in a whoosh, which he surely heard.

She even detected a smirk in his tone when he said, "Afraid I wouldn't meet you in town?"

There was no point in denying it. "Actually — that did occur to me."

He stared at her for a long moment before he sighed and said, "Given our brief conversation, I will allow that you had no way to know that once I accept a job I will see it through to the end."

"So you were about to head into town?"

"Yes."

"Well, then, be glad I've saved you the trouble," she said pertly, and then she recollected her manners and introduced Edna to him, who was quite wide-eyed with her first sight of him. "And my driver, Oliver, is Edna's husband. If you have any luggage you want to put on the coach, Oliver can help you."

He shook his head. "My caretaker transported what we're taking with us to Le Havre yesterday."

She was surprised. So he'd had no second thoughts?

Before he could change his mind, she suggested, "Shall we be off? If we hurry, we can possibly catch ship by this afternoon."

"Highly doubtful," he replied, the smirk back in his tone. "But as you wish."

He turned his horse about and took off down the road, with John and Timothy close behind him. Margaret took a moment to deal with her maid's amazement.

"You can close your mouth now, Edna."

The older woman humphed to cover her blush. "Goodness, I never would have recognized him. And I hope I was just imagining that dangerous air about him."

Margaret sighed. "It wasn't your imagination, but his intimidating manner is to be expected, considering the profession he took up. Just keep in mind he's still Sebastian Townshend."

"Yes, there is his impeccable lineage, and he's quite handsome, too. Or didn't you notice that?"

Margaret would have to be blind to not notice that, but she pretended not to hear Edna's question and focused on the view out the window. Oliver had to crack his whip a few times to keep up with the trio as the morning wore on.

It was a bumpy ride for the most part. The roads, which had been exceptionally good throughout most of France, weren't well maintained in this area, at least not until they reached the main road to Le Havre.

But they were in luck when they arrived at the docks of the old harbor on the northern coast of France. One ship was late departing because its crew had had a bit too much fun carousing the night before. They'd lost their passenger list, too, because of that delay, so they were happy to take on Margaret and her entourage. Even her coach was quickly hefted aboard. Before she knew it, they were sailing out into the channel.

Come what may, Margaret had made her bargain. She just hoped she wouldn't live to regret bringing Sebastian Townshend home to England.

Chapter 8

Sebastian considered most of the jobs he took rather easy, despite how difficult they might appear at first. Apply a little English logic, perhaps a military approach if needed, and voilà, he'd pick up his substantial fees. But for Sebastian there was nothing easy about crossing the channel into English waters.

Standing on the deck of the ship that was taking him back to his homeland brought it all back, the horror of killing his best friend, the surprise on Giles's face as he dropped to the ground. It was still so vivid in his mind. He'd had so many nightmares about that day that changed his life so drastically. So many times he'd wondered if he could have done something differently to prevent it.

Fall was ending and the chill of winter was already creeping in, particularly out on the water. He could feel the damp chill even under his greatcoat, which flapped in the wind on the deck. He didn't like traveling in winter, didn't like his ruins at this time of the year either.

He usually took a sojourn during these months in southern France or Italy. It wasn't necessary for him to work year-round with the fees he commanded. In another few days he would have departed northern France, and Margaret Landor probably wouldn't have heard of The Raven. She would have continued on her way home alone — to find what, when she got there?

He frowned and glanced at her farther down the deck, where she stood gazing out to sea as well. The late afternoon sun added golden highlights to her light brown hair. He'd rather not have found out how pretty that looked.

She'd been wearing a bonnet earlier, but the wind had caught it and whipped it across the deck and over the railing on the other side. The face she'd made as she watched it fly beyond her reach had been rather amusing. And she hadn't gone to fetch another bonnet, despite the brisk wind playing havoc with her hair.

When the last of her chignon tumbled down and her long hair was flying every which way, she'd simply grasped the lot of it in her fist and held it tightly to her chest. That wasn't how most vain, aristocratic women behaved, which was rather odd. Most ladies were concerned with their appearance at all times, but apparently Margaret wasn't one of them.

He'd hoped to avoid discourse with Lady Margaret for most of their short journey. She seemed to prefer it that way. But there was pertinent information he needed from her before they reached home, a few things he had to impart to her as well. He approached her now to get it over with.

"You may not have considered this," he said, drawing her attention, "but my presence will need to remain unknown for several days while I ascertain the situation. The only way to do that is to abide in your house, with your servants sworn to secrecy, in case any of them happen to recognize me. I assume you will accommodate us?"

She was frowning by the time he finished. He guessed she hadn't planned on putting them up, had possibly thought her involvement was done. Bring him home and leave the rest to him, as it were.

She took a moment, he supposed to grasp all the implications of having a bachelor as a guest, then surprisingly didn't offer a single argument about it. "Certainly," she said.

"You should remember White Oaks. You were there for my sister's engagement party."

He wondered at her sudden blush, until he remembered the last time he'd seen her. "Yes," he replied. "As I recall, it had a nice garden."

Her blush deepened and was accompanied by a glare now. He nearly laughed. Apparently proper Margaret Landor would rather not remember how impulsive and improper she'd been as a child. Or maybe she still liked breaking rules but just didn't want anyone to know about it.

He decided to let her off the hook. "We should have no trouble keeping out of each other's way, since I also recall that White Oaks was nearly as big as Edgewood."

"Bigger," she rejoined with a tight little smirk, yet another indication of her competitive nature. "My father did some renovating after Eleanor ran off. And I added a conservatory off of the dining room when I decided I'd like to garden year-round rather than just in the warmer months."

"Another gardener?" he replied with a roll of his eyes.

She raised a brow. "You enjoy flowers?"

"Not in the least, but my man John does."

"It's very relaxing, you know," she imparted. "You should try it."

"Flowers tend to die when I'm around them."

She blinked, then made a moue. "That wasn't very funny."

"Was I laughing?"

She snorted. "I believe you've forgotten how to. Tell me, what have you been doing with yourself all these years, aside from building that remarkable reputation for accomplishing impossible tasks? Wasn't it rather — difficult — having your base in France, with Napoleon so annoyed with us?"

He did have to work at not laughing this time. "Annoyed? That's a rather gentle way of expressing the little tyrant's sentiments toward Britain. He had us blockaded from every one of his conquered countries and forced his allies to do the same, whether they wanted to or not. He was planning on invading England, you know, and probably would have, if he hadn't been distracted by the Russians."

"Yes, I know we finally got fed up with the trade blockades and took the war to him," she replied. "But did you get involved at all?"

He shrugged. "A little. My particular talents came in handy during the Peninsular

War, especially since I'm fluent in the French language, so I offered my services."

"You acted as a spy!" she guessed.

"How astute of you. But I wasn't involved for very long, just toward the end, when they forced Napoleon's brother Joseph to flee from Madrid. And I wasn't in France when Napoleon marched across it in 1815, gathering his last army, after his abdication. I had several jobs in Italy that year, didn't even hear about his last effort to regain his throne until he was exiled again. But to answer your question, I bought those ruins only four years ago, after his exile, so no, I haven't experienced any difficulty making my home in France."

"You actually call that pile of stones a home?"

"Slip of the tongue, Lady Margaret. You're right. It's no more than a convenient place where I can be contacted. As it happens, I'm not there often, and rarely at this time of the year. If I hadn't had a delivery to make near there, I probably would have been on my way to Italy by now."

"How fortunate for me that —"

"And unfortunate for me," he cut in. "Now to the matter at hand. I've been away from Kent for eleven years. I need to know what has occurred during that time. Any changes I should be aware of?"

Her look was annoyed for a moment over that "unfortunate" remark, but then she briefly ignored him while she gave the question some thought. Even in the full afternoon light, her eyes were still so dark, the brown in them was barely noticeable. She was still gripping most of her hair to contain it, but a few shorter strands kept floating across her cheek. He wondered if she'd notice if he pushed them behind her ear. Possibly not, she was so deep in thought, but he restrained himself.

She was charming in her dishevelment. Not many women were, but with Margaret, it made her seem more — accessible. She was too pretty by half, actually. And she wasn't even trying to be attractive, far from it. It really did seem as if she couldn't care less how she was perceived, which was quite odd for a woman. Or perhaps she just felt that way when she was around him. Disliking him, she wouldn't put any effort into attracting him, he was sure.

He found her attitude unique. Never before had a woman hated him. He was almost tempted to win her over — not bloody likely.

She finally said, "Aside from the assorted deaths and births in the neighborhood —"

"My grandmother?" he cut in with dread.

"No, no, Abigail is just fine — or was, before I left for the Continent. But she's quite batty now, you know."

"Nonsense —"

"No, really. Her eyesight isn't so good, which might be why she sees things that aren't there. During my time at Edgewood, she was forever finding me to tell me we had intruders in the house, and whispering it, afraid they'd hear her when there was never anyone there."

He actually smiled at the picture that conjured. "Very well, so she's a little batty. She is eighty-seven now, after all. I'd say she's allowed."

Margaret said nothing for a moment, was staring at his lips, which he found quite disconcerting. The smile vanished before he was even aware he'd smiled. Her lips twisted in a moue of mild annoyance before she continued.

"I'm extremely fond of the old bird, but it took me a while to get into her good graces."

"Impossible. She's the sweetest —"

"Not anymore," Margaret cut in. "She took your side, you know. In fact, she hasn't spoken a single word to her son since he disowned you. If she needs to communicate with him a'tall, she sends someone else to do it."

Sebastian was incredulous. He'd never guessed that his father and grandmother would have a falling-out after the duel. They'd always been in accord, agreeing on everything — two minds thinking as one, as it were. More guilt to take to his breast, as if he didn't have enough.

"But as I was saying," Margaret continued again, "Abbie wasn't easy to win over, especially after Douglas gave his conservatory into my care when he learned how much I love to garden. He was trying to assist me out of my mourning, but Abbie didn't see it that way. The conservatory had been her domain, as far as she was concerned, so she felt I was invading her territory. She was quite cantankerous and argumentative about it. But it wasn't too long before she was in there giving me advice instead of snapping at me that I was doing everything wrong. It's a shame she gets so maudlin, though. It's why I still visit so frequently, to cheer her up."

"Maudlin over what?"

"Can't you guess? She misses you. And, deep down, I suspect she's distressed at being so furious with her own son that she refuses to talk to him. She is concerned about his accidents, though she won't let on to him that she is. But she hinted more'n once that you could easily get to the bottom of what's going on and put a stop to it, which convinced me to find you. Then there's Cecil and her complaints that he doesn't visit anymore. He was like a son to her as well, I gather."

"He died?"

She gave him a sour look. "Must you assume that everyone died? No, he's quite well, as far as I know. But he and your father have been estranged since the duel, so he no longer comes to Edgewood."

Sebastian was stricken. Good God, even more guilt to add to his plate.

"She was very fond of him, I think," Margaret added. "But then I'd heard Cecil was more often at Edgewood than his own home when he was a child. And his own mother had died, so he took to Abbie and she to him. At least, that's my take on it, from the things she's said."

Sebastian sighed. "The door to Edgewood is probably going to be barred to me. My father stated clearly enough that I was no longer welcome there."

"That will pose a problem," she agreed, frowning. "Are you sure you can't reconcile with Douglas?"

"Quite. I wasn't aware the duel estranged him from Cecil till you just mentioned it. It was because of Cecil and my father's regard for him that I was given the boot, as it were. The estrangement that followed after I left would only have made my father more furious with me."

"Or made him come to his senses and realize who was more important," she suggested.

He snorted. "You don't understand how it was with my father and Cecil. They were as close as Giles and I were. When you develop a friendship that deep, it becomes a bond of honor. He had to disown me. I'd killed his best friend's only son, and after he forbade me to harm him."

"Then why did you?"

"Good God, you don't really think I meant to, do you? It was a bloody accident."

"What I think is you're trying to find a way out of our bargain," she said stiffly. "There are any number of ways for you to get back in that house. Think of one."

"I have and there aren't. It's your turn."

She glared at him. "Disguise yourself," she ordered.

He raised a brow. "From my own family? I could wear a bloody dress and they'd still recognize these eyes. Try again, Lady Margaret."

She started to laugh. "You, in a dress? Good God, that's priceless. I never would have thought of that."

"You can stop thinking of it right now. It isn't going to happen."

"No, no." She grinned. "Of course not. It wouldn't do a'tall, anyway. Women just don't come in your size —" She burst out laughing again. "My God, I can't get the picture out of my mind now."

"Shall I help you?" he growled, not the least bit amused as he stepped closer to her and reached for her arm.

She leapt back from him. "None of that, now." She scowled at him, her humor gone. Then she sighed. "Very well, there's the most obvious way."

"What obvious way? There is no obvious way."

"Course there is. We could pretend to be married for a while. That would get you in the door. Any husband of mine would be as welcome at Edgewood as I am."

"Have you quite lost your gourd?"

"Certainly not. I've been away for four months. It's quite reasonable that I could have married during that time. And I'm not suggesting that we stay married. Heavens no. And I'm certainly not suggesting we really get married. That isn't necessary a'tall. No one at home will be able to prove or disprove whether we are or aren't married, since the pretend wedding would have taken place on the Continent. Of course we'd have to pretend to divorce afterward, just as soon as you've gotten to the bottom of who or what is causing your father's accidents and you've removed the threat."

He stared at her. Her thought processes quite bowled him over.

Dryly, he said, "Maggie, m'dear, you're overlooking one simple fact. The stigma of a divorce would ruin you, real or not."

"Rubbish. When people learn why I made the sacrifice, I will be quite the heroine."

Sacrifice. To marry him? Now that hurt, 'deed it did. Unfortunately, she probably had the right of it. Posing as her husband, while it wouldn't get him back into the bosom of his family, just might get him inside Edgewood for a visit or two. And that could be all that was necessary. The pot would be stirred — if her suspicions were correct.

He wouldn't care to have her ruined reputation on his conscience, though, so he told her, "It might not be necessary a'tall. I'll need a few days to investigate to see if it is. However, it's a serious charade you are proposing, so I suggest you give it more thought in the meantime." But because that "sacrifice" remark was still fresh in his mind, he needled her further. "Think carefully about whether you're willing even to pretend to be married to a man like me."

She raised a questioning brow. He took a step closer, brushed her cheek with the back of his knuckles. "You'd have to pretend to be in love with me," he said, "and get used to my touching you, kissing you. Perhaps we should practice to see if you're even capable of that kind of pretense."

It took her several moments to grasp what he was implying, and then she blushed vividly. "There will be no practicing or pretending of that sort! Really, Sebastian, you know very well that even mild displays of affection between married couples are kept behind closed doors. I'd always thought that was rather silly, but now I'm bloody well thankful it is so. As for pretending to be in love with you, I'll manage somehow, if it becomes necessary."

Chapter 9

They could have reached port last night, but their captain was new to the task and too timid to continue on after the rain started, obscuring all view. Although the channel was heavily trafficked, a veteran captain would have had no trouble avoiding a collision with sister ships. But it didn't really matter what time of day they docked at Dover, because their destination was only a little farther down the coast.

Margaret was grateful for the extra time, since she wanted to carefully broach to Edna the subject of the possible marriage, so she and Oliver would know to corroborate the wedding story if it became necessary. She hadn't counted on her maid being so scandalized by the very idea.

"You can't do that," Edna had said bluntly.

"Course I can," Margaret told her. "Keep in mind he is Sebastian Townshend."

"Exactly, the disowned son of the Townshends, a family you're quite close to. You would have given him the cold shoulder if you had met him again under normal circumstances. It makes no sense that you'd marry him."

Margaret hadn't thought she'd have to convince Edna of the reasons she might have married Sebastian but trotted out a few. "I never mentioned this to anyone before, not even to Florence who I confided everything to when we were children, but you know I used to be quite fascinated by him — before the duel, of course. But it isn't unreasonable that I might have held a tendre for him all these years and been delighted to meet up with him again. It's also not unreasonable that I thought I could reconcile him and his family. And you mentioned it yourself, how handsome he is, certainly handsome enough to turn any girl's head."

"Not yours," Edna said with a huff.

"No, not mine, but you get the point. I could have fallen in love with him and married him, despite all the reasons I shouldn't. Besides, we haven't yet determined whether we will need to pretend we're married, but if we do, it's for a good cause, Edna. Let's not forget why I went

in search of him in the first place."

Edna had agreed in the end, though grudgingly, and went off to let Oliver know what to expect. Margaret had a few doubts of her own that night, though, especially after recalling Sebastian's warning about his touching and kissing her. She'd let him know she wouldn't tolerate anything of the sort, but — he was a different man these days from the one she'd admired in her youth. He was a mercenary, a man willing to do whatever was necessary to get the job done, so would he abide by any restrictions she set?

She went to sleep with her doubts but woke up with a new resolve, that she, too, could do whatever was necessary to remove Douglas from danger. And if that meant pretending to be Sebastian Townshend's wife, so be it.

She found him on the deck that morning, staring pensively at the English coastline, which was now in view. She'd been gone only four months but had missed her home terribly. How much worse it must have been for him, being away for so many years. Or maybe, as he'd claimed, he just didn't care anymore. Not bloody likely.

The tiers of his greatcoat were flapping in the wind. On any other man the coat might look dashing. On Sebastian it somehow added to his menace. And yet the man was so damned handsome he took her breath away. This attraction that seemed to be growing stronger each time she saw him was going to be a problem. She was sure it harked back to her old fascination with him, but still . . .

She joined him at the rail, though she hesitated to interrupt his introspection, he looked so bleak. So she was surprised when he said, "Henry Raven."

"I beg your pardon?"

"The name I will use while at your house," he said.

She started to laugh. "I'm sorry, but you just don't look like a Henry. Couldn't you come up with something more suitable?"

"Like what? Black Bart?" She couldn't hold back her laughter, which prompted him to add, "You know bloody well Henry is about as noble a name as you can get."

"For a king. Very well, Henry, if you insist. I'll let Edna and Oliver know. I've already warned them we might have to pretend to be married."

"I can imagine that went over well," he said dryly.

She rolled her eyes. "Yes, Edna was quite scandalized. But I convinced her it would be for a good cause, if we find it necessary to go that route, which hasn't been decided yet."

He agreed. "If I find out what I need to know before anyone even knows I'm home, nothing else will be required of you."

"Fair enough."

It was midmorning before they docked and the passengers and animals were let ashore. Sebastian's stallion was especially troublesome in the unloading. John's gelding was placid as usual. But the stallion settled down once he was on solid ground again.

Sebastian didn't. He was struck with melancholy the moment his feet touched English soil. God, he'd missed his country of birth, missed it much more than he'd realized. The bitterness that he lived with, that had been buried so deeply it was simply a part of him, rose up now like black bile to choke his emotions.

He never should have left. Just because his father had disowned him and told him to never darken England's shores again didn't mean he actually had to go. He'd already defied his father in showing up for that duel. What was one more defiance after that? But his guilt had been horrendous.

And it was still present even after all these years, tearing at his gut, ripping at his mind and heart just as badly now as it had back then.

Chapter 10

Margaret loved her home. Three stories of white oak surrounded by flowers — her flowers. She'd planted every one of them. Every springtime, she was like a mother hen waiting for them to bloom.

While the Townshends' home Edgewood was a splendid estate and she'd been offered a permanent home there, it was only because she'd taken to Douglas and Abigail Townshend that she'd felt comfortable there at all. Without a doubt, she still preferred her own home. It was hers. The staff was hers. The history of the house was hers. And it was every bit as splendid as Edgewood.

And goodness, she was glad to be home. Her staff had missed her, too. A few of them ran out the front door to greet her. Her cook, Gussie, was even tearful.

"Finally I won't feel guilty anymore about making my most superb dishes while you aren't here to enjoy them," Gussie told her, then scolded lightly, "You were gone much too long, Lady Margaret."

"It was necessary, to accomplish all I set out to do," Margaret rejoined. "I assume the wine shipment arrived without any trouble?"

"Indeed. I'll even open a bottle tonight to celebrate your homecoming."

No sooner did Gussie go back in the house than Margaret's groom arrived and breathlessly exclaimed, "Thank God, m'lady. Now that beast of yours might behave again."

She was amused. The man was fond of referring to her mare as a beast. She couldn't imagine why. Sweet Tooth was as sweet as her name — when Margaret was around.

"I'll be back to my usual agenda tomorrow," Margaret informed him, "but I'll visit her this afternoon."

"Thank you, m'lady. And she'll be saddled and waiting for you in the morning."

It took a while to speak to each servant. She ignored none of them. And they'd all come out to greet her before she even got in the door. Florence, her housekeeper, was the last to arrive. She was the newest member of the staff, though she'd grown up at White Oaks, too. She'd taken over the housekeeper position five years ago when her mother retired from it. And like Edna, she treated Margaret with a greater familiarity than the rest of the staff. They'd actually played together as children.

While each of the servants had glanced curiously at the two men and the boy accompanying her, some more than once, only Florence asked, "Shall I prepare extra settings at the table tonight? Or rooms?"

"Both," Margaret replied. "I'm going to have guests for a while."

Florence nodded, then leaned closer to whisper, "Is that who I think it is?"

She was looking at Sebastian, of course. Still mounted on his stallion, he'd merely sat there observing the homecoming, his look as inscrutable as ever. Yet there was still that sinister air about him that prohibited discourse and would probably have most people running in the opposite direction if given a choice.

She wasn't even sure what it was about him that made him so — unapproachable. She wasn't shy by any means, but even she felt nervous when she was around him, so she could just imagine how others reacted to him. And no matter how many times she'd spoken to him now, it got no easier.

Margaret pulled Florence aside to answer her. "Yes, it's him. But we need to keep that to ourselves for the time being. He doesn't want anyone to know he's back yet, so we'll oblige him in that regard."

"Not even his family?"

"Especially not his family."

"Why's he back, then?" Florence asked.

Margaret didn't answer, just stared at her housekeeper until Florence finally got the point and humphed, "Fine. Keep it a secret. What do I care? I'll make sure the others keep quiet about him, if it looks like anyone else realizes who he is. They probably won't. I barely recognized him m'self. Goodness, he's — changed."

That was an understatement, but Margaret merely nodded. She felt bad about keeping secrets from Florence. She hadn't even told her friend the real reason she'd gone to Europe because she knew Florence would try to talk her out of it. She'd never been secretive before, never had a reason to be, for that matter. Clandestine just wasn't her cup of tea, just the opposite. She was forthright by nature, sometimes to the point of brazenness.

It had even seemed as if she had sneaked home, and in fact she had. In the last century, Edgeford had grown from a sleepy village to a thriving little town that now supplied most of the needs of the gentry in the surrounding area. It was on the way from Dover to White Oaks, yet they'd avoided it completely, as well as any other homes on the way. She'd suggested that Sebastian ride in the coach as they neared home, in case they passed anyone who might recognize him, but he'd declined and merely told Oliver to follow him. They hadn't stayed on the road for the last half mile.

"Timothy, lad, it's time for you to earn your keep," Margaret heard Sebastian say as she approached him. "John and I will be recognized, but no one knows you, so go around and find out what you can about my family."

Margaret bristled for a moment. She liked the boy, had learned from John how Timothy came to be with them. She didn't like how he was being used, though, and would have taken Sebastian to task if she didn't notice how delighted the lad was to be given such responsibility.

So she said instead, "Come inside first. My housekeeper will show you to your rooms. It's also approaching time for dinner, so you might want to wait until the morning before you begin any investigating."

Timothy had to glance at Sebastian first for his approval before he ran into the house. Margaret turned, caught Sebastian with his brow raised at her.

"You don't think he can handle the task?" he asked.

"He's a bit young to be doing your job, isn't he?" she countered.

"Not a'tall. And part of my job is assigning tasks to whoever is most likely to succeed at them. In this case, he's the only one among us who isn't known here. He's also young enough to pry innocently and have it appear as no more than a child's curiosity. Be assured, Maggie, I'll even put you to work if I deem it necessary."

That sounded rather unsavory, or maybe it was just his tone that made it seem so. Still, she hurried into the house and out of his presence. Being around that man was exhausting, indeed it was. It wasn't just the attraction, which she fought hard to ignore, but the way he made her so nervous, queasy, all aflutter, which in turn roused her defenses and made her argumentative. Good grief, she was the sweetest person! She'd been told so by countless people. But not around him.

Chapter 11

Margaret felt like herself again when she came down to dinner that night. While her traveling clothes had been highly fashionable, they'd also been made of thick, sturdy materials that wouldn't need much care, so they hadn't been very comfortable. Back in soft peach velvet that was sinfully comfortable, well rested after a brief nap, she felt quite capable of dealing with her guests.

She expected all three of them to be waiting for her in the dining room, but only Sebastian was there, seated at the head of her table. The nerve! And he hadn't dressed for dinner. He was wearing a white shirt without a cravat, open at the neck, loose flowing sleeves cuffed at the wrist. He might as well have had an earring and an eye patch on, because that's probably how her servants perceived him.

David, who regularly tended the table and stood waiting by the door, was no doubt shaking in his boots, he looked so nervous. Of course, the wickedly long dagger that Sebastian was using to spear chunks of meat out of the appetizer that had been brought to him was more likely the cause. Her servants knew better than to begin the meal before her arrival. Sebastian must have frightened David into breaking that rule.

Sebastian rose as she entered and pulled out the chair on his right. She would not have chosen a seat so close to him, but it looked like it would be only the two of them dining, and it would seem haughty of her to sit at the other end of the table, forcing them to raise their voices to have any sort of conversation. It was a long table, after all. But she would have to make a point of arriving at the dining room before him while he was in residence.

David hurried forward to fill Margaret's wineglass, then left to fetch her appetizer. She took the moment of privacy to remark to Sebastian, "My housekeeper, Florence, recognized you today. It's likely some of the older servants will as well. We should probably make an announcement about why you wish to remain incognito —"

"That won't be necessary," he cut in. "I've spoken to each of your servants. They'll say nothing."

"You say that with such assurance. Threatened to murder them all in their sleep, did you?"

"Ah, you've set the tone," he replied dryly. "Shall I sharpen my fork?"

She blushed. She had no excuse for being so rude other than her nervousness. She certainly hadn't expected to be alone with him at dinner.

"I apologize. My humor went awry."

"You were trying to make me laugh? I should warn you, then. I don't."

"Rubbish. Everyone laughs. It's human nature. Can't be helped."

"So now I'm not human?"

Margaret gritted her teeth. Odious man. And her appetizer hadn't even arrived yet. This was going to be the longest dinner of her life, she was sure.

In an effort to put the conversation on a proper track, she remarked, "I expected John and Timothy to join us. They weren't hungry?"

"On the contrary," he replied. "But being back in England has had a profound effect on John. Etiquette demands he take his meals with the rest of the servants now. He is my valet, after all."

"I gathered he was more than that."

"Indeed, he and I have been through a lot

together. But there's no point in arguing with him. It's not just England, it's this house. Reminds him of tradition and all that rot. Back in the fold, as it were."

"You don't sound happy that he has reverted to form," she commented.

"I'm not, but you couldn't drag him in here with a horse. And the boy takes his cue from John."

Margaret wasn't happy with John's desertion either. It meant she'd be sharing a lot of meals with Sebastian — alone. She couldn't even invite other guests, not while he remained incognito. She could hope that he wouldn't have to stay hidden for very long. Or she could make an effort to get along with him, despite her dislike. Familiarity breeds indifference, as it were. Not bloody likely, with him.

"By the by, why didn't you want a come-out?" he asked.

Margaret stared at him, wondering how long he'd been mulling that over, to finally ask. There were a lot of circumstances responsible for her current single state, some of them common knowledge that he wouldn't know about due to his long absence. She saw no reason not to tell him.

"It wasn't that I didn't want one," she said. "But when the time was ripe for one, I was still in mourning. I'd just lost my father. I was living in a new home with your father. By the time my mourning period had ended, I had decided I could do without a husband. After all, I'd witnessed the heartache of love gone awry in my sister's case. And having watched your brother and sister-in-law go at it tooth and nail, as it were — well, not a very good recommendation for marriage, that."

"Admit it. You declined a come-out because you think no one will have you."

Was he making an effort to tease her, or did he really think that? It was impossible to tell with him. But it was probably the latter. She doubted the man knew how to tease anymore.

So she snorted. "Rubbish. And I wasn't finished."

"You really decided not to marry?"

"For a brief time I actually did. Those were just the thoughts of a young girl, though. I simply wasn't old enough yet to decide the matter maturely. But by the time I came to my senses and realized I was being silly to be deterred from marriage by my sister's broken heart and your brother and his wife's constant bickering, I was a bit past the prime for a come-out."

"For God's sake, you're only twenty-three. You haven't passed anything."

"Allow me to know what I've passed or not," she replied a bit stiffly.

He sat back, said casually, "I find it hard to believe that in all these years you haven't been courted. Have all the young bucks left the neighborhood?"

"Not a'tall. I've been courted to distraction."

"And none would do?"

"A few might have, but I suppose I've set my standards a bit high. The choice is mine, you see. Were my father still here, he probably would have made some recommendations and I probably would have agreed with him. By having the choice to m'self, I find no need to hurry."

"Then you've chosen to be an old maid?"

She gritted her teeth. The insults were piling up. "Really, Sebastian," she said dryly, "you shouldn't strive to be so charming."

"Yes, I know. Bad habit."

She almost laughed. But that would encourage him to make more outlandish remarks, so she restrained herself.

"As it happens, I'm still being courted," she told him primly.

"Anyone I would know?"

"Possibly. Thomas Peermont, Viscount

Ridgmore's son, you might remember."

"Little Tommy? He was still wearing knickers when I left. He can't be old enough for you."

Her back got a little stiffer. "Not that age matters at this point, but he's only a year younger than I am. And then there's The Honorable Daniel Courtly, whom you probably don't know."

"Courted by a Courtly, how quaint."

She glared at him, but continued, "He and his mother moved here only two years ago. They bought the old Merryweather cottage on the cliffs after Angus Merryweather moved to London to be closer to his grandchildren."

"Never heard of him."

"Didn't think so."

"Just the two?"

"Two is quite enough, when I'm not really interested in either of them."

"So you are determined to be an old maid. Might as well own up to it, Maggie."

"If you must know, I do plan on going to London to broaden my choices. I just don't intend to compete with a gaggle of giggling debutantes."

"How do you intend to avoid that?"

"By attending a few choice parties and proposing to a man who suits me. In another year or two I will feel comfortable doing so."

He raised a brow. "You aren't joking, are you?"

"Not a'tall."

"I think you've been on your own too long, Maggie. It's quite addled your wits."

She smiled tightly. "My wits are just fine, thank you."

"Then you haven't realized that if it gets out, you'll become a laughingstock?"

"And why would it get out?" she countered. "I assure you, I can be quite circumspect. Nor do I intend to propose to every man I meet."

"Just one or two, hell, just one is all it will take. Consider. An earl's daughter proposing marriage. That's too juicy not to spread around."

"Unless the fellow takes me up on the offer, then it would be in his best interest to keep his mouth shut, wouldn't it? You, sir, are much too negative."

"No. I've just learned to view all aspects of a situation. Besides, you're already going to have one mark against you as a divorced woman," he pointed out. "Only second sons might overlook that stigma."

She sighed. "Even if it is, you overlook a prime motive."

"Your lush body?"

She turned crimson, stood up, and threw her napkin down on top of her dessert, which had just arrived. Her footman was blushing, too, and hurrying back out the door. Good God, she couldn't believe Sebastian had said that, and with a servant in the room to hear it!

"You are, without a doubt, the most despicable man I have ever met. I was referring to the title that will pass to my husband's son, much more incentive than a — a —"

"Lush body," he reminded her.

Even more color shot to her cheeks. Without a thought, she picked up her napkin, smeared now with cream and whipped chocolate, and tossed it at his head. Bloody hell, she missed. But at least the chocolate and cream splattered across his forehead, she noticed, on her way out the door.

"Don't run away mad, Maggie," he called after her.

"Go to the devil, you odious man!"

Was that laughter she heard? No, just her imagination. She remembered that Sebastian Townshend had forgotten how to laugh.

Chapter 12

A brisk autumn wind tugged at the skirt of Margaret's riding habit as she walked to the stable. An avid horsewoman, she owned quite a few riding habits, one for each day of the week, and had had to restrain herself from buying even more. Edna had laid out the emerald green one for her today and attached white and green lace streamers to the top hat she wore with it.

She was quite fashionably clad, but there was no one around to appreciate it. She sighed. She'd overslept this morning. She hadn't been able to sleep last night because she'd been so angry with Sebastian and appalled at her own behavior. She still couldn't believe she'd tossed her good breeding out the door and thrown her dinner napkin at him. The man addled her, plain and simple.

When she'd gone downstairs this morning, the house had been quiet. Florence and Gussie had probably gone shopping in Edgeford to restock the pantry, now that she was home. A few pastries had been left in the dining room, and she'd grabbed two and wrapped them in a napkin, one for her and one for her mare Sweet Tooth.

Before she went to Europe, Daniel Courtly had been in the habit of joining her each morning on her ride. She supposed she ought to send word to him that she was home. She'd been gone so long, though, he might have started courting someone else in the neighborhood.

There were a number of ladies still available in their small social circle to whom he might have switched his attention. Actually, the circle wasn't that small anymore. A prime location, close enough to London to make traveling there a short jaunt, but even closer to the coast and the cliffs that offered such magnificent views, the area surrounding Edgeford had received a moderate influx of new neighbors over the years who either built new homes or bought existing properties they could expand. And many of them followed Alberta Dorrien's lead.

For a good fifteen years now, Alberta, with the esteemed title of dowager duchess, had been the social matriarch of the neighborhood, entertaining frequently, including

127

not one but two grand balls each year that drew the ton from London. Margaret had missed Alberta's summer ball this year while she was traveling in Europe. She'd met Daniel at one of Alberta's earlier balls.

She sighed over Daniel. She had been selfish in continuing her friendship with him when she had no intention of marrying him. Although he was quite suitable for a husband, her feelings for him didn't run in that direction. She liked him. She felt they were friends. Their humor was compatible. But he didn't excite her. And so she didn't encourage him, flirt, or otherwise lead him to believe she'd like their relationship to progress to the next stage, which was probably why he'd never made any serious overtures toward her. Perhaps they were just friends and she had only imagined that he'd been courting her.

Ned, the head groomsman, led Sweet Tooth out of the stable as Margaret approached. She was surprised that she didn't need to wait.

"You didn't keep her saddled all this time, did you?" she asked, her tone slightly scolding.

"No, m'lady," he assured her. "Edna sent word that you were coming down."

"Did she?"

Margaret was distracted by her mare, who'd gotten the scent of her and ripped her reins from the groom's hand to reach Margaret sooner. She was nearly butted to the ground by the mare's affection.

"She's really missed you," Ned was saying. "She pined something terrible that first month you were gone. Barely ate. Tried to bite me every time I got near her. I finally had to bribe her with sweets to behave."

Margaret had to do the same, and quickly offered Sweet Tooth both pastries to get her to settle down. It helped only marginally. The mare was scolding her and greeting her in her own unique way.

"I'd suggest you ride her immediately," Ned said. "She's too excited by your return to stay still. Ian will only be a moment. He's saddling up now."

Another of the White Oaks' grooms, Ian was her regular escort, which was necessary because Daniel usually accompanied her on her rides. "I'll just take a quick turn about the grounds to get the wind out of her, and come back for Ian."

"A good idea," Ned agreed and offered Margaret a heft up, which she accepted.

Goodness, she was barely in the saddle when Sweet Tooth took off at a gallop. She loved her horse, but sometimes the mare showed her Thoroughbred breeding too much. She came from a line of prominent racers, so prominent that Margaret was contacted several times a year by breeders who wanted to bring their best studs to the mare. She refused them all. She wasn't going to let her favorite mount become too fat to ride.

She lost her hat on that brief race around the house. At least she didn't lose her perch. It had been close. Sweet Tooth had gone too long without a good ride. Retrieving the hat, but not bothering to attempt to place it back on her head at the right angle, she swung by the front of the house to drop it off before she collected Ian. And got detained.

Daniel was there at her front door knocking when she rode up. His smile was nearly blinding when he saw her.

"Good God, Maggie, I was beginning to think you were never coming home!"

She blushed as she dismounted. Daniel never called her Maggie. Only the people who'd known her for most of her life did. And she couldn't imagine how he'd picked up on her childhood name when she couldn't recall even a single time he'd heard her called that. Which meant he was giving her what he thought was a personal nickname, which was too personal for their relationship. Goodness, what could he have been thinking while she was gone?

Daniel Courtly was a fine-looking man. Blond, blue eyed, with a tall, strapping body. He was quite handsome, actually, more so than she recalled. Perhaps it was the new mustache that he hadn't sported previously. It gave him a somewhat dashing, rakish air.

She smiled. "It's good to see you, Daniel. How did you know I was home?"

"Found out early this morning when I came by. I've been in the habit of stopping by a few times each week just to check if you'd returned. I never expected you to be gone so long!"

"Neither did —"

She didn't get to finish, because she had the breath knocked out of her by his unexpected and highly improper bear hug. A rough one, too. First the horse, now this. So much mauling in one morning was a bit much!

And then she heard the door to the house open, and the most ominous voice said, "I hope you have an innocent reason to be hugging my wife."

Daniel released her instantly. She didn't manage to catch her breath because she lost

131

it again when she saw Sebastian standing on the doorstep, looking as ominous as he'd sounded. She was reminded of how menacing he'd looked when she'd first met him. This was much worse. There was murder in his bright golden eyes, in fact, his very tone had implied that murder would be done if an innocent reason wasn't forthcoming.

Daniel must have drawn the same conclusion, but he was too shocked to answer. He simply stared incredulously at Sebastian as he blushed profusely. Margaret's cheeks were red as well, but with anger. When had they decided that they were going to go the "fake" marriage route? Had she missed something? She could have sworn he'd said he was going to do some investigating before they determined whether it would be necessary to pretend they were married. And, really, shouldn't the final decision have been hers?

"Need help?" Sebastian said into the painful silence, as he slowly walked toward them. "Childhood acquaintance? Old friend of the family? Relative I don't know about?"

Daniel snapped out of it and quickly replied, "Margaret and I are old friends — well, not so old, only a few years. But I was merely welcoming her home."

"Innocent — I suppose," Sebastian allowed as he crossed his arms over his chest, but added, "As a precautionary measure, though, you'll keep your hands to yourself henceforth. It's nothing personal, old chap. I'm merely appalled to discover that I make a jealous husband."

Put that way, Daniel relaxed slightly. He nodded and even courteously extended a hand for introductions. "I'm Daniel Courtly. And you are?"

Sebastian turned his back on them and walked back into the house without answering. So rude! And he'd left Margaret there to do the lying. Good God, she hoped she wouldn't blunder it. She wasn't exactly adept at telling falsehoods.

"I'm sorry, Daniel. His behavior is inexcusable. I'm as appalled as he is to learn of his jealous nature. Never witnessed it before."

"You've married," was all he said, the shocked expression returning to his face. "I don't believe it."

The hurt in his tone made Margaret distinctly uncomfortable. "I find it hard to believe m'self," she assured him. "I didn't leave here with the intention of looking for a husband in Europe. It was love at first sight, yes, indeed, that's exactly what it was. Quite unexpected."

"But he's not foreign. He's English. Who is he?"

"Henry Raven."

"Raven? I'm not familiar with that name. Where is he from? London?"

She blushed. "I'm not at liberty to say."

"You must be joking."

"No. Let's leave it at that, please. You'll find out more about him soon enough."

"I see — no, I bloody well don't," he said, angrily now. The hurt look on Daniel's face made her feel so guilty, when she really had nothing to feel guilty about, well, other than lying about being married. She could deal much better with his anger.

"I'm devastated if you haven't guessed," he fumed. "I thought — obviously I thought wrong. Bloody hell, I don't even like to ride! I merely took up the habit to be with you."

She was about to remind him that their relationship hadn't progressed far enough to warrant his heated reaction, when he up and left. He even shot her a look of disgust as he mounted his horse and rode off.

Margaret sighed. That had been so unpleasant, and so unnecessary. Blast Sebastian! What could he have been thinking to announce their "marriage" in such a rude way? The news was going to spread now. The visitors would start arriving that very day to wish them well and meet her new husband. And what the devil was she supposed to tell them? Yes, I've married. No, you can't meet my husband, go away. Bloody hell. She was afraid this was going to cause quite a scandal.

Chapter 13

She found Sebastian in the dining room, looking over the selection of pastries laid out on the table, his back to the door.

"When is luncheon served?"

Margaret was nonplussed. How had he known she was there? She'd made no sound as she'd entered the room, had been especially quiet, in fact, so no servants would come out to see if she needed anything.

"The usual time, but you're going to be served a piece of my mind first."

He glanced over his shoulder and raised a brow. "Something wrong?"

How could he look so innocent, as if he hadn't just rearranged her life? A ruse, no doubt, but it wasn't going to work.

"What could be wrong? You just dashed that young man's hopes, and most brutally. That was not the way to break the news to a man I've long been friends with. And about that news, how dare you change your mind about . . . our *marriage* without warning me first? I specifically recall —"

"Settle down, Maggie," he cut in.

He'd turned to face her and popped a small cream puff in his mouth, then licked his fingers — slowly. Good God. Her stomach fluttered oddly, her pulse quickened. Thoughts deserted her as she stared at his mouth.

"Don't do that," he snapped.

She blinked. "What?"

"Bloody hell," he said and turned back toward the table.

With his back to her again, her senses returned to normal, as did her thoughts. She wasn't sure what had just happened, but she had a feeling it wouldn't be wise to dwell on it. He'd managed to distract her from her anger for a moment, but she still wanted an answer from him.

"That nonsense about you being jealous —" she began.

"Was nonsense," he replied, turning back around to face her.

"I know, but why did you do that? What was the point? And why are we suddenly 'married' when you weren't even sure it would be necessary?"

"Timothy was very productive this morning. Now that I do deem it necessary to enact the farce, which was your suggestion, I might add, it was crucial that I stop you from making any blunders before the news spread."

"I don't make blunders," she replied stiffly.

"In the usual sense, you probably don't," he allowed magnanimously. "But I was referring to your saying something to Courtly that would lead him to believe nothing has changed between you two, when in fact our 'marriage' changes everything. Are you getting the point yet, Maggie? If we're going to go through with this, you don't want to leave a doubting Thomas in the wings who could come forward later to denounce us."

"It's doubtful I would have said anything of the nature you're implying. My relationship with Daniel wasn't that close."

"It was close enough for him to put his hands all over you."

She blushed furiously. "That was no more than he claimed. He was welcoming me home."

"A handshake would have sufficed," he pointed out dryly. "Be that as it may, I merely made sure in the quickest way possible that no doubts would arise later. As it happens, I was looking for you to tell you what Timothy found out. Finding you in the embrace of another man, well, I actually thought it was too late, that you already might have blundered. Mentioning our 'marriage' was a calculated risk at that point but the only way to set the stage for our deception."

"A handshake and introduction wouldn't have sufficed?" she shot back.

He actually started to smile. No, surely it was her imagination. "Sorry, not my way," he said.

"No, your way is to shake things up and get everyone's emotions in a tangle."

He shrugged. "Habit. Works very well in my line of work. People tend to say things they wouldn't otherwise say, when they're angry."

She glared. "I'm not your mark, Sebastian, so don't use those tactics on me."

"But you exhibit such magnificent beauty when you're angry, Maggie." His golden eyes roamed up and down her body. "Hard to resist."

"What rubbish." She snorted and stomped angrily out of the room.

But she didn't go very far. She was at the foot of the stairs when she realized he hadn't told her why he'd deemed their pretend marriage necessary. He'd known she would come back, the odious man, because he was standing where she'd left him, facing the door and popping another cream puff into his mouth.

She glanced away before she could see him lick his fingers and stared at the floor as she began to pace it. "What was Timothy's report?" she demanded.

"You might want to hear it firsthand. He's pumped up proud of his deception."

"Where is he?"

"Where else would a young boy be this time of the day? And while you're there, tell your kitchen staff I'm ready for lunch."

She bristled at the order but left to find Timothy in the kitchen. It looked like the boy had just finished eating, so she suggested, "Come for a ride with me, Tim. I've still to exercise my mare, and Ian has a horse saddled that you can use. You can be my escort."

He beamed. The boy really did like being assigned new responsibilities. Odd for a child his age, when most would rather be off playing.

They rode toward Edgewood and stopped on a knoll overlooking Sebastian's ancestral home.

"So what did you find out this morning that disturbed Sebastian?" she began.

"He didn't look disturbed."

"He never looks disturbed about anything, which is beside the point. What did you learn?"

"Well, I was in the stable down there asking for a job. Couldn't get hired, though. All the jobs were taken. One of the grooms was French. Seemed very out of place, him. Wouldn't talk at all except to tell me to get lost."

"That disturbed Sebastian?"

"No, didn't even mention that to him."

Margaret rolled her eyes and decided to let Timothy tell his tale without interrupting him. "Go on."

"Well, I was about to leave and go ask at the kitchen for work, when the big lord himself walked in and started saddling his horse. None of the other grooms came forward to do it for him, so I hurried over and offered to help, just like I worked there. Didn't think he'd know the difference, and he didn't."

"That was rather ingenious of you."

Timothy grinned. "I thought so. Well, I started chattering a bunch, 'bout this and that, nothing personal, mind you, just enough to make him relax and not really hear me, if you know what I mean. Then I mentioned his sons, told him I'd heard he had two fine ones. He definitely heard that.

Got all stiff. Could have chilled milk next to him, he got so cold-like."

"That's all? He didn't say anything?"

"Oh, he did. He said I'd heard wrong, that he only had one son. The other was dead."

And dead men weren't admitted through the front door, Margaret thought. Good God, it must have hurt Sebastian to hear that. Then again, maybe he really didn't care, as he'd said. But he'd been right. The estrangement had escalated severely if Douglas now considered Sebastian dead to him. He wouldn't be welcome, except as her husband. And even that was going to be highly uncomfortable. She could well lose her own welcome if she brought the "dead" son home to Edgewood.

Chapter 14

Sebastian blended well with the shadows, a knack he'd developed long ago. The moon was making only sporadic appearances through a bank of gray clouds that were moving rather rapidly overhead. But he'd taken that into account when he'd decided to wear his dark gray greatcoat, which covered him from neck to boots, and was less discernible than his black one on nights when there were no shadows. The air smelled and felt as if there were going to be a downpour at some point during the night, but not, he hoped, while he was skulking around the grounds of Edgewood.

His old home was still well lit at that hour of the evening. He had to be a masochist to come here and watch his family through the windows, knowing he was not welcome to join them.

He leaned against the tree he and Denton had often climbed as children. One summer they'd dragged boards up there and put together a little hut. It had been a nice hideaway until Denton had brought up one too many things to decorate it with, and the main branch supporting it had cracked. They were lucky the limb had fallen slowly and had dropped them rather gently on the ground. But it had frightened their father enough for him to forbid them to make another tree house.

That old tree was outside the dining room where his family was currently gathered. For once his expression wasn't so inscrutable. Pain, regret, anger — they were all there for anyone to see, his guard completely gone as he stared at his father through the windows.

Douglas hadn't changed greatly. He wore a half century of years very well. His hair was still as pitch-black as Sebastian's. If there was any gray in it, it wasn't noticeable at that distance. His grandmother, Abigail, had changed a lot. Her hair was snow-white now, her shoulders more bent than they used to be. She still wore her hair in the old style. On her it looked good.

God, he'd missed that old woman. She'd been more than just their grandmother. She'd been everything to them after their mother died when Sebastian was nine.

Proud, regal, but warm and loving. She didn't look so warm and loving now. She spoke readily with Denton, but no smiles crossed her lips. And not one glance was directed toward the head of the table.

Douglas sat there alone. Abigail ate at the other end. Denton kept her company there. He'd changed greatly as well. He had begun looking dissipated before Sebastian had left. He looked more so now, haggard, almost downtrodden. Juliette hadn't made an appearance yet, but they obviously hadn't waited for her.

The distance between his father and his grandmother at that table was telling. It was not a happy scene he was watching. A tightness welled in his chest. So much he had to account for. And so much more that he hadn't even known he was responsible for. His family was no longer a family, they were just people who lived in the same house. All of the warmth was gone.

The contrast was tearing him apart. He remembered other dinners so clearly. Giles had been there more often than not, and even his father, Cecil, had been a regular guest. There had been laughter, revelry. Abigail had often been teased mercilessly and she'd loved it. And they'd all sat close together. The table had been smaller, and all the chairs had been filled. There had never been a lull in the conversation, or in the laughter. It had been a place you wanted to be, not a place to quickly escape from — as it seemed to be now.

Douglas left the table first. He said something to Denton in parting, but he barely even glanced at his mother. Sebastian moved farther down the side of the house until he was outside Douglas's study. It was where his father usually retired for a few hours after dinner. Cecil had always joined him there when he and Giles had come for dinner. The two old friends never lacked for discourse, and their laughter frequently traveled through the large house.

The draperies hadn't been closed in the room. Several lamps had been lit earlier. Douglas entered the room and closed the door. He poured a glass of brandy and brought the bottle and glass with him to his desk. He sat down behind it and downed the entire glass, then poured another. Alone there, unaware that he was being watched, he let his shoulders slump. He lit a cigar, but he didn't smoke it. He picked up a paper on his desk, but he didn't read it. His head dropped back against the chair.

It was apparent that he had become a man with nothing to look forward to, with nothing to hold his interest, no friends to share in the joys of life — no joys to share. He wasn't just alone in that room, he was alone with himself.

The tightness increased in Sebastian's chest. He'd done this to his father, made him a shell of the man he used to be. All these years and he hadn't known that Douglas had become as empty inside as he was. They were so similar.

It was no wonder they'd all taken to Margaret while she lived with them. She'd probably brought life to the house with her incessant chatter.

A while later, Sebastian lay on his bed, arms crossed behind his head. He hadn't undressed, had known sleep would be a long time in coming that night and he'd probably have to fetch another bottle of brandy from downstairs to help it along. He'd barely touched the first one, though, his thoughts so deep that he kept forgetting to drink it.

Dead. His father had told Timothy that he was dead. Figuratively, of course, but even so, had a gravestone been put up for him? He had assumed, once he came face-to-face with his father, that they'd have words. Harsh ones, probably, but at least he would have an opportunity to express his concerns, or rather, Margaret's concerns, and possibly work with Douglas to unravel the suspicions that had been raised.

That assumption had been made before he knew about his father's estrangement from Cecil and his own mother, and that his enmity toward his eldest son had increased rather than dissipated with the passing years, to the point where Douglas wouldn't even admit that Sebastian was still alive. Dead. And he'd thought his own bitterness couldn't be matched.

What he was looking at was an insurmountable wall. He couldn't break it. Margaret possibly could. She'd been accepted into the bosom of his family. She was close enough to Douglas that she'd gone above and beyond in her effort to "save" him, if he really needed saving. Maybe he needed saving only from himself. Bloody hell.

Sebastian would have liked to blame his father for this current state of affairs, but he couldn't. All of it, every reaction and result thereafter, could rest only on his own shoulders.

He snarled as he got back up, disgusted with himself for rehashing what couldn't be changed. He went in search of Margaret. They needed to finalize a plan so he could quickly accomplish what she'd hired him for and return to France.

She had refused to have dinner with him that night, which was why he'd gone to Edgewood instead. He wasn't surprised. His behavior the previous night had been reprehensible. Deliberately reprehensible, but still, he hadn't needed to be quite so insulting to get her to maintain her distance. She seemed to be having no trouble a'tall keeping her enmity high on her list of priorities without any help from him. Perhaps it was the other way around. He needed a reason to keep his hands off of her.

There it was, the crux of the problem. She'd walked into the dining room last night looking so incredibly soft and enticing in her peach velvet gown, and his attraction to her had instantly turned into lusty desire. She shouldn't be able to tempt him like that. Her dislike of him should have been enough to put him off, but instead it was having the opposite effect.

He rapped on her bedroom door. There was light coming from under it, indicating she hadn't retired yet. It was nearly a minute before she opened the door, though. The fluffy white robe she was clutching close to her throat suggested she'd kept him waiting while she put it on. Her hair floated loosely around it, very dark in the dim lamplight behind her. She was looking too bloody soft again, turning his thoughts in an intimate direction. Was she wearing anything under that robe?

"It's rather late," she said. "What do you want, Sebastian?"

Her curt, no-nonsense tone got his mind out from under her robe. "We need to discuss tomorrow's agenda," he told her.

"It can't wait until the morning?"

"No. Waiting led to that unpleasant scene with Courtly today. I gathered from your splendid tirade afterward that you'd rather avoid any more like that."

She made a tsking sound. "Very well, I'll meet you in the parlor."

"Don't be absurd, Maggie. We're married. Your servants won't raise a brow if you invite me into your room. They'll expect it, actually."

"I told my housekeeper, Florence, about the marriage so she can turn away any well-wishing visitors tomorrow that we aren't ready to deal with, but the rest of my servants aren't aware of our supposed —"

"Yes, they are."

She glared at him for taking that liberty upon himself but opened the door wider and walked back into her room to put some distance between them. She secured her robe more fully, tying it about her waist. Her hair was longer than he'd realized. Having seen it tossed about on the ship, it had been hard to tell that it reached her hips. Easy enough to see now since she was still giving him her back.

Her room was a surprise. He would have expected someone of Margaret's gruff temperament to prefer dark, masculine colors to match her aggressive nature, but her walls were papered in pink roses, her vanity draped in white lace, her large bed covered with a lilac spread and fluffy silk pillows. The velvet drapes were a darker, bold shade of pink.

Numerous chairs were scattered about the room, upholstered in the same theme. Her plump reading chair was in purple and pink flowers, the seat of her desk chair in dark purple and red. The carpet was a red and pink floral swirl in a typical motif. The large bookcase that covered half of one wall was overstuffed with books attesting to his suspicion that she was also a bluestocking. All the wood in the furnishings was white oak. And there were flowers everywhere, in large vases on the floor, small vases on the tables, in pots near the covered windows, giving the room a pleasant scent. The woman really did like to garden.

Her desk was a working desk, cluttered with household account books and receipts, a few framed pictures, one of her sister Eleanor, whom he recognized. Sadness swept over him as he thought about her death. She'd been a charming young woman and so happy about her engagement to Giles. It bothered him that Margaret blamed him for her death.

Margaret's back stiffened perceptibly when she heard him close the door behind him. She turned to face him. The white lace of her nightgown was revealed at the top opening of her robe. He was glad to see it. Imagining her naked under that robe would have kept him awake the rest of the night.

"We seem to be progressing rather rapidly, to have reached this point already," she commented, her tone still showing her annoyance with him. "Weren't you going to do some investigating first?"

He strolled across the room. He was heading to the comfortable-looking reading chair behind her, but when she scurried so quickly out of his way, he changed his mind and continued in her direction instead.

"A waste of time," he said, "now that news of your marriage will be making the rounds. And I've taken the liberty of sending one of your servants to Edgewood with the news of your return . . . with a husband."

"You take far too many liberties," she replied, still retreating from him.

"You hired me and will be paying a princely sum for my efforts to find out if there's a plot against my father. Don't quibble over the way I do my job. Now, in the morning, send a note to my father that you'll be coming by for a visit with your husband."

That got her to stop moving. "Am I to warn him who I married?"

"No, let's get me in the door before he finds out. Otherwise, we might not find him home a'tall."

"You really think he'd just leave, so he doesn't have to deal with seeing you again?"

"Either that, or he will simply inform you that while you are still welcome, your husband isn't, which will defeat the purpose of this farce."

She sighed. "Very well. So once we arrive, what exactly do we tell them? How did we meet? Where did we marry?"

"In which country did you stay the longest during your travels?"

"My visits to Germany and Italy were about equal in length."

"I spend a good deal of time in Italy, so

that will do. We were staying at the same hotel. You recognized me and refreshed my memory of who you are. I was immediately charmed and began a whirlwind courtship that swept you off your feet, and we were married two weeks later."

"Oh, my, that soon?"

"My plan was to not give you enough time to recall all the reasons why you probably shouldn't marry me."

"Smart man," she rejoined with a nod. "But I prefer the simplicity of love conquers all obstacles, so that wouldn't have been an issue. At least, that's what I will tell your father."

"It may not be necessary to say anything to him a'tall."

"Why not?"

"Because he probably won't stay in a room with me longer than it takes him to see me."

"You really think he'll walk away without saying a single word to you?"

"You think he won't, after what he said to Timothy?" he rejoined.

Her expression changed. Good God, was that sympathy for him that she was exhibiting? When she despised him? No, that would be too much of a contradiction. Of course, his situation was pathetic. Anyone with a soft heart might pity him.

"Careful, Maggie," he warned. "You don't want to start liking me."

She scowled at him and pointed a finger toward the door. "You've apprised me of the course you have set in motion, now you can leave. I won't tolerate any more of your insults."

He didn't move. "How the deuce do you perceive an insult in what I just said?"

"To imply that I could like you after everything you have done is an insult to me."

"All that rubbish you've laid at my door, eh?" he replied sardonically. "Half of which I decline responsibility for. But that reminds me, do you still have those two letters from your sister?"

She blinked at the change in subject. "Why?"

"I'd like to look them over," he said. "Do you still have them?"

"Yes, actually." She moved to the writing desk set up in a corner of the room, opened a drawer, and retrieved the letters. "I'm not sure why I kept the first one," she remarked as she returned and handed the letters to him. "It really isn't legible it's so tear-stained. Why do you want to see these?"

"I find it odd, the manner in which she

left. Three years after Giles's death. Three years was ample time to recover from her grief. To up and leave without telling anyone implies a new reason for doing so, not the one you assumed."

"The second letter doesn't suggest that."

"No, but the first might."

She shook her head at him. "Look at it. There's nothing to see."

He did. Practically every word on the page had been smudged or washed away, as if Eleanor had cried buckets while writing it. But as he'd hoped, there were a few letters intact, not many, but he might be able to decipher a word or two if he tried.

"I'll keep these for a bit if you don't mind, to study them."

"If you must. Just remember to return them. Now if you don't mind, the hour is late."

"You know, Maggie," he said, brushing a lock of hair back from her cheek, "you're going to have to pretend to adore me when others are around. You did marry me, after all. Do you need me to help you practice?"

She sputtered, jumping back out of his reach and pointing a finger toward her door again. "I'll manage — somehow. Now get out!"

He shrugged his broad shoulders. "Suit

yourself. But if you change your mind —"

"Out!"

He obliged, though his inclination was to push her a little harder. He wasn't sure what it was about Maggie, but he was surprised to find he enjoyed riling her.

Chapter 15

Margaret had been forced to turn her callers away that day, and there had been a slew of them. Even the dowager duchess had come by for a look at her new husband. The news had traveled fast through the neighborhood, and, according to Florence, everyone was asking who was Henry Raven, where was he from, and how had he won an earl's daughter's hand in marriage? But she refused to lie any more than she had to.

It had stormed through the night and briefly at midmorning. There was a new bank of storm clouds on the horizon late that afternoon. There was no telling which way they'd blow, but she hoped they'd blow back out to sea before reaching shore. Visiting in the rain wasn't just unpleasant, it was in bad taste, putting one's host on the spot to offer accommodations until the weather cleared.

Edgewood wasn't on the cliffs, but it was

close enough that the sea could be seen from its upper floors with an unobstructed view. Margaret had enjoyed those views while she lived there, especially in the early morning when she could watch the sun rise on the water. White Oaks was farther inland, with no view of the coast at all.

Margaret sighed, sitting on the seat across from Sebastian in the coach. "All this subterfuge is quite distasteful," she remarked. "There's still time to reconsider and simply make a clean breast of it."

"The truth isn't always successful. In this case it won't wash a'tall. You said it yourself, Maggie, that my father considers his accidents just that, accidents. If you try to tell him his life is in danger, he'll laugh at you. If he hears it from me, he'll see it as an excuse for me to get back in his good graces. I'm not about to be accused of that, when it bloody well isn't true."

She winced at his new tone, detecting the underlying bitterness in it. She'd heard it before. He usually concealed it, but occasionally it slipped out. Did he really see himself as the condemned innocent in the tragedy he'd set in motion? Or did he despise himself for the chain reaction that followed his dalliance with Juliette?

A crack of thunder accompanied their arrival. Margaret frowned and glanced at the sky as Sebastian helped her from the coach. "We should beg off, come back tomorrow. It's really bad form to call when it's raining."

He raised a brow. "Getting cold feet, Maggie?"

"No," she said with a huff. "But I don't want to muck up their entryway, or have them feel obliged to ask us to stay over due to the weather."

"Your shoes aren't muddy, and you do want an invitation to stay. Kindly keep in mind why you dragged me back to England. I need more than a brief visit to observe what's going on in there and determine if your suspicions are accurate. The weather we've been experiencing these last two days couldn't have been more ideal if I'd ordered it."

Before she could reply, the front door opened. Henry Hobbs, Edgewood's butler, stood there. Oh, dear, another Henry. And Mr. Hobbs wasn't new, he'd been the Edgewood butler for more than thirty years. He was a tall man with a beaked nose and sharp gray eyes. He recognized Sebastian immediately, no doubt about it.

Which was why Margaret quickly announced, "Mr. Hobbs, I believe you know my husband, Sebastian Townshend."

"Husband?" Mr. Hobbs said incredulously, and then he cracked a slight grin. "Very well, we're due for a new storm."

He opened the door wide. Margaret chose to ignore the storm remark as if she didn't know what it implied and asked as she entered, "Is Abigail receiving today?"

"She's in the music room. Lord love her, she thinks she still knows how to play the pianoforte, when she can't see the keys anymore."

The music could be heard now, and indeed it was quite a discordant racket. "And Lord Townshend?"

"Not back from his afternoon ride yet, rather late, actually. I wasn't informed of any detours he had intended to make, but he was aware you were stopping by, so I expect him soon."

"We'll visit with Abbie, then, until Douglas returns."

"Tea, Lady Margaret?"

"That would be pleasant, thank you."

Margaret moved on toward the music room. Sebastian hadn't said a single word yet, but he didn't follow her immediately. Hobbs hadn't walked away to order the tea, either.

Sebastian said quietly, "It's good to see you again, Hobbs."

"And it's very good to see you as well, my lord."

"Bring some brandy with that tea. I have a feeling I'm going to need a stiff drink this afternoon."

Chapter 16

Margaret waited until the last discordant note was played and Abigail put her hands in her lap. Carefully, so she didn't startle her, she said, "Abbie, I've finally returned home. I hope you haven't missed me too much."

It took a moment for Abigail to locate her, standing by the door. She was looking well. Her snow-white hair was worn in a high piled style from the last century, but it went very well with her old-fashioned clothes from the same century. The clothes weren't old, just the style. Many old dames like Abigail scoffed at the new trends that were more suited for young women.

"Is that you, Margaret? What do you mean, miss you? Weren't you here just last week?"

"Well, no, I've been gone four months. To Europe, remember?"

"Ah, yes. Now I recall I did miss you, you

dratted gel. Come here and give us a hug. You know our garden has gone to ruin since you've been gone."

Margaret winced as she complied with the request. Abigail wasn't referring to her trip, but to her move back home. It was a standard statement every time she visited, a not so subtle chiding for abandoning Abbie, which was how the old girl saw Margaret's return to her family home, White Oaks. Abigail's conservatory was doing just fine. Margaret had trained the man hired to take over the care of it herself, before she left.

"I'll have a look before I leave," Margaret said, as she did each time she visited.

"See that you do."

"A look at what?" Sebastian asked as he entered the room.

"Who's that?" Abigail demanded, squinting her amber eyes toward the door.

Margaret gave Sebastian a moment to answer but sighed when he said nothing. And obviously Abigail wasn't going to recognize him when she could barely see him.

"I've married, Abbie," Margaret said.

"Married? Without inviting me to the wedding?"

The hurt tone made Margaret wince yet again. "It happened on the Continent. It was a whirlwind romance," she quickly explained. "There were time constraints, of course, since I was touring and not staying in any one place for very long. So decisions had to be made quickly. But really, it didn't take more'n a few weeks for us to be sure we were well suited for each other."

"She's lying, Abigail," Sebastian put in. "She forced me to follow her across half of Europe before she finally said yes."

Margaret glared at him. For that briefest moment when he said she was lying, she'd thought he was going to make a clean breast of it. Dratted man.

Abigail was still squinting at him and frowning. She finally concluded, "He looks like a rogue. Are you sure he's not here to rob us, Maggie?"

Margaret grinned at Sebastian, "Well . . ."

"Yes, she's sure," Sebastian said in what could almost be called a growl.

"I'll have the silverware put away, just in case," Abigail said.

He rolled his eyes at that point. Margaret was having a hard time not laughing. Some of the things that came out of Abigail's mouth were quite hilarious, because she wasn't joking. She meant them.

But since the old girl still didn't recognize him, Margaret said with a grin, "You might want to have a closer look at this rogue, Abbie. You were the one who suggested I bring him home."

"I did no such thing —"

"I married Sebastian, Abbie."

Abigail's smile came slowly, then turned brilliant. "Is that really you, Sebby?"

Sebastian instantly looked appalled. "Good God, not if you're going to call me that."

Abigail giggled. She actually giggled! And launched herself across the room to hug her long-absent grandson. "Thank the Lord you've returned. I know you can put a stop to these threats to your father's life."

"You don't need to worry about it any further, Grandmother. I'll find out if there's any real threat."

"You see, Maggie?" Abigail crowed. "I told you Sebastian would take care of it."

Margaret wasn't going to mention she was having to pay him to do so when Abigail was so happy that he was home.

"Shall we adjourn to the parlor for this reunion?" Margaret suggested. "Mr. Hobbs is fetching tea."

"Where's my cane?" Abigail demanded.

Margaret retrieved it where it was hooked on the end of the pianoforte, then helped Abigail out of the room. The old girl didn't use the cane very often. In fact, she probably didn't really need it but merely liked having it in hand so she could raise it to make her points, which she frequently did. They were just entering the parlor when Margaret heard . . .

"Good God, what are you doing here?"

It was Denton, Sebastian's brother. His eyes looked a bit bloodshot, but that was nothing new. He often overimbibed and wore the effects of it the next day. His valet took good care of him otherwise, though, for he was impeccably dressed as usual in a soft brown day coat, his cravat tied precisely. Denton never relaxed his dress, even when at home.

In comparison, Sebastian wasn't looking at all roguish today, contrary to Abigail's remark. John had made sure he was looking up to snuff for this family reunion, though Margaret had noticed him tugging at the tightly tied white cravat a time or two and guessed he hadn't worn one in years! Seeing the brothers together, she was reminded of the Sebastian she'd known before his exile. Thankfully, The Raven was absent.

It was Abigail who answered Denton's question. While her hearing wasn't much better than her eyesight these days, Denton's voice had been loud with surprise.

"Sebastian's home, Denton," Abigail said

in delight. "And he has some wonderful news."

"What news?"

"He's married our Maggie!" Abigail exclaimed.

Denton's expression wasn't one of shock, it could more aptly be described as crushed. Margaret groaned. She'd forgotten about Denton's tendre for her, inappropriate as it was. He had a wife, after all, one he didn't like much, but regardless, Margaret had taken a hard stand with Denton as soon as she'd realized that his feelings for her were leaning in the wrong direction.

The feeling certainly wasn't mutual. Although she liked Denton well enough since he was part of her temporary family, she considered him weak. Countless times she'd watched Juliette walk all over him. He might be handsome as sin, even more so than his brother, but she felt no attraction to him whatsoever.

But even Douglas sensed Denton's feelings for her and had remarked once in a melancholy mood that he wished Denton would correct his mistakes and get a proper wife. She'd known he meant her, though she'd remained silent at the time. It was just after she'd told him she was moving back home. She'd been sure he just wanted an excuse to get her to stay in the family. They were very close by then. She'd become like the daughter he'd never had.

"Shall we adjourn to the parlor for explanations?" Margaret suggested. "Tea is on the way."

She didn't wait for the brothers' compliance as she escorted Abigail into the parlor and got her settled in her favorite chair. Sebastian and Denton didn't follow, however, so she left Abigail with the excuse that she'd see what was keeping the tea. She then rushed back out to the hallway and the confrontation that was occurring there.

"Does Father know yet?" Denton was asking.

"No."

"You think this is going to make a difference, don't you?" Denton demanded.

"Actually, I know it won't."

"Is there a problem, Denton?" Margaret asked pointedly as she joined them.

Denton sighed. "I'm having a bit of trouble believing you could marry him, if you must know. He killed your sister's fiancé," he reminded her.

"Ex-fiancé. It's rather hard to dismiss the fact that Giles ended his engagement to my sister when he married your wife — before you did, of course."

Denton flushed with color. So did Margaret, for that matter, for stating that so frankly.

Sebastian intervened. "I didn't give Margaret much choice in the matter."

"I beg your pardon?" Denton said stiffly, obviously misunderstanding his brother's words.

"What he means," Margaret said with a tsk, "is he quite swept me off my feet, not giving me much time to think of anything other than how charming he is."

"Deliberately, m'dear," Sebastian said, bestowing a devilishly suggestive smile on her.

"We met in Italy, Denton," Margaret continued. "We were staying at the same hotel. I couldn't very well ignore him, considering my close association with his family. I'd known him for most of my life, after all. And after we got reacquainted, well, the past seemed just that, far in the past. I got to know the man he is today — quite well."

That brought on another blush. She couldn't believe she'd said that and what it implied. "That is to say," she amended, "I have no regrets that I married him."

"Now that, m'dear, is deserving of a response."

She wasn't expecting Sebastian to pull her into his arms and hug her, but he did just that. A bloody bear hug. Feeling the whole length of him pressed firmly against her shot the color even higher in her cheeks. And there was that odd fluttering in her stomach again. Why did she have to like being held by him?

She tried to get out of his arms, but he just tightened his grip and whispered in her ear, "You're doing wonderfully. Don't muck it up with maidenly airs. I'm going to kiss you now for Denton's benefit. Just play along."

"Wait," she gasped, but he didn't.

It was no brief kiss he gave her. It was absolutely inappropriate for public view, even if their only audience was his brother. With his arms still firmly around her, his lips slanted across hers like hot velvet, so possessive that her will succumbed completely to his. Clear down to her toes she felt that kiss. And good God, the taste of him when his tongue slipped just beyond her lips and pushed against her clenched teeth.

He let her go with a chuckle. She was sure it was because she'd gritted her teeth in her effort to resist what he'd made her feel, and he knew that. It sounded natural, though, that chuckle. And then she realized he'd actually chuckled. What an actor he was! Could he fake any emotion at will like that?

She started to move away from him but suddenly realized that her knees were weak! She clenched all her muscles, closed her eyes, and took a deep breath, pulling herself under control again. When she opened her eyes, she found both men staring at her, and she felt herself blushing again. This just wouldn't do!

"Really, Sebastian, behave yourself in public," she scolded lightly.

"Impossible, m'dear. We're still newly-weds," he said with a grin.

A grin! She was beginning to see why he'd once been called a charmer. His golden eyes gazed at her knowingly, as if they shared some secret, which they did! But that wasn't the impression he was trying to give Denton, she was sure. No, he was being "naughty" for Denton's benefit, to fix in his mind that their marriage was thriving in every way.

Rubbing it in, because Denton's marriage was such a disaster? No, she didn't think he held any grudges against his brother. Then again, how would she know?

None of the Townshends other than Abigail had ever spoken to her about Sebastian. And the one time she had mentioned his name when Denton and Douglas had been present, the atmosphere in the room had turned icy. Definitely a touchy subject, which she'd never broached again. Abigail had talked about him all the time, but nothing relevant, merely reminiscing about his childhood and how much she missed him.

Denton didn't appear to be pleased by anything he'd just heard and witnessed. In fact, he was looking quite angry and making no effort to hide it.

"You should leave, before Father returns," he said in a frosty tone.

Sebastian raised a brow at him. "Why? I haven't come here to be reinstated in the family."

"Then why are you here?"

"To see Grandmother, of course," Sebastian replied. "Ever since Maggie managed to drag me back here, I've been fighting the urge to come see the old girl. And since —"

Sebastian didn't finish. The front door burst open and a frantic fellow rushed in to shout at Denton, "Another accident, m'lord! We found 'im by the side o' the road, lying in a ditch full o' rainwater."

Denton paled. So did Margaret, until she heard Douglas complaining outside the door in an annoyed but weak voice, "Blister it, man, I can walk."

"We tried that, m'lord," someone said. "You bleedin' well toppled over again."

Douglas Townshend didn't get his way and was carried in by two men, one at his feet, the other with a good grasp on his shoulders. He was filthy and wet. And dripping blood from somewhere . . .

"What happened?" Sebastian asked before Margaret could. His tone was deceptively neutral, but she could almost feel the tension pouring off of him.

Douglas replied, his voice just as weak as it had first sounded, though some annoyance was still detected, "Fell off my bloody horse — I suppose." And then looking up directly at Sebastian, he asked, "Who are you?"

Chapter 17

It was as if a gravestone rose up out of the floor right there in the entryway. That was certainly the feeling that Margaret got, so she could just imagine what Sebastian must be feeling, standing there looking at his father who refused even to recognize that he existed anymore. She would have been devastated. He probably was, too, yet not a single inflection crossed his features to show it, his emotions were so well contained.

Sebastian didn't answer, which was probably fortunate. Anything he might have said — "your ex-son, a ghost, your worst nightmare" — would undoubtedly have sounded sarcastic or chilling.

The tension was killing her, so she began, "Douglas," only to be cut off.

"Is that you, Maggie?" Douglas asked.

Margaret was too incredulous to answer for a moment. He didn't recognize her? Then he hadn't recognized Sebastian either!

"I'm seeing two of you," Douglas said haltingly, "and you're a bit blurry around the edges."

Before she could reply, the fellow who'd rushed in with news of the accident whispered at her side, " 'E's burning up with fever, m'lady. Ye can feel the 'eat pouring off o' 'im."

Margaret nodded. She was rather good in emergencies and didn't hesitate to direct the men carrying Douglas toward the stairs. Walking next to them, she assured Douglas, "Yes, I'm Maggie."

"Thought so," he replied so softly she barely heard him. His voice was getting weaker. "You'll stay? Want to hear all about your trip and the fellow who managed to win your heart."

"Certain—"

She didn't finish. His head fell back against the man carrying him. He'd fainted.

"He did that twice on the way here," she heard from one of the men carrying him, detecting a slight French accent. "The monsieur, he's not staying awake long. Likely the fever," the fellow added when Margaret stared at the blood dripping under Douglas.

"Someone send for the doctor, please."

"Already sent for, m'lady," the other man

carrying Douglas quickly assured her. " 'E should be 'ere shortly."

With no more orders to give, her hands began to tremble. Douglas's fever worried her, but his bleeding frightened her. It wasn't a steady stream, but it was definitely leaving a trail behind him. And until she knew the extent of that wound, she wouldn't rest easy. She followed the men upstairs to help get Douglas settled.

The blood concerned Sebastian as well. As soon as Margaret was out of hearing range, he turned to the remaining man, the one who'd announced the accident. He caught sight of Denton, though, which gave him pause.

His brother was also staring at the trail of blood on the floor and looking quite horrified. He didn't recall Denton's being squeamish at the sight of blood. While that could account for his pallor, Sebastian didn't think so. Denton had gone as pale as a ghost the moment he'd learned of the accident. He almost looked as if he were in shock.

"Snap out of it," he told his brother a bit harshly. "Go see that water gets heated and sent upstairs. Bandages as well. And send up a few more men to help get Father out of those wet clothes."

Denton finally glanced at him, nodded, and hurried off toward the kitchen.

Alone with the remaining fellow, Sebastian gave him his full attention. Not surprisingly, the man took a few steps back from him. Sebastian was used to that. When The Raven appeared, all other birds flew away, so to speak. Not that he wanted to frighten the man. He'd simply lost his knack for putting people at ease.

"What's your name? And who found my father?"

"Yer the disowned son? The one that — ?"

The man didn't finish and took yet another step back. He wasn't just looking wary now, but downright frightened. Sebastian sighed.

"Yes, him. Now you are?"

"Robert Cantel, m'lord. I've been gardening 'ere for five years now. We moved to the west section o' the grounds about mid-afternoon, to do the trimming there. We work in groups. Couldn't see yer father so far away there in the ditch, but could make out 'is 'orse standing there alone through the trees."

"Where exactly was this?"

"Where the property butts up against White Oaks land, by the edge o' the road leading into Edgeford Town. Figured 'e was either coming or going from Edgeford when he took the fall and landed in the ditch."

"Where's he bleeding from?" Sebastian asked.

"Nasty gash on the back o' 'is 'ead. Turned the water in the ditch all pink, it did."

"So he lost a lot of it?"

"Looks to be."

"I'd like you to show me exactly where he was found."

Robert glanced up the stairs first, as if hoping one of his companions would appear so he could pawn off the task. Sebastian usually had the patience to deal with the fear he inspired, but not today.

"Now."

The threat wasn't in his tone. He'd said the word quite softly. It was definitely in his expression, which promised mayhem if the fellow didn't start moving immediately. Fear shot the man out the door. He barely glanced back to make sure Sebastian was following.

Sebastian knew the general location the gardener had mentioned. It was about a ten-minute walk, which didn't warrant getting a horse from the stables. He could have let Robert go about his business, but he wanted to be sure of the exact spot. And he might have more questions and didn't want to have to chase the man down later to answer them.

Exactly where Douglas had taken his fall was obvious, though. The rainwater was puddled in the ditch that ran alongside the road, about four inches deep. Sebastian could see evidence of the blood, which hadn't been completely diluted yet.

There were trees along that stretch of the road, on both sides, all the way up to Edgewood at the end. Many branches crossed the road, shading it. There was also a narrow woods along this western edge of the property that stretched around to the thicker woods to the north — where The Dueling Rock was located.

Sebastian abruptly pulled himself away from that thought. It was reputed that Edgewood as well as the old village of Edgeford that had long ago been attached to it got their names from this stretch of woods. The Townshends had owned the village back then. They still owned most of the land the town of Edgeford sat on.

The old tree closest to where Douglas had fallen did have some lower branches behind it and one on the side. None of them were close enough to the road to obstruct passage, but a couple bent low enough to

180

the ground that if Douglas's horse had veered off the road for some reason, Douglas could have been knocked out of the saddle by the branch near the ditch and then rolled down into it.

He examined the area closely, the slope from the road to the ditch and the puddle. There were many footprints, but those probably belonged to the men who'd found Douglas. If there had been any hoofprints going in that direction, the evidence had been trampled away by the rescue party. The cause of Douglas's head injury was evident, a jagged rock just barely sticking out of the water, big enough to do damage if Douglas's head had hit it directly.

Having examined the scene, Sebastian was satisfied that his father's injury had been an accident. Which didn't mean someone hadn't been there to cause the accident. Only Douglas would be able to rule out that possibility, so no firm conclusion could be drawn until his father regained consciousness long enough to talk.

Chapter 18

Douglas did indeed have a nasty gash on the back of his head. Four stitches had been required, an extra one due to the swelling. Thankfully, he hadn't woken up for the plying of that needle.

Dr. Culden was less concerned about the wound than the fever that caused Douglas to keep passing out. Culden, who was gentry by birth, had become a doctor by choice. He knew them all personally and had been Margaret's doctor since she was a child.

By all accounts, it appeared that Douglas had lain unconscious in that cold puddle of water for close to an hour. Dr. Culden couldn't determine whether the fever was from an infection or a chill he'd caught from the water. The current fear was that he would slip into a state from which he wouldn't awaken.

"I've seen it before," Dr. Culden told Margaret before he left. "Not often, surely, but I had one patient who didn't wake up for three weeks, and another who never woke up."

"Never?"

"Died, that poor woman."

"From lack of nourishment?" Margaret asked.

"No, we forced hearty liquids down her throat with a funnel, but it wasn't enough. Just wasted away eventually, about a year later. Head wound caused it."

Margaret shouldn't have asked. Good God, how ghastly, and just what she didn't need to hear at that point. That wasn't going to happen to Douglas. She wouldn't allow it.

"Now, I don't mean to alarm you, Margaret. Douglas is a strong, healthy man. I'm sure he'll come to," he continued. "He's been weakened by the blood loss. That alone could account for his passing out. We'll likely know more about his condition by this evening. I'll return tonight."

"Thank you."

"He'll need constant attention for the time being, though. Station one of the maids at his bedside. If he wakes up and tries to get out of bed, he could fall and injure himself further. And when he does wake, if I know Douglas and I do, he won't want to stay in bed. But he must. You're probably the only one he'll listen to, Margaret. I hope you're staying here for the duration?"

"Well, I — certainly, if you think it's necessary."

"I do."

He gave her further instructions on how to deal with the fever, commonsense things she already knew. With Douglas settled for the moment, she went in search of Abigail. She had to be apprised of the situation, if Denton hadn't already told her. He probably hadn't. He didn't like delivering bad news. Neither did she, but someone had to.

Abbie was no longer in the parlor, though the evidence was there that she'd had tea. She was probably quite put out that Margaret and Sebastian hadn't returned to visit with her. Then again, she might have forgotten all about it by now.

Margaret was told Abigail had gone up to her room to prepare for dinner. To take a nap was more likely. So Margaret knocked softly on the door in case she was sleeping.

"Come in!" she heard from the other side.

She did. Abigail was at her desk, using a looking glass to try and make out the words in a letter she'd received.

"I thought you might be sleeping," Margaret began.

"I don't take afternoon naps anymore. Sleeping my life away is not a good idea at my age."

Margaret would have grinned if she weren't so worried. Abigail might think she had given up napping, but in fact she nodded off quite often while sitting in a chair, then refused to admit she'd fallen asleep when she was woken. Just resting her eyes was her usual excuse. Everyone was kind enough not to mention the snoring.

"We need to talk, Abbie," Margaret said and pulled up a chair near the desk.

"Splendid. You know I love chatting with you, m'dear, and we've time for a nice long one before dinner."

"I'm afraid I have some bad news. Douglas had an accident."

"Thank goodness Sebastian is home now! He'll take care of it."

"Well, this one has had a serious consequence — no, no, he's all right," she quickly added when some of the color drained from Abigail's face. "But he's got a very high fever."

Abigail frowned. "He's had fevers before. Everyone gets the fevers, gel."

"But Dr. Culden isn't sure what's causing

this one yet. Douglas took a bad fall and gashed his head. But worse, he landed in a puddle of water, and who knows how long he lay there. The water probably wasn't frigid, but there's definitely a chill wind out there today with the rain we've been having."

"You're implying something. Don't beat around the bush, gel. Spit it out."

"This may not be a simple fever. He's been unable to stay awake for more than a few minutes. He keeps passing out. And his vision was blurred, seriously blurred. He didn't recognize me at first. And he didn't recognize Sebastian at all."

"Deliberately, d'you think?"

"Well, that's certainly possible, but I really don't think so."

Abigail humphed. "Which doesn't mean that foolish boy of mine will talk to Sebby when he does recognize him."

Margaret was familiar with the nickname that only Abigail used for Sebastian, yet it was still jarring to hear it again, now that she knew the man. Sebastian Townshend was definitely not a Sebby anymore.

"Which reminds me," Abigail continued. "Is Sebby back yet? I couldn't find him any-where earlier and I still have so much to talk to him about."

"I'm sure he is —" Margaret paused

when Abigail stood up and headed toward the door. "Wait a minute, Abbie. What about Douglas? He's going to need constant attention for a few days, and distraction once he wakes, to keep him in bed. The doctor was adamant about that. He must remain in bed."

"And?"

Margaret hesitated a moment, but it wasn't the first time she had tried to mend the breach between mother and son. And this time she had a better reason for it.

"I think it would do him a world of good if you would visit him during his convalescence and actually speak to him, after he wakes, of course. Nothing to upset him, mind you."

"Yes, yes, I suppose I can call a temporary truce and talk to that fool again — for now."

Margaret hadn't expected such easy compliance. But Abigail's impatience was obvious. She probably would have agreed to anything just to end the conversation so she could go find Sebastian.

"That's splendid, Abbie! We won't want to upset him, though. Just trivial subjects. Nothing unpleasant."

"You must be joking, gel. What other subjects are there around here but unpleasant ones?"

Chapter 19

Sebastian was about to introduce one of those unpleasant subjects to his brother right about then. Denton hadn't been around after he returned from examining the site of the accident. He'd come back for the doctor's evaluation, though, and before he could make himself scarce again, Sebastian put an arm around his shoulder and steered him outside where they could talk without interruption.

"Why do I feel as if I'm being forced to have a conversation with you, Sebastian?" Denton asked, staring pointedly at the hand still on his shoulder.

"Because you are."

"You can bloody well let go of me now," Denton replied stiffly.

"I was joking," Sebastian said, releasing him when they reached the old tree on the side of the house where they'd made that tree house so long ago.

"Sure you were," Denton said curtly. "Gone all this time, but you haven't changed, have you? And where did you go? How many times I thought I'd see you in London, but I never did. Did you actually leave the country?"

"Yes, and I had no intention of ever coming back. I've been living on the Continent, no place in particular, really. I travel a lot, since my jobs tend to take me to all corners of Europe."

"Jobs? You actually work for a living?"

Sebastian had to laugh at Denton's appalled look, a typical reaction of the privileged gentry. "What did you think I was going to do to survive when I left here with nothing?"

Denton flushed with color. "I assumed, well, actually, I didn't assume anything, but I certainly didn't think you'd be taking on common jobs."

"There's nothing common about what I do. People pay me a lot of money to accomplish what they can't manage to do on their own."

"Such as?"

Sebastian shrugged. "Retrieving stolen valuables, righting wrongs, resolving differences, extracting innocents from incarceration. A little of this and that. I've become

189

what you might call a mercenary. Now it's your turn. Your attitude is rather defensive for a reunion, Denton. Why is that?"

Denton raked a hand through his black hair. There were actually a few gray hairs at his temples, which were not really noticeable unless you were looking closely. His amber eyes were bloodshot, which was very noticeable, and had dark circles under them. Denton's eyes had never been quite as bright as Sebastian's, more on the brown side. His skin was pale, too pale, as if he rarely went outdoors. There was a small scar on his cheek, another on his brow, neither of which had been there the last time Sebastian had seen him. All in all, Denton looked too dissipated by half, exhausted, like a man who overindulged his vices too frequently. He was a year younger than Sebastian, yet he actually looked like the elder brother now.

Denton finally sighed. "It's just a shock, seeing you again. I never expected to."

"Neither did I expect to see you again," Sebastian said. Then offhandedly he added, "I find I've missed you."

"Liar," Denton almost snarled. "You never had time for me. We were never close."

"I know. I'm sorry for that," Sebastian

said sincerely. "But you weren't easy to get close to. You built your resentments too early."

"Why in the bloody hell are you bringing that up? It's done, under the bridge, as it were. You can't change the past, Seb."

"I suppose not," Sebastian agreed. "But if that's not causing your defensiveness, what is?"

Denton appeared incredulous. "Good God, you show up. That's enough right there by itself, ain't it? But then Father has to be carried in the house, hurt so bad he can't even see straight. And Maggie married you. I still can't believe that. You fall in the pigsty and still come out smelling like a bloody rose, don't you? I'm having a hard time assimilating it all, and I was already a nervous wreck before you even got here. So what the hell did you expect, a laugh and a hug?"

"I didn't expect to find that you're in love with my wife, or married to Giles's wife," Sebastian said in a hard tone. "Where is that jade, anyway?"

Denton blanched at his bluntness but said, "Don't come home after eleven years and start making assumptions, when you know nothing about what's gone on here."

"Then why don't you tell me, and start

with how you ended up married to the adulteress who instigated the duel that wrecked my life?"

"She didn't instigate anything," Denton said. "She swore that you —"

"She lied," Sebastian cut in.

"Be that as it may, you weren't here to say otherwise, and she managed to convince me at the time. She was lonely and depressed living with Cecil, who was totally shattered after Giles's death. I had begun visiting her to cheer her up."

"It took marriage to cheer her up, I suppose?"

Denton blushed. "No, I was just going to set her up as my mistress, and did, but — things happen. She was enceinte."

Sebastian raised a brow, actually surprised. "You have a child?"

Denton's complexion reddened even more vividly. "No, she lost it."

"Of course," Sebastian said dryly.

Denton glared at him. "That was my own response, if you must know. But I've made my bed. I'm dealing with it as best I can."

Which didn't seem to be at all, Sebastian concluded, but he'd been harsh enough, so didn't say so. "You mentioned already being a nervous wreck. Why?"

Denton sighed. "Because Juliette is in

London shopping. Happens every time she goes. She spends atrocious amounts of money when she's there, frivolously. Father goes through the roof when he gets the bills."

"Then why don't you go with her to put a curb on her extravagance?"

"Because when I do, we end up causing a scene that titillates the gossips for months. Father objects to that even more."

"One of your fights?"

"I see Maggie has filled you in."

"Hardly. She didn't say what you fight about."

"The question should be what we don't fight about. That list would be much shorter."

Sebastian shook his head. He was having a hard time grasping all the implications Denton's attitude raised. He'd expected, under the circumstances, for Denton at least to profess an undying love for his wife, his excuse for keeping her. But apparently no one liked Juliette, not even her husband. So why were they still married?

He didn't really expect an answer, but he asked anyway, "Why haven't you divorced her?"

Denton exploded vehemently, "Good God, after eleven years you come home with a flimsy excuse and immediately start stirring the pot. Well, I've news for you. My wife and I are none of your bloody business."

"I disagree," Sebastian said darkly. "Your wife caused me to kill my best friend and lose the life I'd known up to that point."

He hadn't meant to show the new side of him, at least not to his brother. But he could tell by Denton's brief look of wariness that he just had.

He shook off the air of menace he could so easily assume and even offered somewhat of a smile. He said mildly, "I debated on letting Maggie come home a'tall. Her place is with me now, and my place isn't here. But I've missed Abbie. I wanted this chance to see her again before it's too late. Her advanced age puts a narrow window on that opportunity. If you want to call that a flimsy reason, so be it."

Abashed, Denton said, "Sorry. It appears you'll have plenty of time to visit with Grandmother now. Are you going to stay until Father recovers? Culden wants Maggie to play nurse. Figures Father will at least listen to her about remaining in bed till he's better."

"I haven't thought that far ahead. I expected to have to fight my way in to see

Abbie. I didn't expect Father to be so delirious he didn't even recognize me."

"Rather a stroke of . . ."

Denton didn't finish, causing Sebastian to laugh shortly. "Bad luck? Well, I doubt I'll be here long in any case. When do you expect your wife back?"

"In a few days, possibly the end of the week." Then suspiciously, "Why?"

Sebastian shrugged offhandedly. "I may leave before then. I'm not sure I can come face-to-face with that woman again — without killing her."

"That's nothing to joke about, Seb."

"I wasn't joking," Sebastian said simply. "By the by, what happened to your leg to cause a limp?"

Whether it was his remark about his wife or the mention of the limp, Denton walked away without answering. Sebastian let him go. They both had enough to think about for the moment.

Chapter 20

Edna arrived late that afternoon with several of Margaret's trunks full of clothes. Apparently Sebastian had sent word that they would be staying at Edgewood for a while. Margaret had been given her old room. It was a large room, much more space than she needed, but having spent four years in it during her stay here, she felt quite comfortable and at home there.

She had time to change clothes before dinner. Most of her wardrobe was in the pale pastels of maidenhood that were popular among young debutantes, but she did own a few gowns in more mature colors, which she wore at home when she wasn't expecting company. Now that she was "married," it would be appropriate to wear the darker colors. She actually preferred them, since most dark colors seemed to make her hair appear a lighter, more fashionable shade. Her hair was certainly not her best feature. Blonde was fashionable. Sandy brown was nondescript.

Edna knew her well and had packed all of those darker shades for her stay at Edgewood, including several that were appropriate for dinner. Margaret chose a deep sapphire blue gown, fashionably low cut with tiny puffs off the shoulders and tight sleeves to the wrists. She hadn't particularly cared for the waistless empire style the French had made so popular during Napoleon's reign and had been glad to see the return of tight waists and shapely skirts. Her tiny waist was one of her best features, after all, but she'd rarely gotten to show that off until the fashions had recently changed. She had Edna leave a few tendrils of hair curled and dangling to her shoulders. Contrasted with the deep blue of the gown, they appeared almost blonde in the bright lamplight.

"And where will your husband be sleeping while you're here?" Edna wanted to know.

Margaret noted the disapproval in her maid's voice but kept her answer light, replying, "Wherever he used to sleep, I imagine. They've given me my old room here, I'm sure they did the same for him. Married couples in our circles don't usually share the same room. You know that."

Edna humphed. "Just be careful in this charade you're playing, Maggie. Don't let that man take any liberties that he wouldn't otherwise be allowed, just because you're pretending to be married to him."

"You worry too much," Margaret replied. "He's here to find out what's really going on, no more than that. And he knows I don't really like him. I was quite frank with him about that."

"Good. That should keep him from getting any inappropriate ideas."

Margaret might have agreed, if Sebastian hadn't kissed her for Denton's benefit earlier, but she wasn't about to mention that to Edna.

Margaret rushed through the rest of her preparations, wanting to check on Douglas again before she went downstairs. He still hadn't woken up again. That was starting to worry her, but she'd wait and see what Dr. Culden had to say about it when he returned. Douglas's fever seemed no higher, but then it had been very high to begin with and still was. The two maids she had set to take turns sitting with him were to summon her immediately when he woke, no matter the hour. Until he did wake, she wouldn't be able to get Dr. Culden's "worse" complication out of her mind.

She hadn't seen Sebastian again after the doctor left earlier. He was waiting for her, though, at the bottom of the stairs. The way his eyes moved over her as she descended made her feel quite self-conscious. Usually when a man looked at her like that she felt nothing out of the ordinary. When Sebastian did it she felt far too much.

"You look lovely, m'dear."

"There's no need to begin the performance until you have an audience," she huffed.

She started to pass him. His hand caught her arm and pulled her back against his chest. His words fell by her ear.

"I trust you'll do better with your performance once we have an audience?"

"Actually," she said with a smile, "I've decided that you're due a bit of tartness for embarrassing me with that kiss in the hallway. You know very well that was inappropriate, no matter the reason."

"Kindly remember that we're still newlyweds."

"And what has that to do with holding grudges?" she demanded.

"Everything, m'dear," he replied. "As a recent bride, you would be much too interested in lovemaking to hold them for very long."

She gasped and started to sputter, but she snapped her mouth shut when she noticed his grin. He was grinning again! This house was having an odd effect on him, she decided.

With a huff, she jerked her arm back from him and entered the dining room. Denton and Abigail were already there, and Abigail wasn't looking too happy.

The very moment she noticed Margaret she said, "I've a bone to pick with you, gel. Sebastian wasn't downstairs like you said. I searched all over, couldn't find —"

"I'm right here, Grandmother," Sebastian cut in as he followed Margaret into the room.

"Thank goodness! I was beginning to think I imagined your return, Sebby."

Abigail patted the seat of the chair beside her. Sebastian obliged, though he sighed when his grandmother used that nickname again. Margaret took the seat next to Denton farther down the table while grandmother and grandson got reacquainted.

Her anger had been on the rise with that "newlywed" remark, sure that Sebastian was going to use that excuse to his advantage, not hers. But hearing him sigh over his childhood name did temper that considerably. She couldn't help but smile as she remembered the appalled look on his face when Abigail had called him Sebby.

Margaret noticed that Denton was wearing quite a dour expression as he watched his brother. "Buck up, Denton," she said. "Don't begrudge him this reunion."

"I don't. It's actually good to see him again. Never thought I would feel this way, you know. And — well, never thought I'd say this either, but I've missed him. We may not have been the best of chums, but Sebastian was always there if help was needed, if you know what I mean."

"You could depend on him?"

"Exactly."

"Then why the gloomy look?"

He rolled his eyes. "You have to ask? I still can't believe you married him. Him of all people."

"I never would have imagined it m'self," she agreed. "And if you must know, I didn't warm to him immediately when we met in Italy. But he was a familiar face from home, so I was loath to give him the cold shoulder completely."

"You would have?"

"Certainly."

"Because Father disowned him?"

"Oh, no, not a'tall. Because my sister

would still be here, alive, if Sebastian hadn't killed Giles."

"Ah, a deeper grudge than I thought. And yet you married him anyway."

Hearing it put that way, Margaret winced. "Well, he's still the charming man he used to be." She almost choked over that lie, but it did get her point across. "I fell in love with the new him, not the old him. It's bloody hard to differentiate between the two now."

Denton shook his head sadly. "You know I'd hoped —"

Margaret quickly cut him off with the warning, "Don't say something you'll later regret." Her tone had been rather sharp. She curbed it with a smile and patted his hand. "I find I'm pleased to be part of this family again. You know I love Douglas and Abbie. I'm even fond of you. It worries me now that I may not be welcome a'tall when Douglas recovers and finds out Sebastian is here and that I've wed him. We'll have to wait and see."

"Nonsense. You know my father thinks of you as the daughter he never had. He's not going to blame you for succumbing to Seb's charm. Just the opposite will be more like it. Another mark against my brother, as it were."

Margaret sighed. She hadn't thought of that. Not that it mattered, when Sebastian had no intention of staying in England after he finished the job she'd brought him here to do. It still amazed her that Douglas had had yet another accident, and right when she returned home.

"There weren't any other accidents while I was in Europe, were there?" she asked.

"Now that you mention it, there was one. Father fell out of bed."

"What?!"

She said it too loud, drawing Sebastian's attention. She shook her head just the tiniest bit, to let him know it was nothing to be concerned about, then turned her attention back to Denton. "You were joking, right?"

"Perhaps I phrased it wrong, but no. He got out of bed, twisted his foot, and fell to the side. Scraped his back up pretty good on the bed frame. And his ankle was sprained for a couple weeks. He blamed it on the rug by his bed, that it was bunched up and he put his foot down on it wrong."

"I see."

That really did sound like only clumsiness on Douglas's part. She simply couldn't imagine anyone sneaking into his room to make a mess of his rug in the hopes he'd fall and hurt himself. That was far too far-fetched — or the plan of someone who wasn't quite right in the head anymore.

With Douglas absent, Margaret rearranged the seating so that they were all seated together at Abigail's end of the table.

Sebastian seemed to be on his best behavior, no doubt for Abigail's sake. But what a contrast! He wasn't pulling out any long-bladed daggers here as he'd done at her dining table. No indeed. Here he looked every bit the aristocrat, at ease, and so bloody handsome it really was hard to keep her eyes off of him.

But for a family reunion, he did more asking than answering, despite everyone's avid curiosity about what he'd been up to these last eleven years. It was amazing how he could speak of his life in Europe and reveal only a little of what he'd done there. The man was as inscrutable as his expression usually was. She'd been hoping she'd learn a thing or two about him, but in fact she probably knew more about him now than his family did.

But while he said little of consequence about himself, he listened raptly to every word his brother and grandmother said. And he watched them and the servants keenly. Margaret reminded herself that he was just doing the job she'd hired him to do, trying to figure out who wanted Douglas dead. Though the odd link in the chain hadn't made an appearance yet. It was certainly going to be interesting to see what transpired when Juliette returned home — and when Douglas woke up.

Chapter 21

Abigail retired shortly after dinner. Sebastian disappeared as well, Margaret hoped to do the job she was paying him for, well, *would be* paying him for. Finding herself alone after Dr. Culden's second visit, which left her with no better news about Douglas's condition, Margaret chose to retire early as well.

It had been quite an eventful day, much more taxing than she'd expected. Trying to juggle the truth with the lies she and Sebastian had concocted in order to carry out their performance without making any mistakes had exhausted her mentally, if not physically.

A hot steamy bath was in order! Edna arranged it before she retired to the room she and Oliver had been given in the servants' quarters. Edgewood had plumbing, but like White Oaks and most households, the pipes didn't reach the upper floors, so water still had to be heated in the kitchen and carried upstairs. Margaret's room did have a small separate room for bathing, or bathroom, as it was gaining popularity in being called, with a nice porcelain tub, which she put to good use that night.

She was just about to nod off, she was so comfortable in the tub, when she heard, "I was hoping you'd be asleep by now so we wouldn't have to have this conversation."

Her eyes flew open. She sank down as low as she could go in the tub to hide. She simply couldn't believe that Sebastian was standing in her doorway and said so. "I don't believe this!"

She hadn't closed the door. She hadn't needed to, since the bedroom door was closed. No one should have entered without knocking, especially him.

"Did I forget to mention we're sharing this room? You know, just like we're married." His tone was excessively dry, as if she'd forgotten their pretense.

"Not all married couples share bedrooms," she replied tartly. "Surely you know that. And we fall into the it's-not-going-to-happen category!"

He sighed. "As I said, I really was hoping this conversation could wait until morning, but if you insist —"

"Just leave, Sebastian. We can discuss this any time but now."

"Well, no, it obviously must be now, since I'm not leaving."

She poked her head over the rim of the tub just enough to see him. "What d'you mean you're not leaving? We have enacted a pretense. That does not give you liberties that would otherwise be denied you. This is not going to work!"

"Be quiet, Maggie. It will work. If you'd put aside your maidenly modesty for a moment and just think about it, how better to keep any doubts about our marriage from arising than by our sleeping in the same room, with the whole household aware of it?"

"This is not going to work!"

"Be quiet, Maggie," he said again. "Separate bedrooms would be fine at your house, not that I would allow them if we were really married, of course —"

"Allow?!" she cut in.

"But everyone here knows we're just guests for the duration," he continued, ignoring her outrage, "that we have no intention of staying long — except my father, who isn't even aware yet that I'm here."

Margaret wasn't going to discuss that either at the moment. She could see his golden gaze trying to make out her shape beneath the bathwater. "For the last time, get out of my bathroom! If we must discuss the sleeping arrangements now, you will kindly let me finish my bath first."

"Kindly?" He started to laugh. "Don't believe I'm capable of that anymore, Maggie. But if it will expedite this discussion —" He turned to leave, then turned back again, his intense golden eyes meeting hers. "You have magnificent breasts, Maggie."

Before she could scream, he closed the door, with himself on the other side of it. Margaret spared a moment to make sure it was going to stay closed, then flew out of the tub. She didn't waste time drying off. She wanted her body covered right away. The pink robe would have to suffice, since she'd left her clothes in the bedroom.

With her robe belted tightly around her waist, she was still somewhat trembling from her outrage. She leaned against the door for a moment, took several deep breaths. He was impossible. How could he make that remark about her breasts? She didn't know how to deal with a man who did and said whatever he pleased. He'd lived alone too long, she feared, away from polite society. He'd forgotten how to behave around a lady. Or he simply didn't care. That was more likely.

She wasn't actually calm yet, but her heart had stopped pounding, so she took one more deep breath and opened the door. She was hoping, she really was, that he'd dredged up some semblance of decency and wouldn't be waiting for her in her bedroom to finish a discussion that they shouldn't *even* be having in the first place. It was a foolish hope.

Sebastian was stretched out on the chaise longue, a fancy piece in soft blue and green quilted silk. It was designed for someone to sit on with her back against the high end and her legs stretched out comfortably, as she enjoyed a good book. It was designed for a woman to do that. She doubted Sebastian's legs would fit even if he weren't now almost lying prone on it, his calves off the end, his feet on the floor.

Both his arms were crossed behind his head. He looked entirely too much "at home," with no intention of leaving. She was determined to put a dent in his current satisfied expression.

She marched over to the chaise, crossed her arms over her chest, and said matter-of-factly, "Did I mention this isn't going to work? Your spending the night here? Don't interrupt me," she snapped when he opened his mouth. "We are pretending a marriage.

We can bloody well pretend you've spent the night in here as well."

He actually appeared to give that some thought, but then he shook his head. "That won't wash, m'dear. Too many servants passing along the corridor out there. One's bound to see me sneaking in and out."

"Rubbish. That is the impression you are striving for, that you have access here at any hour."

"Yes, but not if I'm leaving at night and entering in the morning. Besides, if I'm known to be sleeping here, I won't be given a separate bedroom, will I? So where would you suggest I sleep?"

"Do you really need to ask?" she asked with a tight little smile.

He gave a short bark of laughter. "Sorry, but stables and kennels don't agree with me."

"You aren't being reasonable, Sebastian."

He came off the chaise quickly in one fluid movement. She wasn't sure how he did it, but he was suddenly standing there, towering over her, much, much too close. Nor did he let her get out of his way. He put both his hands on her shoulders, pinning her to the spot.

"Let me put this another way," he said, his tone turned husky. "If you continue to stand here arguing with me, which I believe I mentioned before I find quite stimulating, I'll be sharing that bed with you. I'd wager after a few moments of my persuasion you'd stop arguing about the sleeping arrangements and be involved in something much more pleasurable. So I would suggest that you take this opportunity, while I still have some meager control over the lust you inspire in me, to get your delectable body under those covers over there and out of my sight."

He let go of her so she could do just that. She didn't hesitate, she raced to the bed. But she did pause there to glare back at him.

"You've lost all semblance of sanity," she began, only to be cut off.

"Maggie, don't tempt me," he growled.

She dove under the covers, pulled them up to her chin. Her heart was racing again, her arms and legs trembling. It took nearly ten minutes and the silence that followed for her finally to calm down.

He had possibly waited for just that before he said all too casually, "I'll sleep here on the chaise tonight, but if I wake up in the morning with a stiff neck, we'll be taking turns here."

Margaret shot out of the bed, yanked off the thick bedspread, and tossed it on the floor across the room. It landed rather neatly spread out, she noticed, before she dove back under the sheets she had left to her.

"There," she said huffily, pointing out, "I believe John mentioned to me, when we were discussing the accommodations on the ship, that you both frequently had to sleep on the ground during your travels."

"Not on the floor of a bedroom," he corrected. "But — you're quite right, that will probably do much better. A pillow?"

"Certainly," she replied primly and tossed one in the direction of the spread. "Anything else?"

"Good God, don't ask such a leading question!" he barked at her.

She blushed and refused to watch him cross over to his new bed on the floor. He said no more. And sometime in the middle of the night, before she finally succumbed to sleep, she realized that he'd managed to end their argument about his sharing her room rather abruptly with his threat of lovemaking. Odious man. She had no doubt that had been his exact intention.

He'd be hearing what she thought about that — but tomorrow. Tonight, she was just thankful he wasn't saying anything else that flayed her senses with more excitement than she could handle.

Chapter 22

Margaret stretched, yawned, and sat up on the edge of her bed. She started to get up, then sat back down and didn't move another muscle as her eyes fell on the man lying on the floor not ten feet away from her.

Sebastian had rolled himself up in the thick bedspread she'd sacrificed for his use. She'd have to tell Edna to find some extra bedding for him — no, what was she thinking? He couldn't stay in her room another night. They were going to have that conversation again, and this time she would have the last word on the subject of sleeping arrangements.

He was lying on his side, still sleeping, one arm outside the cover. Her eyes followed that arm up to his shoulder before she realized both were bare. He'd removed his coat and shirt! She noticed them on the seat of the chair nearest him, quite rumpled now, as if he'd just tossed them there. And what was that with them? Oh, good God, he'd removed his britches too! This was intolerable. It was bad enough he was even in the room, but without his clothes on?!

Margaret shot across the room to her bureau, snatched undergarments and stockings out of the drawers with barely a glance, grabbed a morning dress from her wardrobe, and ran straight to the bathroom. With the door closed behind her, she took a few moments to regain her composure, then quickly dressed for the day.

Well, that didn't work very well. She couldn't reach all the bloody buttons on the back of her dress and she was wearing two stockings that didn't match. She poked her head outside the door to make sure Sebastian was still sleeping, then rushed to grab a shawl and her shoes. She'd have to wait until later when Sebastian was gone to change her stockings.

She'd just reached the bedroom door to make her escape when she heard, "Open it and I guarantee you will be scandalized when I make the effort to stop you."

Margaret dropped her forehead against the door and groaned. She understood the threat. But he was all the way across the room. Surely she could get out of there before he reached her. And then chase her

215

down the corridor? Bloody hell. She wouldn't put that past him.

Angry now that he was being utterly unreasonable again in trying to keep her there, she turned about to blast him with a piece of her mind and lost every thought.

He was standing there with his pants back on, thank God, but still no shirt, stockings, or shoes. The expanse of his chest was amazing. He had seemed to be a prime specimen under his clothes, but without them, it was confirmed without a doubt. A Corinthian body, firm muscles, not a speck of excess flesh. A thin mat of dark hair across his chest that didn't travel much lower than that. Tight, firm waist that led to narrow hips before his very long legs began. Thick bunches of muscles in his thighs rippled and smoothed out with each movement he made.

His long black hair had come undone from the tight knot where it was usually contained at his nape. It spread across his shoulders and back. Even when he tossed some of it back with one hand, it fell back to annoy him. He looked quite wild. He looked so handsome she could barely breathe.

She searched frantically for the anger she'd so justifiably felt toward him last night, found it, but still couldn't open her mouth while he was standing there half naked. So she crossed to her bureau to find a pair of stockings that matched, praying he'd be finished dressing by the time she faced him again.

He was, mostly. His shirt on, at least half fastened and tucked into his pants, he was sitting in the chair now putting on his shoes. His hair was still in wild disarray, though, and he simply looked so different like that! Not so in control, certainly not so sinister. She had a brief urge to help him with his hair. Actually, she just wanted to touch it, it looked so soft.

"You need a barber," she said curtly.

"I need a drink," he shot back, then pinned her with his golden eyes. "That was quite possibly the worst night of hell I've ever experienced."

"Muscles aching from the hard floor?" she smirked.

"No, Maggie, aching for you."

Her mouth dropped open. The fluttering in her belly that his words caused actually felt — pleasant. But she forgot to breathe again. What a horrid habit that was starting to be. She swung around, gulped in a deep breath, started to head to the bed to sit down to change her stockings, but quickly vetoed that idea and moved to the chaise longue instead.

By the time she had her own shoes on and stood up to glance at Sebastian, he had finished dressing as well, even had his hair clubbed back again. Much better. At least he looked civilized. But he was just standing there staring at her. Waiting for her to reply to his last outlandish remark? As if she would, she snorted to herself.

Calmly, or at least as calmly as she could manage with his eyes so intent on her, she said, "You really are going to have to be reasonable about this, Sebastian. There simply isn't enough privacy in here for us to share this room."

"I agree."

"Thank God." She went weak with relief.

"But that doesn't solve our dilemma."

He wasn't going to be reasonable after all. She could see that, and it incensed her. "We don't have a dilemma!"

"Be quiet, Maggie."

She glared at him. "Don't you dare start ordering me about again. If I want to chatter for a week, I bloody well will."

"I was referring to your tone, m'dear. Flay me all you like, just do it without shouting. The walls are thick, but they're not that thick."

"Oh," she said nonplussed and with a blush.

"Now, as I was saying," he continued. "I do have another suggestion. But first, tell me, where did you get the kind of money you intend to pay me with?"

"I don't have it, but I can get it. My family owned many properties. I'll just sell a few."

"Unless you're talking about ducal estates, you won't be getting more'n a few thousand pounds for 'properties.' "

She blushed. He was probably right. But she simply hadn't thought that far ahead.

When she didn't answer, he added, "You could pay me off in trade."

She raised a brow at him. "What trade? I have nothing to trade you."

His golden gaze moved over her. "Your body will do."

She drew in her breath sharply. "You are despicable!"

"No, just randy at the moment."

Could her face get any hotter? She'd never in her life been subjected to the sort of things this man said, and he said them as if there was nothing wrong with saying them. The man really had forgotten how to behave in polite society, had far too long been The Raven, uncouth, deadly, a merciless mercenary.

Stiffly, she said, "That's out of the question. I'll get your money."

Was his shrug a little bit disappointed? she wondered, but he merely warned, "Don't make me wait too long proving that you can."

"Or what? You'll leave? Without finishing the job?"

"A job you haven't paid for."

"This is your family," she reminded him. "I shouldn't have to pay you."

"Ex-family. I warned you that they mean nothing to me now."

"Liar," she retorted, and then in an incredulous tone, "Good God, you even said it yourself, that you weren't serious about that price."

"I've changed my mind."

He started walking toward her. Margaret stiffened, but by the time he reached her, she could have been a statue for all the movement she was capable of. She expected the worst. He was looking too damn serious. And such close proximity to him flayed her nerves as it usually did. And quickened her pulse. And shot her anticipation sky-high.

He ran the back of his finger across her cheek. It was the lightest touch, and yet it set afire every nerve in her body and made her feel as if she were melting. How could something so harmless nearly buckle her knees? How could this man affect her so strongly? She simply didn't understand it.

"You do realize that no one will expect you to be a virgin after you obtain your 'divorce'?" he said in too soft a tone. "And it will settle the difficulty we are having with a single room. Think about it, Maggie."

She'd do nothing of the sort. He was mad even to suggest it. But she wasn't about to say that with him standing so close to her that she could feel his body's heat and hear him breathing. She had to remind herself to breathe! And she wanted to step back, she really did, but couldn't seem to move. Fear. That had to be it. He was terrifying her. Yes, that was a much better conclusion to draw than that he excited her beyond anything else she'd ever experienced.

Her silence must have encouraged him because he suddenly caressed her other cheek. Really, so lightly she might not even have noticed if it had been anyone but him touching her.

"You're soft," he murmured. "I wasn't expecting that, as hard-nosed as you are."

She blinked. Teasing her when she was so frazzled she couldn't put two thoughts together? But it allowed her to break the trance she'd been in and stumble away from him — stupid knees still weren't working right.

But the distance let her think clearly again and she was quick to mention, "There is another option, the most commonsense one. You simply return to White Oaks until your father recovers. Make some excuse for doing so. You can't talk to Douglas, anyway, until he regains consciousness. There's really no reason for both of us to take the bedside vigil."

He appeared to give that some thought, then said, "No. I need to be here when Juliette gets back from London. I need to see her reaction to my return. And besides, leaving here now that I've gained entrance defeats the purpose of our 'marriage.' I can't very well push and prod to find out what's been happening here if I'm at White Oaks."

She sighed. "Fine. I'll return home, then, and you do the bedside vigil."

"I don't do bedside vigils. And we don't want my face to be the first thing my father sees when he awakens. That would probably shock him back to unconsciousness. Denton was right in that regard. He'd much prefer you for his nurse."

Margaret gritted her teeth. The man was absolutely impossible to deal with. And absolutely determined to share a room with her, apparently.

She threw up her hands and marched to the door. "Very well, but your bedding will be moved into the bathroom. There is plenty of floor space in there for it, and don't you dare try to insist there isn't. And the door will remain closed between us. And you will knock before entering this room. And I will not discuss it further. That is my last word on it."

She'd reached the door, opened it, and turned to glare at him, daring him to come up with an excuse to refute what she'd just said. He said nothing, was giving her his usual inscrutable look. He'd gotten what he wanted in the end, both of them "appearing" to be sharing the room. He'd thoroughly wracked her emotions and she'd still lost the battle. Odious man.

"And I'm not the least bit hard-nosed!" she added before she closed the door on him. "I merely exercise common sense."

Chapter 23

Douglas's fever was still very high, Dr. Culden stopped by again that morning, and this time even he was starting to look worried after he tried with no success to wake his patient. He wasn't ready to resort to funneling liquid down his throat, but he did order them to feed Douglas the very moment he woke.

To accomplish that, Margaret had a cauldron of soup brought up and set near enough to the fireplace in Douglas's room that it was kept warm. She also had buckets of icy water fetched from the cold cellar to be used for compresses for his brow, which were to be changed regularly.

Dr. Culden had checked Douglas's head wound again and reported that it looked clean and didn't appear to be infected. The swelling hadn't gone down, though. And until they knew otherwise, the fever remained the greater problem. As long as it remained high, Douglas was still in danger.

Margaret spent the morning in his room. He'd certainly had enough sleep, so if he was going to wake, it should be soon, and she wanted to be there when he did.

At midmorning Abigail poked her head around the door. She didn't come into the room, merely squinted at the bed, though she probably couldn't see that Douglas was still sleeping.

"Any change?" she asked.

"No, none yet," Margaret told her.

"I'm not surprised," Abigail said in a disagreeable tone. "He's a stubborn fool even when he's sick."

That remark harked back to Abigail's old bitterness, the reason she and her son hadn't spoken in all these years. Margaret joined her by the door and said quietly, "He doesn't know yet that Sebastian is here. I'd rather keep it that way, until he's feeling up to scratch and able to deal with it."

"Deal with it?" Abigail scoffed. "You mean give Sebby the boot again."

Margaret winced. "That's quite possible. In fact, Sebastian expects it. He's here to visit with you, Abbie, not patch things up with his father."

"Which would be a useless endeavor if he tried," Abigail predicted.

Margaret raised a curious brow. "Do you really think so? After eleven years?"

"Has it been that long? Yes, of course it has. But nothing has occurred to make Douglas change his mind. He wouldn't discuss it back then, why would he now?"

"I'm sure he had his reasons —"

"Don't defend him to me, gel," Abigail cut in. "He was wrong, so wrong. Instead of standing by Sebastian in that unfortunate tragedy, he did what he assumed would be expected of him."

"Sebastian outright defied him and caused a death in doing so. Did you never think that that was the reason Douglas took the stand he did?"

"Sebastian made a mistake. He didn't deserve to be condemned by his own family for it."

"You have a tender heart, Abbie. You see it that way. Obviously Douglas saw it differently. But that's all water under the bridge."

"Water soon to rise again," Abigail said with a snort, then headed back down the corridor.

Margaret sighed and quietly closed the door. Douglas and Abigail were both too stubborn by half. She'd never noticed that trait in Denton. Sebastian, possibly . . .

"Was that my mother?"

"Douglas!" Margaret gasped and swung about, then rushed to the bed to feel his brow. It was still quite hot. "Let's feed you first, before we talk. Doctor's orders."

His eyes were only half opened. She was quite fearful that he would nod off again before she could get some nourishment into him. He tried to sit up to eat. That didn't work, so she stuffed some pillows behind him to prop him up a bit. He reached for the bowl of soup she brought him as well, but when he nearly spilled it, she took it back and started spoon-feeding him herself.

He didn't like being waited on to that extent and demanded between spoonfuls, "Why am I so weak?"

"You lost a good deal of blood, and you're running a nasty fever. Now, shh. We'll talk after you finish this bowl of soup."

He complied, though grudgingly. In fact, he looked about as annoyed as his tone had been. Margaret recalled two times during her stay here when Douglas had been sick and told to stay in bed. It had been like trying to contain a lion in a small cage.

He finished the soup, but by the time he did, his eyes were starting to droop. "Normally I would suggest more sleep, until you feel better," she told him. "But you've had so much of it already . . . Does your head hurt?"

"Like it's splitting in two."

"Oh, dear. Well, I have a powder here for that, one of Dr. Culden's concoctions to relieve the pain. Give me a moment to stir it into some tea for you."

She moved to the table where a tray of tea had been brought for her. "How did you get that wound?" she asked over her shoulder. "Do you remember?"

"I'm not positive," he replied. "I think my horse got spooked by something. I recall I was riding down the road on my way home when he suddenly bolted to the side. Blasted branch there swept me out of the saddle. I think I tumbled a bit. Must have been the slope off the side there. Then a wicked pain in my head. Then nothing. Remind me to cut down those lower branches along the road to the house. They serve no useful purpose."

His tone was grouchy and weak by turns. And his eyes had closed again. Margaret hurried with the tea. She was afraid he was going to pass out again. But at least she'd gotten some food into him first. Dr. Culden had warned that the powder he'd left would make Douglas sleepy as well as ease the pain.

She brought him the tea. He hadn't passed out as she'd feared. His eyes opened again when he sensed her presence by the bed.

"I had the oddest dream," he said after he drank the tea. "I dreamt I woke up and saw my mother sitting in the chair beside my bed. I started to speak to her but then — nothing, complete blackness. I assume I really woke up at that point, or the dream just ended."

"That doesn't sound so odd. I frequently have dreams that end abruptly or switch to something else."

Maggie thought it probably had been Abbie. Had the old girl been so worried about him she'd actually sat beside his bed? Or had Abigail recalled their talk and been willing to speak to him again?

"Yes, but then I had the exact same dream again," Douglas continued. "Except it was Sebastian I saw this time in the chair."

Margaret managed to hide her surprise. She wasn't about to tell him that it was quite possible that neither dream had been a dream.

"Dreams follow no rhyme or reason usually," was all she said in response. "I'm going to send for Dr. Culden," Margaret continued. "He'll want to examine you again now that you're awake. All those medical questions he's so fond of asking, you know."

She started to head to the door, but he said, "Maggie, wait."

Margaret stopped cold, filled with dread. She was afraid he was going to ask her something she wasn't prepared to answer yet.

"I'm glad you're back," he continued, "and sorry this accident has delayed my meeting your husband. Tell me about him. Where'd you meet him? Is he good to you? You're happy with him?"

She smiled in relief that his questions involved only the story she and Sebastian had devised. She turned and gave him the concocted version without mentioning her husband's name. She didn't need to go into more detail, though. He nodded off again before she finished relating the simple facts. She checked him, gently shook his shoulder. It wasn't the natural, restful sleep she'd hoped for. He seemed to have passed out again.

She was actually somewhat relieved and feeling a good deal of guilt because of it. But she did not want to be the one to tell him that Sebastian had come home. He would find that out soon enough, when Sebastian came to talk to him, but not, she hoped, before Douglas had recovered enough to deal with all the unpleasant feelings that confrontation was bound to stir up.

Chapter 24

Margaret summoned a maid to sit with Douglas again, sent a footman after Dr. Culden, then went in search of Sebastian to tell him about her brief conversation with his father. She found him in the conservatory with Abigail. She actually heard the sound of his laughter just before she entered and saw his pleasant expression before he noticed her there.

There was such an amazing difference in him when he was around his grandmother. Obviously, he wanted her to see only the old Sebastian, the one Abigail remembered, not the cold, hardened man he'd become that everyone else had to suffer knowing. She wondered which one he'd show his father when they finally came face-to-face.

"Douglas awoke briefly," she told them. "I managed to feed him before he passed out again."

"Did he mention what caused him to end

up in that ditch?" Sebastian asked.

"Yes. He thinks his horse got spooked and bolted to the side where he was swept out of the saddle by one of the lower branches on the trees there."

"The evidence at the site supports that, though what could possibly spook his horse on a road merely lined with trees I'd like to know."

Abigail had an answer for that. "I heard him tell Denton that his new mare is a bit more skittish than the old one. He mentioned it more'n once," she said, then blushed, having just admitted that while she wouldn't speak to him, she certainly listened, probably to his every word.

Margaret went on to tell them the rest of what had been said and about the dreams Douglas had mentioned. She asked Abigail pointedly, "Did you visit him? Long enough for him to see you there?"

Abigail admitted, "Briefly, early this morning, just as you asked me to. I didn't notice him waking while I was there, though, so I doubt he saw me."

Since Abigail probably wouldn't have noticed his eyes open, especially if they didn't stay open for very long, Margaret concluded, "Well, that's an excellent sign, if he has been waking more than we thought, or at least trying to wake. I'd say that means he's fighting that fever."

Denton came in to fetch his grandmother for a project they were working on. Last night at dinner Abigail had mentioned she was going to take up the hobby of painting again. Every few years she tried her hand at it. And each time she wanted new windows installed in the room that had been set aside upstairs for her hobbies. She blamed the lighting every time for her less than exemplary efforts. Denton was overseeing the remodeling for her.

Margaret apprised Denton of the good news and went over again the brief conversation she'd had with his father. Denton expressed little interest in his father's awakening. "Just a spooked horse? Well, that could happen to anyone," he said, sounding greatly relieved, as if he'd expected something entirely different to have caused the accident.

Sebastian must have noticed his brother's odd reaction, too, because as soon as Denton escorted Abigail out of the room, he asked Margaret, "Was it my imagination, or did Denton's spirits lift at an odd moment of your dissertation?"

"I wouldn't call it odd, when Denton is known for his delayed reactions. He frequently apologizes for his head being in the clouds. Well, that's his usual excuse. Surely you recall that about him?"

"Not in the least."

She was surprised. "Really? He's been like that as long as I've known him."

"Which is how long? From the time you lived here? Since his marriage to Juliette?"

"Well, yes, I suppose you could say that. I didn't know him very well a'tall before my father died and I moved here. We didn't do much socializing then. Father was sickly for an extended period before he died, and before that, Eleanor had kept us a house in mourning for three long years."

He actually winced slightly, just enough for her to notice. Or did she just imagine it?

But he did say, "You've had a hard time of it, haven't you, Maggie?"

The question made her uncomfortable, caused her to snort. "Rubbish. I was a child, more or less. I didn't miss out on anything that has caused me any regrets. Other families have their tragedies. We had ours. I see no difference."

"You had friends?"

"Certainly."

Well, she wasn't going to admit that her current housekeeper, Florence, had probably been her closest friend. He'd see that as a lack, when she didn't view it that way at all. And she had her friends from the private school she'd attended for several years, after her tutor had finished with her. She kept in touch with them. She also knew every other woman in the neighborhood, she'd just never taken to any of them enough to call one a close friend.

"What happened to Denton's leg?"

The abrupt change in subject startled her. "Why don't you ask him?"

"I did," Sebastian replied. "He got all red in the face and — limped off."

"It happened just last year," she told him. "He got so foxed one night, he fell down the stairs. Unfortunately, it happened in the middle of the night, so he wasn't found until morning. By then, he'd lost so much blood he was barely alive. It was quite touch and go for a few days and it took a long time for him to recover."

"Lost blood from what?"

"He broke the banister during the tumble. One of the broken spikes sliced his leg open so badly that it left permanent damage, which accounts for the limp. Actually, I'm not surprised he wouldn't tell you about it. He's quite bitter that he's not a perfect specimen anymore. But don't show him any pity. He bloody well goes through the roof if he suspects you feel sorry for him."

"Why didn't you mention that accident?"

She frowned. "Well, I simply attributed it to Denton's drunkenness."

"Then you don't think it's related to my father's accidents?"

She blinked. "I suppose it could be, it just never occurred to me."

"You said Denton and Juliette fight a lot. Could that fall have been the result of one of their fights?"

She shook her head. "Doubtful. That would mean she left him there to die."

"Perhaps that was her intent."

She wasn't surprised that his thoughts were taking that route. "You think she's going for a tally? How many husbands she can get killed? Come now, that's so far-fetched —"

"You don't really want to know what I think, Maggie."

She would have had to be dense not to realize the subject had just changed drastically again, and to one she didn't want to discuss. His lowered tone suggested it. And his expression, for once not the least bit inscrutable, was far too intense as he stared at her, or more precisely, at her lips.

When he took a step toward her, she

fairly jumped back from him. "I need to return to my vigil," she said quickly.

"Stay put," he warned.

Defying him, she took another step back. "Really, the doctor will be here soon —"

She didn't get to finish, because he yanked her toward him. She glanced down at the hand that had pulled her forward. He'd grabbed a fistful of the pink lawn chemisette she wore under her low-cut dress, which added pleated ruffles to her neck and modestly filled in her bodice. It wasn't the first time he'd done that.

Incredulously, she said, "You did it again! How dare you do that again! Five thousand pounds deducted from your fee for wrinkling my clothes. Now maybe you'll keep your hands to yourself!"

His response was a kiss that wrinkled her toes instead. Margaret didn't try to stop him, probably couldn't have if she thought to. But she was too enthralled to do anything at that moment other than enjoy the sensations inspired by his lips and tongue.

Her teeth hadn't clenched this time. His tongue moved into her mouth as if it belonged there. The fluttering was back in her stomach, too, and even her breasts tingled. A single pulse began to throb between her legs, almost frightening her, but it was so pleasant she didn't know what to make of it.

She'd gripped his shoulders, was afraid she'd fall if she didn't, her knees were so weak. But he was holding her firmly to him, both his arms wrapped around her back. And the feel of his big, hard, muscular body was so exciting . . .

"Are you going to deduct for that, too?" he suddenly asked. "Or maybe add the five thousand back on?"

She wasn't a flirtatious sort, but she'd just been shocked — pleasantly — so she said something she wouldn't ordinarily say. "Maybe I will add it back on. That kiss was rather nice. Would you mind doing it again?"

"Jesus, Maggie," he almost growled before his mouth claimed hers again, ravaging her senses.

He was holding her much tighter now, and heat was starting to radiate between them, so much of it she swore if she wore spectacles they'd be steamed. Never in her life had she guessed that kissing could be like this, could cause such intense feelings . . .

The cough by the door tore them apart. "The dowager duchess has come to call," Mr. Hobbs announced without inflection.

Chapter 25

Margaret blushed deeply upon being discovered in such a compromising embrace by the Townshend butler. The door had been wide open! She hadn't even thought, well, hadn't thought of anything, actually, she'd been so lost in kissing Sebastian.

She swallowed her embarrassment and asked, "Alberta is here to visit with Abigail?"

"With you, Lady Margaret."

"Oh, dear," she said and turned back to Sebastian, only to find that he'd slipped out the back door.

"She's aware of who you married," Mr. Hobbs warned her.

"Word has spread already?"

"Indeed. And she's not alone, as usual. The ladies are all waiting in the parlor. Lord Denton is trying to entertain them. I'm sure he'd appreciate your rescuing him from that duty."

Margaret sighed. She couldn't put Alberta Dorrien off again. Once had been unwise, twice would mean social ruin.

She hurried down the hall to the parlor, stopping only for a moment by a mirror she passed to make sure she still looked presentable. Were her lips a little swollen, a little pinker after that kiss? No, surely it was her imagination. And at least her mauve morning dress with the pink trimming was suitable for receiving a duchess. She did have to straighten the ruffles on her chemisette, though, thanks to Sebastian's manhandling.

She could get through this, she assured herself, she really could. But thinking it was not the same as facing six of the most prominent women in the neighborhood, as well as a few of the less prominent ones. Even her old school chum Beatrice, who had moved to London with her husband several years ago, was there.

Margaret didn't manage to utter a greeting before all eyes turned to her and she began to blush.

Denton made his excuses and escaped the moment she arrived, wincing at her apologetically on his way out the door. Then the ladies began to bombard her with what was on their minds.

"Margaret, how could you?!" was said more than once.

"Really, Maggie, him of all people?"

"There isn't a member of the ton who doesn't know he was given the boot by his own family. And reasonably so. Look what he did, after all."

"Has Douglas forgiven him? Does he even know he's here?"

Oddly enough, the ladies' condemnation of Sebastian raised Margaret's hackles. She found herself wanting to defend him. He could do that well enough on his own, if he'd bother to, but he wasn't present to do so.

"He's changed," she said simply, letting them interpret for themselves whether that was good or bad. "And it didn't take me long a'tall to fall in love with him. A wife must stand by her husband through thick and thin," she reminded them pointedly.

Each of these particular ladies was married or widowed, a couple even had grandchildren. She waited until she saw at least one of them blush slightly before she added, "But no, his father doesn't know yet that Sebastian has returned."

"Douglas hasn't recovered yet?" Alberta asked, indicating that she'd heard of the accident.

"No, his fever lingers."

"It's going to be quite a — surprise, when he finds out."

That was an understatement, but Margaret decided that some optimism was in order and said, "We're hoping it will be a pleasant one."

Abigail arrived to save her from having to answer any more unpleasant questions. If there was one thing Abbie was still quite good at, it was dominating a conversation and keeping it neutral. Though she did mention her delight over Sebastian's return and marriage.

Beatrice, however, cornered Margaret and whispered, "I think it's very brave of you to marry such a blackguard."

Margaret managed not to roll her eyes. Beatrice was considered a very fashionable blonde and an incorrigible gossip. She'd had her London season and had married before it was even over. Already she had two children to show for it.

"Bea, do you even remember Sebastian?" Margaret asked curiously. "As I recall, you moved to Kent with your family not long after he'd already left England. Had you ever met him prior to that?"

"Well, no, actually. But I certainly heard an earful about him this morning when I called on the duchess."

"I can imagine. But there was nothing brave about my marrying him, I do assure you. He is, quite frankly, one of the most handsome men I've ever known. And charming. I really couldn't help but fall in love with him."

"Really? But what about Daniel Courtly? They say he's shattered over this, that he was courting you himself before your trip to Europe, and now's he's gone off to London to nurse a broken heart."

"Nonsense. Daniel and I were just friends. Any courtship involved was purely in his mind. He never once implied he had serious intentions."

"Goodness, I'll need to set a few ladies straight on that, then."

Margaret smiled to herself. She hadn't expected to find a good use for an avid gossip. But then she hadn't expected to be accused of breaking Daniel's heart, either.

The ladies stayed for lunch, of course. The hour was that late, they had to be invited. And they lingered afterward. Margaret had no doubt they were hoping for a look at the black sheep of the family, but he remained conspicuously absent.

Her suspicion was confirmed when Alberta said in parting, "I believe a party is in order. Marrying abroad as you did, we missed the prenuptial festivities. No, no, Maggie, you have your hands full here," she added when Margaret started to look appalled. "I'll see to everything. Say this Friday at my house? And no excuses. You and your husband will be the guests of honor."

"This isn't the best time for a party, because Douglas isn't well enough to attend," Margaret pointed out.

But Alberta was too used to getting her way to agree and simply said, "Nonsense, Douglas might be quite well by then, and if he isn't, he certainly wouldn't want to stand in the way of your new husband's reintroduction to society."

Margaret groaned. There was nothing she could say to that. Mentioning that Sebastian probably wouldn't agree to come was out of the question. You just didn't say things like that to Alberta Dorrien.

But the dowager duchess did surprise her with one final remark, which she whispered. "I haven't seen Abbie look so perky in years. Obviously having her grandson home is responsible, so I do hope all works out well here when Douglas is on his feet again — for her sake."

So did Margaret, with all her heart.

＊ ＊ ＊

Margaret took a break later that afternoon from sitting at Douglas's bedside. He still hadn't awakened, though if he'd done so briefly she might not have noticed, she was so distracted by her own thoughts. Sebastian figured in those thoughts, too prominently.

It wasn't the first time Margaret missed having a mother she could talk to about such things. But hers had died so long ago that she had no memories of her. Eleanor had tried to fill the role from time to time, but she'd been too young herself to know how, and anything of a "mature" nature that she'd tried to impart she'd merely picked up from her friends who didn't know any better either.

So Margaret knew next to nothing about lovemaking that she could state clearly was a fact and not hearsay, other than what she'd gathered from nature. But she knew there was no comparison there. Animals were governed by a different set of rules or no rules, merely instincts. Yet people had choices, and aside from needing children to carry on lines, they still chose to make love regardless. So they must like it or they wouldn't keep doing it.

Would she like it? She blushed, remembering how intrigued she'd been by Sebastian's suggestion of a trade. But she shouldn't even be thinking about it. She knew in her heart it was wrong to trade sex for money. She'd come up with that blasted money for him somehow!

Besides, she didn't even like Sebastian, merely found him handsome. She was attracted by his looks. But she was repelled by his personality. And there were her old reasons for not liking him, a dislike that had been compounded since she'd met him again. And yet, what he made her feel . . . She couldn't deny that those few minutes in his arms had been sublime and more exciting than anything she'd ever experienced.

Her dratted curiosity was urging her to find out more about those exciting feelings. That was the trouble.

Chapter 26

Margaret caught Sebastian just as Mr. Hobbs let him in. She wasn't sure how to break the news to him about Alberta's party, but she did have better news to impart first. But then John followed him in, luggage in hand.

She raised a brow at Sebastian's valet. "Moving in, when we might not be here another night?"

"Optimism, Lady Margaret. I'm full of it."

She grinned, liking his attitude. With Mr. Hobbs taking John off to get him settled, she turned to Sebastian, to find him still standing in the open doorway. "We brought your mare with us from White Oaks. Care to go for a ride before dinner?"

What a wonderful idea! "Yes, actually. That was rather thoughtful of you, to bring Sweet Tooth."

"I have my moments, I suppose."

He said that so dryly she couldn't help but laugh. "If we're not going far, I won't have to change."

"Just out to the cliffs. Timothy has a hankering to see the view and will chaperone us."

"Splendid. Shall we be off, then?"

The ride wasn't long. It actually took only a few minutes since they ended up having a little friendly competition getting there. It was merely a raised brow on her part that started it, but Sebastian had understood perfectly and obliged her. A race to the cliffs, and she won! How exhilarating. She was laughing when he reached her.

"Well done, Maggie," he said as he helped her dismount. "I see now why you ride a Thoroughbred. Of course I wasn't really trying to win," he added with a grin.

"Of course you weren't." She chuckled.

They had dismounted near the edge of the cliff and walked side by side now, leading their horses by the reins. A few hardy wildflowers were surviving the colder season, dotting the grassy area they traversed. Sebastian actually bent down and picked a few, lifted them to his nose, then made a face because they didn't actually smell sweet, merely earthy. But then with a formal bow and a half grin, he presented the bouquet to her.

"Not as pretty as those you cultivate, but —" He ended with a shrug, even seemed a little embarrassed over his offering.

Margaret was charmed. "They're beautiful. Thank you."

They continued their walk, Sebastian glancing out to sea every so often, Margaret glancing at him surreptitiously. She'd never seen this side of him, relaxed and at ease. Well, actually, she had, when he was with his grandmother, but that was different, strictly for Abigail's benefit, because he didn't want to show her The Raven.

"I used to come here as a child and sit for hours watching for ships," Sebastian said.

"Did you really?" She had to laugh. "So did I!"

"I know."

She blinked. "What d'you mean, you know?"

"I saw you here once, scampering about just as our young friend here is doing. I was merely riding past. Don't think you noticed."

"No, I don't recall it," she replied.

They watched Timothy for a moment. The lad noticed and waved at them before tossing a few rocks over the cliff.

With Sebastian behaving so (dare she say

it?) charming, she thought it was a good time to mention Alberta's plans for them. "The duchess is going to give a party for us in a few days. I tried to dissuade her, but she was adamant."

"Us?"

"Yes, a celebration of our marriage for the neighbors to enjoy."

Sebastian didn't even try to hide his groan. Margaret was surprised that was his only reaction. He could simply decide not to go.

She changed the subject before he gave the party too much thought. He was being entirely too — likable today. She really didn't know what to make of it.

"By the by, this is where your father nearly fell off the cliff."

"You never explained the details of the other accidents," Sebastian reminded her, "so you might tell me now."

"Well, your father claimed he was riding along the cliff, as he often did during his morning outings, and the strap on his saddle came loose. The saddle started to slide and him with it. It would have been minor if he weren't so close to the cliff's edge. He went over, caught himself a few feet below on an outcropping, but there was nothing there to get a foothold on or pull himself up with. It wasn't until a half hour later that someone came by and noticed his horse alone there and went to investigate."

Sebastian was frowning now. "The strap came loose, or was it tampered with?"

"That was the first accident. Hearing about it after the fact made it seem not so alarming, since Douglas was found and was unhurt. He must have been terrified at the time, but once rescued, he brushed it off as bad luck so no one thought to check the saddle afterward."

"What else?"

"You know that balcony up on the third floor that your mother had built so she could take her tea up there and enjoy the view? Your father still goes up there occasionally. I did too, for that matter, when I was up early enough to watch the sunrise."

"You're going to get to the point sometime today, correct?"

She could tell from his tone that he was teasing her, but she made a face at him anyway before continuing. "Douglas fell through the floor up there. It just gave way under him. He caught himself on the edge of the hole it made, thank heavens, and pulled himself back up. He could have died from that fall if he hadn't."

"And how did he fob off that near-death

experience?" Sebastian asked.

"He said some of the floorboards must have rotted after so many years of being exposed to the elements. He now has a servant check the balcony floor regularly."

"You realize that is a valid explanation?"

"Yes, of course. But I'd been up there just the day before and there was nothing wrong with the floor, no creaking, no odd-looking boards."

"Anything else?"

"There were a couple of minor falls I'd thought nothing about. Mere bruises he blamed on tripping. Then he was almost run over on one of his trips to London. A passing carriage driving too fast, though the driver never stopped to apologize. Douglas didn't even mention that one. His own driver brought back the news. But that was one accident too many for me. And Juliette and Denton had gone with him to London that time. That was when I finally began to suspect that some skulduggery was afoot and that Juliette and Denton might be involved."

"Well, since nothing you've mentioned can be looked into after all this time, I'll have to use other means to investigate. But enough about that. You really are too single-minded, m'dear. I invited you out here to relax and have a little fun, not to discuss unpleasantries."

She was warmed by that "m'dear" when she shouldn't be. This charming Sebastian really was much too likable.

Chapter 27

Margaret and Sebastian had just returned from their ride and were entering the parlor when she vaguely heard a coach pull up in front of the house. But neither of them could mistake hearing Mr. Hobbs say, "Welcome home, Lady Juliette."

Margaret quickly moved out to the entryway. She certainly wasn't going to warn Juliette that Sebastian had come home. She just wanted to witness the lady's reaction when she first clapped eyes on Sebastian. If Juliette really was trying to get rid of Douglas so she and Denton could inherit their new titles, then the possibility that the elder son might patch things up with his father would definitely put a wrinkle in her plans.

"Hello, Juliette," Margaret said.

Juliette turned and smiled. She was an extremely lovely looking woman. Her blond hair was artfully curled, her figure as trim as ever, her green eyes sparkled. She wore makeup, but only enough to enhance her beauty. She always dressed in the height of fashion, but then she frequently visited the seamstresses in London to assure that.

"Maggie! How good to see you back. I did not expect you to return so soon. If I had gone to Europe, I certainly would not have hurried home. But I would have hurried home from London if I had known you were here."

Juliette hugged her. Margaret expected it. Juliette had actually taken to her during her time at Edgewood. She was aware that Juliette considered her a friend, quite possibly the only one she had in England. The other women in the neighborhood had never forgiven her for her part in The Tragedy. They might not shun her, because she was a Townshend, after all, but they'd never warmed to her. She wondered if Juliette thought that might change once she was an earl's wife and enjoyed a higher rank than many of the neighbors.

Juliette stood back and eagerly asked, "So did you enjoy your trip? And visit all the places in Paris that I mentioned? Come now, I wish to hear . . . every—"

Her words trailed off. Sebastian had come to stand in the parlor doorway. Apparently

Juliette had noticed him and had turned so pale that she could have been witnessing her own death — or seeing it in Sebastian's expression. Margaret turned to glance at him and was taken aback. This was The Raven, cold and deadly. He looked even more menacing than when she'd first met him in those old ruins he called home. It was his eyes. There probably wasn't anyone, with or without an active imagination, who would doubt there was murder in those golden eyes.

Mr. Hobbs must have thought so. Margaret had never seen him move as fast as he did just then, disappearing down the hall. She too felt a distinct urge to leave, and Sebastian wasn't even looking at her. So she could imagine what Juliette must be feeling.

"Run along, Maggie," Sebastian said, his tone even — until he chillingly added, "Denton's wife and I have some unfinished business to discuss."

"Stay, Maggie, please," Juliette whispered urgently at her side.

"Maggie, go!" he bit out.

She bolted up the stairs and hurried to Denton's room, where she pounded on the door.

When he opened it, she simply said, "You might want to go downstairs and prevent your brother from being charged with murder."

"Murder?"

"Your wife is home."

"Bloody hell!" was all he said as he rushed down the corridor.

Margaret followed, though she remained at the top of the stairs. Juliette, seeing her husband coming to rescue her, ran up them herself and into their room.

Margaret heard Denton tell his brother, "You can't kill her."

"Why don't you divorce her, then?" Sebastian demanded.

"You think I don't want to?"

"Well?"

"I can't. So leave it alone, Seb. Please, just leave it alone."

Denton said no more and returned to his room as well. He barely glanced at Margaret in passing. He looked like a defeated man. That was the first time she'd ever heard him say that he wanted quittance from his wife.

Margaret was reluctant to meet Sebastian's gaze as he mounted the stairs. Now would be a good time for her to hide in her own room, but the trouble with that was he'd just follow her. She stared at her feet instead, feeling quite guilty now for calling Denton and cutting short

Sebastian's talk with Juliette.

He lifted her chin, forcing her to meet his eyes. "Why did you do that?" he asked her.

She squirmed but told him honestly, "I was afraid you were going to kill her."

"I wasn't, but how in the bloody hell am I going to get the truth out of her if I can't speak to her alone?"

"It's not as if everyone here doesn't know what you'll be asking her. You don't need privacy for it."

"You're missing the major part of that scenario, Maggie. Having others around will give her the courage to lie. She'll feel safe doing so."

"Oh, I hadn't thought of that," she replied with some embarrassment.

"No, you were too busy thinking you'd hired a murderer," he replied.

A lot of embarrassment now. "You did look like you had murder on your mind," she said in her defense.

"Good to hear, since that was intentional," he said dryly, then sighed. "Very well, a new tactic, then. If it's all been about the bloody title, then let's see how long it takes them to try to kill me."

She didn't like the sound of that, not one bit. "You're going to set yourself up as a target?"

"That is the easiest course of action, since the lady will no doubt go to extremes to make sure I never find her alone now."

"Do you really think your brother is part of this?" she asked him.

"Don't you?"

"Well, yes, I did but that was before I learned that he'd like to divorce her but can't. What d'you suppose is preventing him?"

"Blackmail would be the logical guess, though with that lady, anything is possible. However, you might as well know I never suspected my brother of having harmed our father. He may have harbored some resentments, but not against our father. I believe he resents me because he loves Douglas and felt I was the favored one. On the other hand, I doubt Juliette is alone in this."

"Who, then?"

"Timothy mentioned that one of the grooms in the stable here speaks with a French accent. I checked into that with Hobbs. The chap was hired to work here at Juliette's insistence, right after she married Denton. So he is definitely an acquaintance of hers."

"Or accomplice."

"Exactly. Which could explain how my father had another accident yesterday while

Juliette was in London. Her accomplice could have been hiding behind one of the trees and thrown something out on the road to spook the horse, then removed the evidence."

"People have been known to break their necks falling off horses," she remarked.

"True, though the chance of that is rather bad odds, which leads me to wonder . . ."

"What?"

"If the intention is actually to kill him, or just make it appear so."

"For what purpose? To frighten him?"

Sebastian chuckled without humor. "If so, they're failing miserably. He has to suspect something for that premise to work, but from all that you've told me he seems to suspect nothing. But no, I was thinking along different lines, that perhaps these accidents are meant to frighten Denton instead, which could be the hold Juliette has over him."

"Goodness, I never would have thought of that."

"It's just supposition."

"Have you considered the possibility that Douglas just doesn't want to frighten the rest of us by admitting something is amiss?"

"Actually, I'd guess that is more likely the case, rather than his concluding there's nothing odd about the number of accidents he's recently experienced. My father isn't stupid. We'll have to see what my talk with him turns up."

"If he'll speak to you."

"I don't intend to give him a choice in the matter," he said.

Margaret bit her lip. "I'd really prefer that you wait a day or two to question him until he can regain some of his strength. The fever drained him, as did the loss of blood, and he's barely eaten anything yet to help him recover because he's slept almost all day."

"You really think he'll keep to his bed that long?"

"I think he'll need to follow the doctor's orders for at least a few days."

"Very well. That will give John time to nose about in the lower quarters, I suppose. By the by, Maggie, have you had a chance to think about my suggestion of a trade?"

She gasped at his audacity in bringing that up again, but before she could reply, he drew her to him there at the top of the stairs and kissed her hard, almost angrily. It caught her completely off guard. Considering what they'd been discussing, it was also uncalled for, leaving her to wonder if Sebastian had been thinking about kissing her the whole time without giving her the least clue that he was.

There was no getting out of his hold, either, not that she had any thought in that direction at the moment. He had one hand gripping her derriere, one firmly across her back, and both were pressing her so close to him that she could feel his arousal.

Despite her resolve to resist him, desire rose up in her with alarming swiftness, so it was a few minutes before she managed to break away to give him an answer.

"That suggestion was the most ridiculous thing I've ever heard!"

"In other words, no?"

"Most definitely no."

"Then I'll have to think of some other way to improve my sleeping arrangements," he said idly.

He left her there to wonder what he meant by that.

Chapter 28

There were only two people in the dining room when Margaret arrived, grandmother and grandson. And she caught them laughing. Not for the first time, she thought how incredibly different Sebastian was when he was around Abbie. Like night and day. It made her yearn to know the old Sebastian . . .

Sebastian rose from his seat when he saw her, and Abigail said, "There you are, m'dear," and patted the seat on the other side of her.

Margaret hesitated to take that particular seat, which would put her directly across from Sebastian. But since they were the only three there and quite possibly would remain just three for dinner, she couldn't very well refuse. And besides, Sebastian was courteously holding the chair out for her with an amused expression on his face. It reminded her of how this family used to fight for her attention. Douglas had wanted her to sit near him, Juliette had wanted her to sit near her, and Abigail had wanted the same. And of course those three camps had never sat near each other, so it used to be a matter of who spoke up first when she arrived at the dinner table.

No sooner had she sat down when Sebastian asked Abigail, "You don't hear that?"

"Course I do, but it's just a normal sound in this house, sort of like the pots banging in the kitchen."

"Someone should mention to the two people making this 'normal sound' that they should be more considerate while Douglas is convalescing," Sebastian said.

Abigail chuckled. Margaret couldn't help smiling herself, he'd said that so dryly. The noise, of course, was the muffled shouts of Denton and Juliette fighting upstairs. And Abigail hadn't exaggerated. It really was a normal sound in this house, so normal that half the time the inhabitants didn't notice it. But Sebastian had a point. Douglas needed to rest, and his son and daughter-in-law's shouting at each other down the corridor was definitely going to disturb him.

"I'll speak to them," Margaret offered as she chose one of the two wines the footman came forward to present to her. "I'm sure they can be persuaded to take their battles outside for a few days."

"Not refrain from having them?" Sebastian queried.

Abigail snorted. "That would be asking a bit much. We've all tried — uselessly."

The shouting got louder, indicating that they were coming downstairs. In fact, they could all hear Denton clearly now saying, "I don't give a bloody damn whether you want to face him or not. He's here. Deal with it."

"You will regret this — !"

"I'm sick to death of hearing that as well. Say it again and I may be the one you need to fear."

"You don't care if he knows?" Juliette's voice sounded amazed.

"By God, I may tell him myself."

A laugh, full of scorn. "You won't."

Was Denton actually dragging her downstairs? Yes, he was, which was apparent when he shoved her into the room ahead of him. Juliette jerked her arm out of his grasp, stiffly straightened her clothes, and then, without a glance at the others in the room, took the seat as far away from Abigail's end of the table as she could get, without actually sitting in Douglas's chair.

Surprisingly, though, Denton followed

her and yanked her to her feet. "Forget it. For once we're going to behave like a normal family and actually eat together."

More than one brow rose when he dragged his wife again and shoved her into the chair next to Margaret, then went around the table to sit across from her. Considering Juliette's volatile nature, Margaret was surprised she stayed there. Actually, she did seem a bit intimidated by this new, forceful side of Denton. Usually she walked all over him, held the upper hand, as it were. Perhaps Sebastian's return was giving Denton some long overdue courage.

Abigail, with her usual calm, brought some normalcy to the table, or tried to, by asking Juliette about her trip to London. Juliette didn't take the hint, though, that it was time to behave.

"That city is filthy," she replied scornfully. "I do not know why I continue to subject myself. I would go to Paris to shop instead, but I have been denied that pleasure."

"Your Paris that you so frequently glorify is no better," Denton countered. "Traipse through the gutters and you'll get doused with piss no matter which big city you're in."

His wife gasped at his slur on her beloved

city. "You were not in Paris long enough to appreciate — !"

"I was there long enough to be glad I'm never going back — and neither are you. You spend enough money on this side of the channel. We're not going to add a shopping spree in France to the extravagance you practice."

"Perhaps if you were not so stubborn in your denials, then I would not be so extravagant," Juliette purred.

The remark caused Denton to flush brightly, indicating more than one double entendre. What exactly had he denied her to earn the punishment of her extravagance? Certainly not a mere trip to France. So perhaps the "denials" referred to his refutation of something Juliette considered the truth? Then again, she may not even have meant denials per se. While her English was remarkably good, she still occasionally used a wrong word merely because she was off a little on the definition of it.

Abigail tried once more to introduce a topic everyone could partake of. The dowager duchess's upcoming party for the newlyweds worked nicely. Margaret had mentioned it to her after the ladies had left today. And Denton must have already warned his wife about the marriage, since she showed no surprise upon hearing about it now.

Sebastian merely raised a brow at Margaret. While the dinner conversation consisted of speculating about the guest list and a little gossip about a few of the names mentioned, Margaret couldn't help but notice that Sebastian participated in none of it. He hadn't said a word since Juliette's arrival. But he watched Margaret like a hawk. And, while she was seated opposite him, she took pains not to glance directly at him even once.

When the footman brought dessert, the table fell silent, but it was not an uncomfortable silence. One of the cook's favored specialties, dessert was a rich creamy chocolate topped with mounds of fluffy cream that everyone dug into with gusto. It was very similar to the concoction Margaret had nearly tossed at Sebastian's head the first night they'd dined together at her home. The memory caused her to look up at him, spoon in mouth, to find his eyes hot on her. Had she said the silence wasn't uncomfortable? It just got extremely so for her.

Edna was in Margaret's room to help her undress, but Margaret dismissed her maid the moment her hard-to-reach fastenings were seen to. She was afraid Edna would notice her nervousness and figure out the cause. Edna had already huffed and mumbled that afternoon about the inappropriateness of Sebastian's sleeping in there, even though she'd brought in the extra bedding and dumped it in the bathroom. She and Oliver were the only two who knew the "marriage" was a farce.

The hour was still early. Margaret was dressed for bed in her most becoming nightgown, a lacy blue sheath she had bought in Paris on her tour. She was surprised Edna had included it in the few things she'd brought over from White Oaks, but she'd noticed it last night. She was also surprised that after Edna's grousing earlier that day, she hadn't removed it from Margaret's choices.

It was the first time she'd ever worn it because after she'd bought it, it had seemed too expensive to sleep in. It was certainly too thin to wear at that time of year, even if a fire was burning in the hearth. It was sheer, with just touches of lace, revealing much more than it should have.

After glancing in the mirror, she found herself blushing and feeling more nervous than she'd been before she'd put on the gown. So she quickly changed into a serviceable white cotton gown that buttoned to her neck and wasn't the least bit enticing. She was not going to be obvious in her anticipation of Sebastian's lovemaking.

Having come to that decision, she also turned off all the lamps, spread the fire so it lost its glow, and buried herself deep under her covers. She was going to be asleep when Sebastian chose to retire. Well, she could hope . . .

Chapter 29

The house was quiet as Sebastian moved through it. God, he missed Giles. Every room in this house reminded him of his friend. He missed his father, too, for that matter, the father he used to have before he had lost his love and respect.

He'd briefly sat next to Douglas's bed late last night, when thoughts of Margaret sleeping so close drove him out of her room for a while. He'd noted the gray hair blending with the black. Natural enough. Denton had more gray, which was unnatural at his age. What the hell could have caused it? Stupid question. He was married to Juliette. She could cause anyone to go prematurely gray.

His father should have remarried. Watching him through the window the other night, he'd found him a damn lonely man. He had a younger son he'd never been all that proud of, a daughter-in-law he didn't like, a mother who wouldn't talk to him, a best friend who had severed their relationship, and an older son he considered dead who wasn't dead. He had no one he could talk to anymore about anything that mattered. At least Sebastian had John.

Why had his father never married again? Didn't want to bring a gentle lady into a house of strife? Or maybe he did want to. He recalled the brief story Margaret had told him. She had suggested that Douglas marry her and then laughed, but maybe she hadn't really been joking. Maybe Douglas had given her reason to believe he was interested . . .

The thought disturbed him for a moment, until he recalled that Denton also seemed to be enamored of Margaret, and that thought thoroughly infuriated him. She'd lived in this house for four years. What exactly had happened here during that time?

It didn't take but a moment for him to doubt that his father's feelings had run in that direction. Douglas wasn't too old for her, but he would have seen it as taking advantage of his ward, since she might have been obliged to agree out of gratitude. He was too honorable to have done that. But Denton, married to an adulteress whom he fought with constantly, had he sought solace in his father's beautiful ward? Well, he couldn't have her . . .

He went upstairs and found Margaret's room completely dark. He swiped one of the lamps from out in the corridor and placed it on the table in the room. He approached her bed. She was sleeping, or trying to give him that impression. Bloody hell.

He removed his coat, tossed it over the nearest chair, but then noticed the blue material already piled on the seat of it. He fingered it, lifted it, and raised a brow. Glancing at Margaret again, he almost laughed when he saw what she chose to wear to bed instead. That was a message if he'd ever seen one, about as loud a no as he'd ever heard. He approached her bed anyway.

What had caused her blushes tonight at dinner, then? He could have sworn she was going to take him up on his offer. Had she been remembering their kiss? Had she been feeling nothing more than simple embarrassment?

He was having a deuced hard time figuring out the lady. She had professed to dislike him right up front, yet she dealt with him in a straightforward manner. He'd seen no sign of any real dislike. And any anger she'd displayed had been temporary and induced by him at the time. It had had nothing to do with the past. Perhaps she'd said she disliked him because she thought she ought to feel that way?

She was attracted to him — he'd sensed it more than once — yet she fought it. Because of her sister? Margaret was logical about most things, but about that she wasn't. Silly reasoning. He could accept the blame when it was his. But he had doubts that Eleanor had run away for the assumed reasons. He'd studied her letter briefly, long enough to decipher a name in it: Juliette. Everything, it seemed, pointed back to Juliette.

And their "marriage" had been at Margaret's suggestion. She'd come up with the idea damned quickly, too. He could make more out of that, though he probably shouldn't. Everything she did or agreed to do stemmed from her desire to "save" Douglas, after all. And she had every confidence that Sebastian would see to that.

He sat down on the edge of her bed for a moment, just a moment. She wouldn't know, was sleeping soundly. But even in sleep, she had a profound and immediate effect on his body. Once again he felt the lust for her that had tormented him last night. He groaned. Apparently he couldn't get this close to her and not want her. It was happening every bloody time now since he'd first tasted her. He needed to get this lust out of the way, and soon, so he could concentrate on the job he was there to do.

She continued to sleep, curled in a ball, buried deep under her covers, her long hair spread out on the pillow behind her. Even in the dim light that reached across the room, the brown of her hair gleamed with golden streaks. He wanted to gather it in his hands, rub it against his face. That wouldn't suffice, when he wanted to do a hell of a lot more than that.

He should take himself off to the cold bathroom where she'd no doubt arranged bedding for him. And spend another painful night thinking of her warm, lush body? He didn't move. He'd be a cad to take advantage of her. He bloody well knew that. The old Sebastian wouldn't have, but The Raven would. . . .

Chapter 30

Margaret lay in bed concentrating on her breathing. If only she had fallen asleep before Sebastian arrived, but she hadn't, and now it was taking her every conscious effort to keep her breathing sounding natural, to keep from holding her breath as was her habit when she was around him.

She had heard him move about the room but hadn't yet heard him close himself in his small sleeping area. She'd cracked her eyes open just once, to see that he'd brought a light into the room. She wasn't going to risk trying it again to find out what was taking him so long to retire.

She knew precisely when he came to stand beside her bed. She even guessed why. It was her fault. All day she'd been wondering what making love with him would be like, and somehow he'd figured out what she was thinking.

The bed dipped. Oh, God, he'd sat down

on it! Should she turn in that direction? Would that be natural? Maybe she should snore. No, she didn't know how to fake a snore. If she tried, he'd probably laugh and know she wasn't asleep.

He was staring at her. She felt it and would be blushing soon if he didn't stop it. Was the light bright enough for him to notice? If she blushed now, she'd never forgive herself. Breathe, blast it!

Her nerves were going to shatter soon. She was going to get up and start screeching at him for putting her in such a state of high anticipation.

"If you're sleeping, you won't hear this, will you, Maggie?"

His voice actually had a calming effect on her. It was very quiet, so she knew he wasn't trying to wake her. She relaxed somewhat. He was going to tell her what was on his mind and she wouldn't have to respond. That was fine. As long as he didn't say something that made her laugh, she could get through this and then he'd go away.

"You won't feel this, either, or you might think you're dreaming. Would you like a nice dream, Maggie?"

Her anticipation shot sky-high again, and her breathing stopped altogether. He'd slipped his arm under her covers. The cotton of her nightgown wasn't thin, but it wasn't thick enough to prevent her feeling the heat of his hand on her hip. Now would be the time to wake up and stop him.

"You prevaricate when there's no need to. You liked me kissing you. There's so much more to it, pleasure of the kind you can't begin to imagine."

Her dratted curiosity was back! Why did he have to say that? And his hand hadn't stayed put. Her knees had already been bent toward him in her curled sleeping position. Now his hand moved down along her upper thigh to them, found that her nightgown was raised to that point, and dipped under her gown — then straight back up the middle between her thighs.

Margaret was sure she was going to pass out if his fingers didn't stop moving in the direction they'd taken. They didn't. They reached the junction between her legs and slowly slid inside there.

Her eyes flew open and were caught by the golden glow in his. He didn't stop what he was doing now that he knew she was awake. And she couldn't get out the words to insist that he stop, didn't really want to say them because she was too mesmerized by the pleasure he'd mentioned, which she was definitely feeling some of, a lot of . . .

He whipped the covers off her, slipped his other hand behind her neck, and drew her across his lap and up his chest to kiss her. The heat and passion in that kiss shot delicious sensations throughout her body. She heard a groan of pleasure. Was it his? Hers? She was crushed against him, but again, she wasn't sure who was responsible, since she was now holding him as tightly as he was holding her. And the heated pleasure, good God, it seemed to be coming from everywhere, from his mouth, from the feel of his body, from his fingers and what they were doing, pressed so deeply inside her.

The taste and scent of him was like a heady wine that had instantly intoxicated her. She was quite giddy, flushed with heat, and utterly mesmerized by each new sensation he provoked. And with his kisses he continued to dominate her, sucking the will from her, his tongue meshed with hers so erotically.

She couldn't guess how long he held her like that, spreading the pleasure along her senses, drawing her into the sensual storm he'd created. But suddenly he rolled them over, lifting her gown. He pulled on the loose knot at her throat and whisked the gown off her completely.

Her hair cascaded around her in wild disarray, but he gently pushed it back, clearing a path on her neck for his mouth. Scorching heat there, near her ear. He took a moment to tug on the lobe with his teeth. Shivers spread across her shoulders and followed the trail of his mouth down to her breasts. His hand plumped up one globe, feeding it to his mouth. She gasped more than once as his tongue laved across her nipple, playing with it, then his teeth scraped across the tip, giving her a jolt of sensation deep in her loins.

He was caressing her even as his mouth spread the fire. And she was aware of every touch because his fingers were so hot, or seemed to be. So was his body, pressed to her side. Immediately she felt chilled when she lost that heat.

She opened her eyes to find him standing beside the bed looking down at her as he methodically removed his shirt. There was such warmth in his eyes as they moved over her body that she didn't doubt he liked what he was seeing, and that kept her from blushing. Nor did he take his gaze from her when one button gave him trouble. He merely ripped it off, tossed it aside, and then tossed the shirt as well. His chest was so wide. Her eyes were probably as admiring as his had been as she took her fill of the view he was giving her. She really did like seeing his bare skin. And she'd get to touch it now . . .

She began to blush when he started unfastening his pants. She held his eyes at that point, afraid to glance lower, but she was caught by the intensity of his gaze. He'd taken a risk, moving away from her, giving her a chance to regain her wits if she'd temporarily lost them and point a finger at the door. She had lost them, but then, she'd also decided to leave this night to fate, and fate seemed to be leaning in his direction.

And then the chance was gone. He rejoined her on the bed, let her feel the length of him pressed to her side as he kissed her again, deeply, with sublime expertise. It was a highly erotic moment for her, feeling so much male skin all at once. She curled toward him of her own volition, wrapping her arms around his neck, felt his hand curve over her side, around her hip, then pull one of her legs over his, giving her even more access to him.

There was a hard protuberance pressed against her belly, then with a brief adjustment, it slid along the crevice between her legs. Hot, hard, slick from her own excitement, he grasped her buttocks and glided her slowly along that length, back and forth, building a sweet tension that made her anxious and thrilled her at the same time. All the while his kiss got hotter, more possessive, more demanding of a response, and hers was growing wilder with each beat of her heart.

Suddenly he moved on top of her, rolling his hips over so he didn't lose his position. Her arms and legs seemed to move of their own accord, twining about him. And there was a new pressure, very subtle at first, very enticing . . .

"Say yes, Maggie," he whispered against her lips.

"No," she gasped.

"Very well, as long as we both know you meant yes."

She did, she just couldn't bring herself to say it. And the pressure was increasing. So was the tension. If something didn't happen soon, she felt she would explode.

"But I'll get that yes out of you later."

The promise made her shiver, it was said so deeply. He wouldn't. She just couldn't see herself being that complacent about lovemaking. But it didn't matter. As he'd guessed, he had her full agreement already.

And then it happened, what she assumed she'd been waiting for, a tearing that surprised her into opening her eyes briefly. It hadn't hurt, but it hadn't been all that pleasant, either. Yet no sooner did that thought flit across her mind than he sank deeply into her, and she knew that was what she'd been waiting for. Heat rushed through her, recharged, coalesced, then erupted.

"Good God, yes!" she gasped without thought as wave after wave of the most exquisite pleasure pulsed in her loins.

She heard his chuckle, entirely too triumphant, but she supposed that was all right, because he kissed her again as well, quite possessively. And thrust against her a few more times, prolonging her pleasure and gaining his own.

He said no more, but his lips rained tender kisses across her face before he moved to her side again. And he still wasn't done with her. He pulled her half onto his chest, his arm around her, his hand caressing her ever so gently. It was a divine place to be just then. Sated, lusciously content, she fell asleep almost instantly.

Chapter 31

If night and day weren't already clearly defined as being opposites, Margaret was shown a new difference that morning. Whereas during the night she had been in complete accord with what was happening between her and Sebastian, the morning roused in her self-reproach and some flaming blushes. She sat on the edge of her bed, refusing to look behind her where Sebastian lay sleeping. She stared instead at the clothes scattered on the floor by her feet, his clothes. Tidy he wasn't. And a button that had rolled and come to rest in the middle of the room gleamed brightly in the morning light. The image returned of him ripping it off . . .

She quickly found her nightgown where he'd tossed it aside and covered herself while she swept up his clothes and dumped them on the chair, then gathered her own clothing for the day. She hoped it was early enough for her to dress and leave the room before Edna arrived to help, but she had no idea what time it was. And no such luck. The soft knock came, and as usual, Edna poked her head around the door to see if Margaret was awake yet. She couldn't miss the lump in the bed, or that Margaret wasn't in it.

She quickly summoned her maid into the bathroom with her. Edna might assume that Margaret had slept in the bathroom instead. No, Edna's frown said she didn't think that a'tall, especially when she glanced at the pile of bedding, which was exactly as she'd left it.

With a pointed glare, Edna demanded, "Have you lost all your good sense?"

Margaret sighed. "No, just a bit of it. I won't lie. My curiosity got the better of me. But we're supposed to be married, and we will be getting a divorce, so no real harm was done."

Edna humphed, "Unless you get yourself with child."

"A child! Don't even . . ."

Margaret didn't finish. The thought of a child, Sebastian's child, gave her such pause, she realized it quite thrilled her for a moment. How she'd love to be a mother and hold her own baby in her arms. Her only regret about not having married yet was that she had no little ones of her own.

"I think we should go home so this sharing of rooms doesn't need to be part of the pretense," Edna suggested reasonably. "We don't live so far away that you can't come here each day to check on the earl."

Margaret bit her lip in indecision. "You're right, of course, except Sebastian has his foot in the door. This is where he needs to be to accomplish what I hired him for, and until Douglas kicks him out again . . . no, we'll stay here as long as we're welcome. But what happened last night isn't going to happen again. I've already rethought the matter."

"Some sense at last," Edna said, her tone still disapproving. "And you might want to hurry dressing. The doctor is downstairs and wants to speak to you. And Abigail is waiting to go on that trip to Edgeford you promised her."

"Goodness, why didn't you say so?" Margaret said, and hurried downstairs as soon as she was presentable.

Sebastian had set a new plan in motion. It would probably be his only chance to get Juliette alone. He didn't expect to be welcome in Edgewood beyond tomorrow, since he was going to speak to his father in the morning. His gut instinct guessed a quick eviction thereafter. His gravestone, which Douglas had erected in his mind, would be the deciding factor. So he had concluded it would be today or never if he was going to get any answers, and never didn't suit him.

He had been the one to suggest that Margaret and his grandmother enjoy a shopping expedition to Edgeford today, to take their minds off of Douglas for a little while. As soon as they left, Denton was going to be summoned to the stable at John's insistence. Sleeping powder mixed with sugar would at least make it appear that something was wrong with Denton's horse to keep him there for a short while. And that would leave his prey temporarily alone. He was counting on her returning to her room as soon as Denton left the house, rather than risk running into Sebastian before Denton got back from the stables.

Juliette didn't disappoint him. She opened the door to her room without thinking to check inside it first. Sebastian closed the door for her.

"Dieu!" she gasped, swung around, then gasped again. "Get out! Get out now or I scream!"

She was already doing that, at least her

voice was above shouting level. Ironically, her many loud fights with Denton meant that no one would pay any attention to it.

But in case she didn't realize that, he said, "Do so and I might have to put my hands around your neck for a little silence."

She glanced about frantically, probably for a weapon to use in holding him at bay. She should have moved out of his reach instead, but she didn't, which made it a simple matter to grasp her and shove her up against the wall, one hand about her throat to hold her there.

"Denton swore you would not kill me!" she said with some defiance, glaring up at him.

"After eleven years' absence, Denton doesn't know me very well."

That simple statement, which was quite true, put the fear in her eyes, but her tone was still defiant when she demanded, "What do you want?"

"Answers. You're going to tell me why you manipulated that duel between Giles and me."

"But I did not — !"

He squeezed her neck just hard enough to cut her off. "Let's get something clear before this goes any farther. I said answers, not lies or denials. We both know what happened in London. You instigated that rendezvous between us for an ulterior motive. What was it?"

There was a long moment of silence. She was determined not to answer him. His patience was occasionally his salvation. Much as he'd like just to break her neck, he refrained. But he did despise her, he was surprised at how much. In his mind, she was single-handedly responsible for destroying the life he'd known. And there was nothing he regretted more than having sex with her that night in London. He wasn't even sure what he'd seen in her, other than an easy conquest. He hadn't much cared where he found his gratification in those days. The ignorance of youth.

His own silence was the catalyst. She probably feared that more than his threats; at least it opened a can of spoiled beans.

"It — it was to punish him! He begs me to marry him, then he acts as if he were ashamed he did so. He hid me in London. Hid me while he went to confess what he had done to his father and his fiancée. As if it were such a horrible thing he had done. I was furious with him. I never should have agreed to marry such a coward."

Oddly, it sounded like the truth, something a selfish, self-centered woman would do. But he reminded himself that he didn't know her well enough to judge that. And her eyes were telling him something different. There was calculation in them, but also frantic thought, suggesting she could be weaving lies as they came to her. But again, he simply didn't know her well enough to be sure either way.

"So you get your husband killed just because you think you made a mistake?" Sebastian tried again.

"No! That duel was not supposed to happen. You English, you overreact to such things."

"Then what did you think would happen, when you told him you'd slept with his best friend?"

"I told you, it was just to punish him, to shame him. I thought you might fight, you and him, and you, being the bigger, would hurt him a little. No more than that. It was what I felt he deserved. Not death. I never wanted that."

"And what I would feel mattered not at all in your scheme of things? You merely used me as a tool to teach your husband a lesson?"

She actually flushed. Contrived? He didn't think so, but he had no way of knowing for sure.

"It sounds terrible, I know," she said. "You — you were just a means to an end, yes. I am sorry for that. But I have a terrible temper and my anger was guiding me. I did not think beyond that."

"You rarely think about anything but yourself, do you, m'dear?" Denton remarked, having just opened the door.

Sebastian glanced over his shoulder and saw that his brother appeared perfectly calm. "How much did you hear?"

"Enough to say I was given quite a different version of what happened between you two."

"Ah, yes, that I was the seducer. Of course, she couldn't give me that version when she and I know better. I think I would have been much more inclined to believe she was overcome with lust for me and couldn't help herself."

"Wounded, are you?"

"Yes, I believe so."

"Bastards! The both of you!" Juliette snarled over their English humor, then at her husband. "I could not tell you I was punishing Giles. You are my husband. I did not want you to think I would do the same to you!"

Denton lifted a brow at her. "But haven't you? In so many ways?"

Instead of answering, she pulled at Sebastian's fingers, which were still around her neck. He didn't want to let go. He had a dozen more questions for her but knew he wouldn't get the answers now — unless Denton was ready to talk.

He let go of Juliette. She immediately ran over to Denton and slapped him as hard as she could. "Do not ever let him near me again!"

Denton fingered his cheek, but he didn't seem the least bit surprised by the violence. Sebastian sighed. He suspected he'd learned absolutely nothing, other than lies — and that his brother's marriage was made in hell. Margaret had definitely been right about that.

He crossed to the door. Juliette scurried out of his way. He was done with her. He asked his brother for the second time that day, "Why don't you divorce her?"

Denton said nothing. Juliette did. She laughed and taunted her husband. "Go ahead and tell him. What is the worst he can do? Kill you? How many times you've wished for death instead of marriage to me. Now is your chance, chéri."

"Shut up, Julie!"

She just laughed harder. Sebastian reached for the door. He'd heard enough to make him want to kill someone, so it was a good time to leave.

But before he left them to go at each other's throats again verbally, he warned, "My father has had one too many accidents. If he has another, I'll be back, and one of you will pay for it."

"Seb —" Denton began to refute what had just been implied, but Sebastian closed the door.

If he heard another excuse or lie he'd probably go through the roof. Frustration he didn't deal with well. Actually, now might be a good time to visit that French groom in the stables. That ought to be a brutal enough encounter to relieve some of his frustration.

Chapter 32

Margaret noticed Sebastian in the parlor when she and Abigail returned from Edgeford. Abigail didn't catch sight of him and went straight upstairs, but Margaret joined Sebastian. She wasn't sure if he'd spoken to Dr. Culden earlier or knew yet that his father's condition had improved.

But he seemed to have been waiting for her and said, "Ah, there you are, Maggie."

He started to approach her. She positioned herself so that a table stood between them, but that didn't work. Sebastian walked around it. So she quickly related her news to get his mind off pursuing her.

"Douglas's fever broke last night," she told him. "The maid had to wake some of the footmen to help her change his bedding. He's been awake numerous times today, though he's still quite weak. Will you wait a day or so before talking with him? Should I let him know you're here? I've avoided him myself. I think he suspects, or remembers, seeing you in the hall, and he's going to ask me pointedly —"

He kissed her to silence. It worked very well, stirring quite potent memories of the night before.

"You chatter too much," he said as if providing an excuse for kissing her. "Tell him whatever you like, if you can be sure it won't hinder his recovery."

Margaret drew herself up stiffly and said, "Don't do that again, please."

"What?"

"The kissing," she whispered primly.

He sighed. "Back to square one, are we?"

"It's a matter of prudence. I'm going to have a difficult time explaining a divorce, or getting married, for that matter, if I have a child who people believe can claim the title which, due to our lies, would not legally be his."

Deep down, she was actually hoping Sebastian had an answer for that, that he'd marry her for real if it came to that. He didn't.

He nodded, though he did say, "One could wish you weren't quite so astute, Maggie. One could even wish you didn't think so bloody much. Very well, I'll keep my hands off of you. And I'll speak to my father now."

She wasn't expecting that or for him to leave the room immediately to go upstairs. She followed him slowly, worried that it was still too soon for a confrontation between him and his father, but was hesitant to stop him, when for all she knew Douglas might be delighted by his return.

She drew up short in the corridor, when she saw Sebastian standing outside his father's door. He glanced at her but said nothing. There was an odd look in his eyes that she didn't recognize. Was he worried? Anxious? Both emotions seemed beneath him. He was a bulwark. He was The Raven. And he entered the room abruptly now and closed the door behind him.

Margaret bit her lip. She ought to join him. Her presence might make a difference. But she didn't think Sebastian would want her support right now. He might be willing to reveal emotions that he wouldn't reveal if she were present. Besides, he would have been the first to suggest it if he thought she could help. She went back downstairs, fervently wishing him luck.

Douglas was sleeping. Sebastian was almost relieved, a reprieve, as it were. Except he wasn't going to leave. He didn't think his wait would be long. Douglas was propped up in his bed. He'd been awake and reading, the book laying on his thigh, his hand still on it.

The maid who was sitting across the room said nothing when he entered and left quickly at his nod toward the door. Sebastian took the chair by the bed, but he didn't stay in it long. He paced some. He was more nervous than he'd expected. No other man alive could inspire that emotion in him. But his father could.

The fight he'd had with Anton in the stable earlier had turned out to be quite satisfying, despite the fact that the man seemed vaguely familiar to him and he couldn't figure out why. He didn't get any answers from the chap about the accidents. Very loyal to Juliette, he was. And he'd put up a good defense. The stocky Frenchman had held his own nicely, giving Sebastian a splendid workout.

Thinking of that relaxed Sebastian a little, allowing him to put his defenses in place, one by one. When he was finally ready, he turned back toward the bed, intending to wake Douglas, only to find his father's eyes on him. For how long? Douglas should have spoken, asked what he was doing there, anything. That he'd said nothing indicated he had no intention of talking to Sebastian at all. The gravestone . . .

"I'm not dead," Sebastian almost snarled. "I'm not a dream, either. Nor am I here by choice. So don't worry, I'll leave just as soon as I can assure Maggie that you aren't going to exit your room, trip over a cord, and fall down the bloody stairs."

"What the devil are you talking about?"

"Well, that's something," Sebastian said dryly. "At least you talk to ghosts."

"Sebastian."

The warning note worked very well, harked back to his youth. It was all Douglas had ever needed to do with his sons, simply say their names in that particular tone, and they felt reprimanded enough to end any argument or excuses they had lined up.

"Beg pardon," Sebastian said. "I'll make an effort to stick to the facts, one of which is, Margaret's trip to Europe wasn't to tour and shop as she let on. It was expressly to find me and convince me to come here."

"Why?"

"I'm getting to that. She had no luck in convincing me, since I swore never to return to England. She managed to trick me, though, into taking the job, which she's already paid handsomely for. So I'll see it through until I can assure her that she's just a silly woman with an overactive imagination. If you will cooperate long enough for me to do that, then I can get the hell out of here and we'll both be left in peace again."

"I could have sworn you mentioned facts," Douglas said coldly. "When are you going to get to them?"

Sebastian withered a little more inside. His father was now wearing the exact same expression he'd worn the night he told Sebastian to get out and to never darken England's shores again. Had he really thought there could be a reconciliation? Good God, what a fool he was.

"Fact. Margaret thinks you're in danger."

"Rubbish."

"It's her opinion. Not mine, and obviously not yours. But it's why she hired men to find me, and when that didn't work, why she spent four months trying to find me in Europe herself. She had it set in her mind that I can solve whatever is afoot here. I believe Abigail gave her the notion. Margaret thought I would volunteer to do so. She was wrong in that. She's probably wrong in her other suspicions as well. But that's what I'm here to find out."

Douglas actually began to look interested. "What sort of danger?"

"Fact. You've had considerably more than a fair share of accidents recently."

His father flushed slightly, which Sebastian found interesting, but Douglas merely replied, "Nothing untoward."

Had his father paused a little too long there in saying that? "Fact. You live in a house with a viperous bitch capable of anything."

Douglas sighed. "Can't very well dispute that."

"Fact. Denton would actually like to divorce his wife but says he can't. She has some sort of hold over him that ties his hands. Do you know what that is?"

"No, and you've found out more than I ever could. He won't discuss his wife with me a'tall."

"Defensive, is he? With you?"

"Yes, extremely so where she is concerned."

"And your conclusion?"

"He's ashamed of her. He's ashamed of himself for getting involved with her. He did offer to leave. I selfishly talked him out of it. He's all —"

There was a brief pause, which goaded Sebastian to finish, "— all you have left?"

Douglas dropped his head back like a man in defeat, then winced when his wound hit the headboard. "I was going to say all my mother has left. This would be a house of silence if it were only she and I here. She won't talk to me, you know."

"So I've heard."

"Denton keeps her company. I'm grateful for that. And Margaret was a godsend while she was with us."

"Are you in love with your ward?" Sebastian asked pointedly.

Douglas blinked, then scowled. "What claptrap is that? She's a wonderful girl, but she's young enough to be my daughter."

"So? When did age ever stop a man from — ?"

"That's quite enough, Sebastian. I can't imagine where you got that notion from, but it couldn't be more off the mark. I felt compassion for her when she first came here. She'd just lost her father. But I was never attracted to her in the way you're implying. She was like a breath of fresh air. She brought normalcy back to this house. More'n once I actually hoped Denton would —"

"Seduce her?"

"No!" Douglas burst out, then with a sigh, "I had hoped she might provide him the incentive to fix his 'mistake,' but it was obvious she wasn't interested in him that way. To be honest, I was just looking for a way to keep her in the family, so to speak. We were all gloomy when she moved back to White Oaks after she came of age."

It was apparent that no one had yet told Douglas who Margaret had married. Sebastian would as soon keep it that way until after he was gone. Douglas wouldn't hear of it from Abigail, since she didn't talk to him. It was doubtful that Juliette would visit him. Denton was the only one who was likely to mention it. He'd have to have another talk with his brother.

It wasn't that the "marriage" seemed to be no longer needed as a bridge, since Douglas was cooperating enough at least to discuss the situation with him. But he'd never intended to leave without making a clean breast of it. And considering his father's wish to have Margaret in the family, it wasn't likely to go over well that he hadn't really married her. In fact, the thought of having Douglas find that out now made him feel distinctly uncomfortable.

"Other than the obvious reasons why Juliette would want to be part of this family, wealth, title, et cetera, can you think of anything else, anything a'tall, that would make her want to stay here, when she apparently doesn't like England?"

Douglas frowned. "What are you implying?"

"Perhaps a grudge against the Townshends?"

"You mean of the vengeful sort?"

"Yes."

"I can't imagine why," Douglas replied. "I'd never heard of her before —"

Sebastian cut him off abruptly. "We can get through this in a civilized manner as long as you don't bring up that part of our history. Now it occurs to me that I never heard her family name. Have you?"

"Yes, but it was unfamiliar. Poussin, I believe it was, or something like that. I only heard it once."

Sebastian had met a lot of people in France, but no one by that name. On the other hand, if Juliette's motive was revenge, it was doubtful she would have given her real family name to any of them.

It occurred to him to ask, "Have you ever been to France? Perhaps you could have met her family, offended or harmed them in some way without realizing it?"

"You are gadding up the wrong tree. I know it's considered a rounding off of the education, as it were, but I never took the tour. I was too interested in getting a commitment from your mother at the time to want to be out of the country. And I married her with unseemly haste."

Sebastian had never heard that before. Ordinarily he wouldn't pry, but this trip to Edgewood would very likely be the last time he ever saw his father. "Why?" he asked baldly.

Douglas shrugged. "Had to. And no, not for the first reason that might come to mind. She was the prime catch of the season, and I fell in love with her the same day I clapped eyes on her. But her being the prime catch, there were also more'n a half dozen other young bucks trying to win her hand. It was a bloody nerve-racking time, waiting for her to decide who the lucky chap would be."

Sebastian smiled. Like Denton, he'd put his mother on a pedestal; she'd died when they were so young. They had their memories of her. She was the angel, the Madonna, all that was good and gracious. It was rather a surprise to learn she'd been a typical female of her day, wanting to squeeze out every bit of enjoyment from being so popular. It made her seem more real to him — and made him miss her all the more. And he guessed he had his answer now to why his father had never remarried. The look that had come over him when he mentioned his wife said it all. He still loved her, too much to consider letting another woman take her place.

"I'll let you rest for now," Sebastian said. "Don't want to tire you out while you're still recovering. I'll return later to finish discussing your accidents."

"I told you —"

"And I didn't buy it," Sebastian cut in, to his father's chagrin. "So give some thought to the truth when we meet again."

He crossed to the door. He expected a few more rebuttals before he reached it, but Douglas remained silent, which was odd. Or perhaps their conversation had exhausted him more than he let on.

Sebastian opened the door and said without turning back, "Thank you for revealing what you did about my mother. I wasn't expecting that — all things considered."

Chapter 33

Abigail met Timothy that afternoon for the first time, and not surprisingly, since the boy had such a quirky sense of humor, the old girl took to him as if he were a member of the family. "We'll keep him," she told Margaret in a decisive manner.

Margaret didn't have the heart to tell her she couldn't just keep him. But Timothy, that cheeky scamp, thought it was hilarious, and he was pleased to keep Abigail company, entertaining her with tales of France. She had a feeling he'd never experienced a grandmother before.

Margaret didn't stay long to listen to them. She was too anxious to be good company herself, was a bundle of nerves, actually, waiting to hear what had transpired in Douglas's room. To that end, she lingered at the top of the stairs, arranging and rearranging the vase of flowers on the table nearby. She didn't want to miss Sebastian when he left his father.

He abruptly came out of the room. The menacing expression on his face, one The Raven often sported, gave her no clue. He'd been in there an awfully long time, but that might not indicate anything significant. For all she knew, Douglas could have been sleeping most of that time . . .

As soon as he spotted her, he walked over to her and said, "Let's go for a ride," then grasped her hand and started down the stairs, pulling her along with him.

"Let's not," she said to his back, wanting an immediate answer to the question that had her on tenterhooks.

He didn't take the hint and merely said, "Our horses need the exercise, whether we do or not," and continued to drag her out of the house.

She gave up at that point and just tried to keep up with him, since he wasn't letting go of her hand. Dragging her across the lawn wasn't very civilized, but come to think of it, no one could accuse Sebastian of being civilized, so it was pointless to mention it.

In the stable the grooms all quickly made themselves scarce, something Sebastian was undoubtedly used to, since he began saddling his horse without calling for assistance. One groom did show up, however, and almost belligerently asked Margaret if she needed anything. The Frenchman. His accent was so slight she might not have noticed it if she hadn't recently been in France. But before she could answer, she got a better look at him in the dim light and gasped.

"Goodness. You look like you fell asleep in one of the stalls and woke up with the horse standing on you," she said with some natural concern. His face was severely swollen and bruised.

"It was exactly that, mademoiselle. Thank you for noticing."

His sarcastic tone suggested there was no truth in his reply, but beyond that, she didn't care for his attitude at all. So she was relieved, as well as embarrassed, when Sebastian came up behind her.

"Go away," he told the fellow coldly. "I'll see to the lady's needs."

The fellow looked at Sebastian with such loathing that Margaret was sure he was going to make some inappropriate remark about the "lady's needs," which was why she found herself blushing. But once the groom glanced at her, he must have changed his mind. She could get him fired, after all. So he merely shrugged and ambled off.

"So rude," she mumbled to herself.

"To be expected," Sebastian replied and moved along the remaining stalls to find her mare.

She followed him, then waited while he went to fetch her a sidesaddle. When he returned and began strapping the saddle on Sweet Tooth, she finally noticed his swollen knuckles.

"You did that to the Frenchman?" she guessed.

He shrugged. "He threw the first punch. I merely enjoyed what followed."

She humphed. "Learn anything from him?"

"Nothing a'tall," he replied. "Though I suspect he sent word to Juliette in London, which brought her back so quickly. It was a splendid fight, though."

She rolled her eyes. "I'm not surprised you'd think so. The winner does usually have that opinion. Er, that is, you did win, correct?"

He actually chuckled. "Does it look like I lost?"

She was surprised by his moment of humor, about as rare as a hailstorm in summer. Come and gone though so quickly, she could have imagined it.

It didn't take him long to finish with the

horses, and a quick toss landed her in the saddle. A bit too quick, as if he was loath to touch her, but since that couldn't possibly be the case, she didn't dwell on it.

A few moments later, he was galloping out of the stable. She had no trouble keeping up until she suspected where he was going and then she slowed her pace deliberately, almost halted and turned about. She couldn't imagine why he'd want to go there, of all places.

She'd been there once before, as a child. She and Florence had thought it a lark. She didn't doubt every child in the neighborhood had thought the same at one time or another and went there at least once. Morbid curiosity. Adults weren't the only ones who had it.

Her own curiosity decided the matter and brought her through the trees to the renowned clearing. No grass or even weeds ever grew in the narrow twenty-foot stretch. Trees, bushes, and other thick foliage grew all around it, blocking it from the wood path that passed nearby. Grass even grew up to a point, then stopped, outlining the strip of dirt. It wasn't because it got trampled so much. It was rare a duel got fought there now. It was more like all the blood spilled there over the years had blighted the area. A morbid thought to go with her morbid curiosity.

Sebastian had dismounted, was standing in the middle of that strip of dirt. He wore the expression of a man in pain. What was amazing was that she could see it clearly. He wasn't trying to hide it, or if he was, he was experiencing too much pain to manage it.

She felt torn herself. She had the strongest urge to go to him and put her arms around him, to offer what comfort she could. There was no feeling of satisfaction, or thought that he deserved this pain. From the moment she'd believed him, that Giles's death had been an accident, she'd stopped blaming him for Eleanor's death. He was still responsible for dividing a family she was very fond of, but that was between him and his father, and had nothing to do with her sister.

She realized that she really had no reason to hate Sebastian anymore, though that didn't mean she liked him. Well, actually, she must like him a little or she wouldn't have let her attraction to him rule the order of the day, or night, as it were. But she didn't like The Raven. No getting around that. The Raven was too abrasive, high-handed, cold, and downright intimidating at times.

She wouldn't be having these thoughts if she didn't know there was another side to Sebastian, the side he rarely revealed, the side she might like too much if she wasn't careful. Fortunately, since the man had absolutely no intention of remaining in England after his job was done, she didn't need to worry about that.

She shouldn't ask, but she did anyway, "Why did you come here?"

"I'm getting soft."

She was taken aback by his odd answer. "Is that such a bad thing?"

He didn't answer, or look at her, leading her to conclude that in his mind it was. Were the memories he had of this place supposed to keep him cold and uncaring? Bitter was more like it, and that wasn't a good emotion.

"I don't suppose you reconciled with your father?" she finally asked.

"There will be no reconciliation."

That clipped response annoyed her, enough to demand, "Who did he get to see after all these years? His son? Or The Raven?"

He finally glanced at her. "I don't know why you're determined to separate the two. There is just one me, molded by the life I've made for myself."

"Rubbish. Tell that to your grandmother when you laugh with her. She gets to see the man you used to be, the one you came here to trample back into the dust."

"He's an illusion," he replied. "Speaking of which, I'd as soon my father not know about our temporary 'marriage.' "

Now that surprised a frown from her. "But that was the whole point of it."

"We're beyond that point. I'm in the door and, for the moment, not being asked to leave."

She tsked at him and pointed out, "Everything for you has to be steeped in intrigue, when the plain and simple truth still works wonders."

"Not all the time it doesn't, and when it doesn't, you're left with dead ends. Intrigue, as you put it, gives you more options. And I'd prefer the option of not being around when he finds out about it."

"Why?"

"Because I find that I can't lie to him. I thought I could, but I can't."

She blinked. "So you'll tell him that we aren't really married?" She bit her lip. "Well, I don't suppose it needs to go any farther than him. I'm sure he'll understand once he knows why we perpetrated the farce."

He shook his head at her, warned, "You'd then have to explain to him all the reasons why you hate me and won't have me, because mark my words, he'll insist we put 'truth' to the word 'married.' "

"Nonsense."

"You don't think so? Even if he didn't have the moral fiber that would insist on that solution, consider this. He wants you in the family, Maggie. It would be the perfect excuse to see it happen."

She was overcome with a myriad of emotions, and appallingly, one of them was a burst of excitement at the thought of having to marry Sebastian for real. She must be insane! All the intrigue, which was so against her nature, was getting to her. No other excuse for it.

"How do you hope to prevent him from hearing that we married, then? He's not going to remain in his room much longer. Someone's bound to mention it."

"Not necessarily. Abigail and Denton won't. I've spoken to them, as well as the servants. And according to my grandmother, Juliette rarely talks to him either. So that leaves you."

She made a moue, then said stiffly, "I'm not going to instigate this forced marriage you are predicting, I assure you. I don't agree it would come to that, but it certainly won't be on my head. Now, must we discuss this here of all places? Or did you want to talk about the duel?"

"No."

"Then why — ?"

"Maggie, you talk too much."

She gritted her teeth in exasperation. "We could have had this discussion somewhere not so morbid. Why here?"

"Because it was the only place I could think of where I wouldn't be tempted to toss up your skirt in the grass."

Chapter 34

Margaret couldn't speak for a moment. An image came into her mind, lying on soft grass, Sebastian beside her, leaning over her, tenderness in his eyes just before he . . .

The image shattered abruptly. She'd never seen tenderness in his eyes, at least not when he looked at her. At Abigail, yes, she'd seen it once, enough to know he was capable of tenderness. He wouldn't have feigned that emotion, not for his grandmother, anyway.

She turned her back to him and told him quite primly, "I must insist that you refrain from saying things like that, Sebastian."

"You can insist all you like."

She gritted her teeth. "But it won't do a bloody bit of good?"

"I always knew you were a smart girl."

She drew in her breath sharply. Was the man actually teasing her? She glanced over her shoulder at him, but his expression hadn't changed. The morbid setting was still governing that.

"We could have had this conversation at Edgewood," she pointed out stiffly.

"At this time of day? There was no place with guaranteed privacy — other than your room. Are you inviting me back into your room, Maggie?"

That question, asked in a lower timbre, held much more meaning than she cared to address. It also warned her that he wasn't going to honor her request to keep his hands off her.

Why had she expected him to come to his senses and realize how great a risk they'd taken last night? He was a man who took risks, after all. They were part of his life. Apparently, getting himself trapped in a real marriage was a risk he was willing to take.

"You will need to spend your remaining nights at Edgewood sleeping somewhere other than my room," she said pointedly.

"Not a chance."

She sighed loudly in frustration. "Then we'll need to come up with a reason why you're going to request your own room. A spat will do nicely, one that we don't wish to discuss."

"That won't work."

"Course it will. Civilized people don't pry

into the problems of married couples."

Amazingly, some humor entered his golden eyes. She was sure, well, maybe not so sure. It could have been a trick of the light, she supposed.

But his tone suggested anything but humor when he said, "Do you really think you could keep me away from you if we really were married? When the thought of your lush body under mine has driven me beyond good sense?"

She gasped again, felt her cheeks bloom with bright color. And it wasn't just his words, though they conjured up all sorts of images of the previous glorious night when he'd made love to her. It was what he was making her feel inside, at that very moment. And the way he was looking at her . . . no humor now in his eyes, but some very intense heat. Despite where they were, despite her resolve, she knew without a doubt that she would succumb to the temptations he presented if he approached her. She was that powerfully attracted to him.

Desperately latching onto anything that would tamp down the desire that had arisen between them, she took the perfect opening he'd given her.

"You'd actually force yourself on me if I were seriously angry with you?" she asked with the outrage his comment deserved.

"If we really were married, Maggie, we wouldn't be having spats," he replied. "We'd be spending too much time in bed to argue."

She couldn't believe how much that promise appealed to her. She really was out of her league with The Raven, and he was definitely The Raven right now, using skills to chip away at her resolve that she couldn't hope to resist.

All she could do was fall back on indignation, which she had to try hard to muster. "Odious man, that did not answer my question."

"But the answer is twofold. No, I wouldn't force you against your will, I'd manipulate your will so that it matched mine. I'm adept at that, even if I have been making a muck of other things since we got here."

Margaret wished she could refute his confidence that he could manipulate her sensually. Even for a moment she'd like to refute it, just to put a dent in his colossal ego. But since he might see that as a dare and feel the need to prove his point, she opted for good sense over pride and refrained.

"What muck are you talking about? What hasn't gone as you intended?"

320

Sebastian told her about his frustrating conversation with Juliette. When he was done, Margaret said thoughtfully, "Well, there you have it, a case of revenge netting more than she bargained for."

"Perhaps," he replied. "I understand why Juliette would want to marry Denton after Giles died. She needed a husband, and once I was disowned, Denton became a good candidate, being an earl's heir. Now they appear to loathe each other, but she might be willing to wait for Denton's inheritance. The question is why does he remain married to her when he's told me he'd love to quit the marriage?" Sebastian shook his head. "For all their animosity toward each other, they seem to be connected in some intimate way, as if they're both guarding the same secret. By the by, my father is also hiding something."

Margaret blinked, incredulous. Douglas, like Abigail, was too straightforward to harbor secrets.

"What d'you mean, hiding?"

"Nothing that I can put my finger on exactly. It's just that when he told me the same thing he told you about the accidents, he actually seemed a tad embarrassed about it. There was also a not so brief pause."

"Indicating?"

"My guess would be that he wasn't quite sure which answer to give me."

She tsked. "He's just recovering from an extreme fever. Any pauses in his speech might be related to his health. He could have been out of breath. He could have been dealing with pain from his wound. That hasn't completely healed yet. He could simply have been too weak for the type of interrogation you're capable of."

"I've considered all that, Maggie. But I'm going with my gut instinct. He's hiding something. And as soon as we know what that is, I think your fears will be put to rest and I can get the hell out of here."

Chapter 35

Margaret wasn't reassured by Sebastian's final account. In fact, his "get the hell out of here" put quite a damper on her mood for the rest of the day. He hated being in England. He had never pretended otherwise. She had a feeling that even if he had been able to reconcile with Douglas, he'd still feel the same way. He'd made another life for himself, one that was at odds with his role in society here in England.

The trouble was, she had started hoping that he might feel differently. She wasn't sure when she did, but it had definitely been in the last couple of days when her hopes had been so high that he and his father could make amends. Then he might want to stay. Then he might want . . .

She pushed those thoughts away. Who was she kidding? The man would make a terrible husband, at least for her. She had enjoyed her own independence too long to want to succumb to such a high-handed man. She liked making her own decisions. She liked having complete control over her life. Someone like him would take all that from her. It would be his way or no way. He would probably even drag her off to Europe if she were foolish enough to marry him for real.

A small voice in her head asked if that would be so bad, if she'd really mind where she lived as long as it was with him. The thought thrilled and terrified her at once, so she quickly shoved it away. No, a real marriage to Sebastian was out of the question. Not that he was asking her. Not that he'd given any indication that he wanted more than a brief sojourn in her bed. She'd tried to read more into his interest in her. She had to stop doing that.

There was no safe place in Edgewood where she could be assured that Sebastian wouldn't misbehave. He'd kissed her in the entryway, in the parlor, at the top of the stairs, and in her room. The only thing she could be slightly sure of was that there was at least safety in numbers. So she spent the rest of the afternoon with Abigail, and before dinner, well, she simply couldn't avoid visiting Douglas any longer.

She dreaded it, though. She stood outside

his door for nearly five minutes, she was so nervous. She might have managed to carry off "the lie" with the others, but Douglas was different. Sebastian had put it aptly today when he admitted he couldn't lie to his father. She found she felt the same way. Douglas represented a parental figure. She never would have considered lying to her own father.

She took a deep breath, put on a smile, and knocked on his door. The maid let her in. He was awake. She'd been hoping for a reprieve, that he wouldn't be. Ah, well. Not many of her hopes had been realized lately.

He was propped up in his bed. He put down the book that he'd been reading. A lamp had been lit next to him, even though there was still a little late afternoon light coming in through the windows. No sunlight, though. A thick bank of clouds had arrived just as she and Sebastian had left The Dueling Rock.

"Maggie, have you been avoiding me?"

She sighed as she sat down in the chair next to his bed. "Yes, actually, but then you know how I am. Once I start chattering, there's no end to it. I have been reminded of that quite frequently lately," she added with a frown. "But Dr. Culden stressed that rest for you right now is extremely important. I just didn't want to disturb your rest, or I would have come to see you sooner."

"Nonsense. If I rest anymore I will grow roots in this bed."

She grinned. "I know you can't tolerate inactivity, but you really must try for a few more days at least. How is your wound?"

"Tolerable at this point."

"You had us all quite worried."

He raised a brow at her. "And you even prior to this last accident? Maggie, why the devil didn't you come to me with your fears? You didn't have to gallivant across Europe to find him."

She blushed at the scolding, but she was also surprised he'd made reference to Sebastian. Was he actually willing to talk about him? Not that she wanted to. Heavens, no, that could lead to what Sebastian wanted to avoid.

She had to think fast to keep the subject neutral, without mention of the "marriage." "I'm sorry if his presence has upset you, Douglas. But I did come to you, if you'll recall."

"And I assured you there was nothing unusual to be concerned about with the accidents."

"Yes, you did. But I'm afraid I imagined otherwise. Nothing I could put my finger on, mind you, just nagging 'feelings' that something wasn't quite right." She was doubtful that he would leave it at that when his frown appeared, so she added abruptly, "He's very good at investigation. It's part and parcel of what he does now. I merely thought he might be able to, well, at least put my misgivings to rest."

He sighed but reached for her hand so he could pat it. "I could wish you had simply believed me on the matter, but it's all right, m'dear. You needn't feel guilty about bringing him here."

She managed not to blink. Did she look guilty? She must for him to have drawn that conclusion.

She tried to look relieved and gave him another smile. "I can assure you he's not going to stay. You needn't worry about that. He didn't want to come here. I had to somewhat coerce him."

Oddly, he sighed again, as if that wasn't what he'd hoped to hear. "I'm not surprised," he said, then, "How did you find him?"

She agonized for a moment about telling him the truth. She wished she knew what Sebastian had told him, but that dratted man didn't relate much of their conversation. However, she was sure that he hadn't mentioned anything about their supposed marriage, so she opted for the truth herself.

"It was actually rather funny," she admitted. "I went to him to find him. Yes, I know that doesn't make sense, but you see, he uses a different name in Europe. He's known simply as The Raven. Quite a glowing reputation he has, actually, for getting things done. Never fails to complete a job successfully."

"Never?" Douglas asked with interest.

"Indeed. Rather sterling, his reputation."

"What exactly is it that he does, aside from investigation? Or is that it?"

She frowned. "You know, I never asked for a full description. I assumed he is somewhat of a mercenary, you know, people go to him when all else fails, that sort of thing. I merely assumed that he took on all manner of jobs, though he is particular. Won't work for a woman," she said in disgust. "Which was why I had to coerce him, as I mentioned. Perhaps you can ask him." At his renewed frown, she stood up to make a quick exit and amended, "Or not. But goodness, I've talked your ear off as usual. Your dinner will be here soon, and I must change for mine. I'll return in the morning."

She was almost out the door. She heard him call her name to come back, but she decided on prudence and pretended not to hear him. Her heart was pounding. She probably shouldn't have revealed as much as she had about Sebastian. He might not have wanted his father to know about The Raven.

Her dratted nervous chatter. It was going to be her undoing one of these days.

Chapter 36

Margaret slammed her fork down on the table, glowered at Sebastian and warned sharply, "Don't talk to me!" Thus was the scene set for their "spat" at dinner that night. Sebastian made no remark. He merely sighed and rolled his eyes at his grandmother to indicate it wasn't his fault that Margaret was suddenly annoyed with him.

Juliette wasn't there to smirk about it. Denton had mentioned she was suffering from a headache and wouldn't be dining with them this evening. Which was too bad, Margaret thought. She would have at least provided a distraction. The dinner was entirely too quiet with Margaret supposedly stewing too much to contribute to the conversation.

She left early so the others could relax and finish their dinner without the tension she'd raised. After such a gloomy day, thoughts and weather both, she wanted a nice hot bath to while away in for an hour or so. At least her plan had worked, and Sebastian now had his "reason" to request his own room. He should have done so sooner, the dratted man.

Bubbles were in order, lots of them. And some scented oil. Edna knew her well and had packed the "essentials," as Margaret called them, even for such a short stay.

Actually, they seemed to have come to a dead end as far as Sebastian's strategy was concerned. Of course, it would probably take a little time to arrange an "accident" for him, if Juliette thought to go that route. Margaret really didn't like him setting himself up for that. Of course, he'd be expecting it, would have the advantage, but still . . .

Maybe it was time for some bluntness instead of strategies. Juliette might open up more with her — no, she'd see Margaret as being in the enemy camp now. Denton? Now there was a thought. Not having known before that he'd like to divorce his wife, she'd never asked him about it herself. If she could approach the subject carefully with him . . . She'd have to give that some thought.

The bathwater was perfect. Edna had seen to that before she'd left. Margaret slid slowly into the water, letting the oil and bubbles caress her skin before she lay back in the tub, closed her eyes, and relaxed, with only her head and arms out of the water.

A brazier in the corner kept the room toasty warm. There were no drafts to disturb the tranquil mood she sought — and then there was.

She opened her eyes to see if Edna had come back for something. No indeed. Sebastian was standing halfway between the tub and the door he'd just opened. He was already removing his coat.

She didn't gasp or dive under the water as she'd done the last time he'd intruded on her privacy while bathing, but she did point a stiff finger at the door. "I gave you the perfect excuse to ask for your own room," she reminded him. "What the devil are you doing in here again?"

"You set up the story, m'dear. I'm going to finish it for you," he told her. "This is the part where we make up."

She didn't need further explanation. It was in his eyes, which were locked with hers, containing enough heat to sear her. It was in his movements as he sensually seduced her as he undressed. Tell him to get out. Tell him now! The words wouldn't come out. She'd had her chance but lost it as she became transfixed, watching him remove his clothes, piece by piece.

The play of light across his muscles and skin was hypnotic. He was so bloody strong, just how much was in every line of his body. She didn't mind that, rather liked it. Her eyes moved over him at her leisure. There was so much to admire, so much to thrill her, too. He wasn't undressing in a rush this time, he was letting her have her fill of him.

When he was finally naked, she realized, incredulously, that he wasn't going to take her out of the tub, he was going to join her in it. He did just that, and she only just managed to get her feet out of the way in time before he sat down at the other end of the tub. The water rose accordingly, some even lapped over the side while he positioned himself, then taking her hands, he slid her forward until she was almost touching his chest.

She looked at her scrunched knees, quite in the way, and asked, "Do you think this is wise?"

"Good God, yes!" he said as he grasped her head and brought her mouth to his for a searing kiss.

She didn't much care about strange positions after that, but he went on to promise her, "We'll manage, Maggie," and he proceeded to show her how.

And they did manage quite splendidly. It certainly wasn't how she, with her small bit of experience, would have imagined making love in a bathtub, but after he slid down a little and sat her in his lap, it didn't seem so strange. He even cushioned her knees against his shoulders to make her more comfortable, not that she would have noticed much discomfort when her anticipation was so high.

He gave her his queue to hang on to and she laughed. He licked bubbles off her nipples. She laughed again. But she stopped laughing when he ran his hands up her legs from the backs of her knees to her thighs, and then higher. She gasped and shivered from the delicious sensations.

"Cold, Maggie?" Sebastian asked in a husky voice. "Let me warm you up." He leaned forward and kissed her hotly, plunging his tongue into her mouth. When he entered her completely, all she felt was exquisite pleasure. So deeply did he penetrate her, and with such ease, that she let out a cry. Gripping her hips with both hands, he rocked her against him. The water lapped against them and she let her head fall back as she moaned with pleasure. He caught one of her nipples carefully between his teeth. She gasped and climaxed immediately with a tiny scream. A few more hard thrusts later, which sent water flying everywhere, and he joined her in that supreme pleasure.

She smiled down at him with a depth of feeling she'd rarely experienced. Water dripped from his brow. She leaned forward and licked it off, not even wondering at her own boldness. The look he returned wasn't just filled with his own satisfaction. She saw it clearly this time — there was tenderness in his eyes. For her. And, as she sighed with happiness, she couldn't begin to describe how wonderful that made her feel.

Chapter 37

Sebastian wouldn't let her touch a towel. He dried her off himself, every inch of her. Margaret didn't object. When he picked her up and carried her to bed she might have told him it was unnecessary, but she rather liked his arms around her, so she didn't say a word.

He didn't join her in the bed, though. He actually went back to clean up the mess they'd made in the bathroom. He might have thought she'd be asleep before he finished. Perhaps he'd hoped so. But she wasn't. She wasn't the least bit tired, and she managed to keep all thoughts of his imminent departure far from her mind.

He smiled when he joined her in the bed and pulled her close to him, so she could snuggle with his arm around her. While she wasn't going to castigate herself over her complete about-face, at least not yet, she did have something on her mind that he might not be pleased about.

"I have a confession to make," she told him.

"Must you?" he asked dryly. "I'm damned pleased with you at the moment, Maggie. You aren't going to change that, are you?"

"Possibly," she said. "You see, I visited with Douglas this afternoon. We talked about you, well, that is to say, I talked about you."

"You told him about The Raven?" he guessed.

She cringed. "Yes. I'm sorry. I didn't think you wanted to keep that secret, but then it occurred to me that you might, but well, I thought of that too late and —"

"You aren't going to run on and on again, are you?" he cut in.

She pinched his side. "As it happens, yes I was. Are you very angry?"

"Not a'tall," he replied. "I'm not proud of the name I've earned, but I'm not ashamed of it, either. It was never my intention to garner such a reputation. But I really don't care if he knows or not. You didn't mention our 'marriage' to him, did you?"

"Certainly not," she said indignantly as she sat up. "I may become scatterbrained occasionally, but I don't forget important conversations and decisions of that sort. If he hears of it, it won't be from me. But you do realize that he won't stay more'n another day or two in his bed, if even that? He's regaining strength rapidly now, and his wound is mending."

"And your point?"

She wondered if he said things like that just to annoy her. "You know very well what it is. I managed to tell him about my 'husband' without mentioning your name. And he hasn't associated my bringing you back here with my having a husband now. But it's bound to occur to him soon that he doesn't know who I married and he'll end up asking someone. And there's the dowager duchess's party tomorrow night, which is expressly to honor the 'newlyweds.' He might even be up to attending and —"

He silenced her with a hard, demanding kiss. "You made your point admirably, m'dear. I'll have to see what I can do about wrapping this up tomorrow to put your concerns to rest, which will end my job here. I'll speak with him again in the morning, so I can be on my way before noon."

She didn't gasp. She wasn't sure how she managed not to. Just like that? Here's your answer, good-bye? And there wasn't a single thing she could say to keep him here — nothing that he'd want to hear.

Somehow she hadn't thought that would be his answer. It put a definite damper on her mood. She lay back down but turned on her side away from him. That caused him to lean up now and turn her back to face him.

"What?" he asked curiously.

"I —" She could have said that the thought of him leaving disturbed her, but he might read more into that than she wanted. She found her voice through the lump in her throat and was proud of how calm she sounded as she mentioned, "I haven't paid you yet."

"Don't be ridiculous, Maggie. I never intended to take your money."

That jolted her out of her despair. "You didn't? You had me agonizing over your suggestion of a trade when you —"

"It worked, didn't it?" he cut in, giving her his devilish smile.

There was no holding back that gasp, or her retaliation as she shoved him out of her bed. "You're not just an odious man, you're a — a — a really odious man! And you can spend the night where you deserve to be," she added, pointing a stiff finger at the bathroom.

He sighed. "Just as well. A man could get used to —"

"Don't say it!" she warned furiously with heated cheeks.

He started to but must have changed his mind. But was that a wistful look she saw in his eyes as he glanced at the now empty spot in the bed beside her? He didn't stay long enough for her to credit that possibility as more than her imagination.

Chapter 38

Margaret was sleeping soundly. Sebastian tried not to wake her as he dressed that morning. He'd found his trunk tucked into the corner. John likely hadn't had the nerve to unpack it, or hadn't been able to get past Edna to do so.

He stopped by her bed, shoved his hands in his pockets to temper the urge to touch her. He'd never had any trouble saying good-bye to women. He knew bloody well it was going to be different this time.

As soon as he'd realized he might be heading for the nearest ship today, he'd known he had to put some distance between himself and Margaret, emotional distance. Getting her angry at him again last night had been easy enough to do and had given him that distance. He regretted it, though, and not because he had a stiff back from sleeping on the bathroom floor again. The damned woman had gotten under his skin. He'd never felt so attracted to and intrigued by a woman, and yet so at ease with her. God, she certainly was beautiful and had a delectable body, but he also admired her spunk and her willingness to eschew the silly social conventions that kept so many women tied up in knots. Still, she was a lady through and through, sprung from the same world of traditional good manners, honor, and gentility that he'd once belonged to, but was no longer a part of, he reminded himself. He quickly walked out of the room before he ended up with even more regrets.

There was no sound coming from his father's room as he passed it. He didn't stop. He needed to talk to John before he confronted Douglas again. He found him in the kitchen, sharing a cup of tea with an old acquaintance.

The room had been quite noisy, since it was a natural gathering place for the servants, even those who didn't work there. A collective hush descended as soon as Sebastian entered. John's friend immediately departed. So did everyone else, except the cook who was too busy to notice the mass exodus.

John rolled his eyes at the door through which the servants had beat a hasty retreat and remarked with a chuckle, "I see you haven't lost your touch."

"Being treated like a pariah has its uses, but let's go outside anyway."

John nodded and followed him out the side door and around to the back lawn, past the hedged terrace and away from the gardeners. Edgewood had no fewer than five men who kept the grounds immaculate.

"I hope you've found out more than I have," Sebastian began. "Some of these people have known me since I was a child and they still won't open up."

"That's probably more the class difference, m—"

"If you say 'm'lord', I may sock you."

John gave a short burst of laughter but allowed, "I have to admit it didn't take long to revert to form, but I'll try to restrain myself."

"Thank you. So what have you found out?"

"Unfortunately, not much. No one I talked to thought any of the accidents were out of the ordinary."

"Not even the number of them?"

"No. They were spread across too many months to draw notice. Not that any have been forgotten. I heard a number of different accidents described and with the usual remarks you might expect, that he was helped in, or limped in, or limped to his room under his own steam, or limped for a few days then was right as rain, or —"

"Why was he limping so frequently? Are you sure they were talking about my father and not Denton?"

"Yes," John said, then shrugged. "I didn't think much of it. People get hurt, they tend to limp around, even if there's nothing wrong with their legs. I remember the time I cracked a rib. I limped in order to pamper that side. So did you when —"

"I get the point," Sebastian said, then sighed. "You'll notice I'm grasping at straws here. I need something, anything really, that I can allude to that will make my father think I know more than I do."

John frowned thoughtfully, then perked up. "Damn me, I did forget one thing."

"Thank God."

John winced at that. "Well, it has nothing to do with the accidents, and it was from long ago, before your brother even married, but you will find it most interesting —"

"Not until you spit it out I won't," Sebastian interrupted impatiently.

John coughed, continuing, "The account is from one of the gardeners, chap named Peter. He was working off to the side of the front road when he noticed your brother coming down it, on his way home from Edgeford. Nothing unusual in that. Your brother was a frequent customer in the Edgeford tavern and everyone knew it."

"So?"

"Peter then spotted another horse galloping toward your brother, tearing across the lawn on the other side from the direction of the Wemyss estate. Peter remembered he was annoyed, thinking he'd have to repair the lawn over there, so he was glaring at the rider until he recognized it was a lady. She shouted at Lord Denton to stop. He did, but only until she reached him, then he continued along the road as if he didn't want to talk to her, forcing her to ride along with him. It was obvious they were having some sort of argument. Peter admitted it was Lady Juliette, though he didn't know that at the time."

"Fighting even before they married?" Sebastian said. "I'm not sure that's relevant, nor does it even surprise me at this point that —"

"I wasn't finished," John cut in this time. "When they passed Peter, he heard Juliette say, and I quote, 'I got rid of my brother for you. I got rid of your brother for you. You'll damn well —' "

"What?"

"That was it. Unfortunately, he missed the rest of what was said when a bee got too close to him and he had to fight it off."

"Bloody hell. Did he at least tell my father what he'd heard?"

"I did think to ask that, but you know how servants are. They don't want to stir up any fuss that they might end up taking the blame for. He admitted he did give it some thought, that it preyed on his mind for a while. But then Juliette became a member of the family and that settled it in Peter's mind to forget about it."

Sebastian stopped, frowning. "So much for her 'punishing Giles' excuse."

"You'd already guessed that was a lie."

"Yes, but it's nice to have it confirmed. Not that I care anymore what her bloody motive was. I just want to get this wrapped up and be gone."

"You don't think her remarks implicate your brother?"

"Yes, they appear to, but I'm going with my gut instinct on this one, and that's that Denton isn't involved. I do think he's guilty about something, and I wouldn't mind finding out what, but not if it means staying here any longer."

"Then I should begin packing?"

Sebastian paused only a moment. "Yes."

Chapter 39

Sebastian wasn't expecting much cooperation on this second meeting with his father.
He'd had the upper hand on the first go-
round, the element of surprise, since
Douglas hadn't known he'd returned to
England. His father's condition, being barely
recovered, had also made it easier to avoid
any discussion of the past. Neither element
was going to be present today.

He knocked. The maid didn't let him in,
Douglas's call did. A quick glance about the
room showed that his father was alone. And
no longer in bed.

"Where's the maid?" Sebastian asked.

"Don't need a watchdog any longer. I can
reach the bellpull m'self if necessary."

"And your valet?"

Douglas was standing in front of the
mirror, tying his own cravat. Even Sebastian
didn't attempt those fancy knots on his
own, though it was rare that he dressed that

formally anymore to need John's expertise in the matter.

"Dismissed him years ago and never bothered to hire another. Found I prefer to dress m'self," Douglas said before he turned away from the mirror to give Sebastian his attention. "Beating about the bush, are you?"

Was it that obvious? The question didn't embarrass him, but he didn't like that his father could still read him so well. "No, just judging for myself how well you are."

"Before you attempt to walk all over me again?" Douglas said pointedly.

Now that embarrassed him. It also warned Sebastian that his father had recovered more of his strength than the family realized. So much for having another advantage. In fact, if he didn't quickly introduce the topic he'd come there to raise, he had a feeling they'd be discussing the door and how he should make use of it.

"I wasn't expecting you to ignore your doctor's advice," Sebastian said.

"Nor have I — for the most part. But aside from the occasional headache, I'm feeling up to scratch. That infernal weakness is gone, so there's no reason for me to warm the bed any longer."

Sebastian guessed that his father had

been getting dressed actually to leave his room. Bloody hell. Margaret was right, someone was going to mention her marriage to him in passing, with the assumption that he already knew about it. While she would be able to carry through on the farce as she'd intended, he hadn't expected old feelings to arise that would prevent him from doing the same.

Seeing his father like this, without the animosity that had come between them, reminded him too much of the closeness they'd shared before he'd left England.

He'd never lied to his father, never had a reason to. He would have found the very idea ludicrous. Sebastian wasn't that man anymore, but then — he was. It was a bloody strange feeling that didn't sit well with him a'tall.

"But you didn't come to inquire after my health, did you?" Douglas continued.

"No, and I'll be frank. I want to be on a ship sailing to France before the end of the day. You can assure that by simply —"

He couldn't finish, had to turn around. The disappointment he'd just seen in his father's expression — it was wishful thinking on his part. He knew damn well it was. Hope could delude a man. But a tightness still welled up in his chest and stopped the words from coming out.

"I'm not going to discuss my run of bad luck again, Sebastian. You can take my word on it that no outside influence of any sort has been involved. To look for a culprit here is ludicrous."

Too much defensiveness in Douglas's tone, or Sebastian might have let it go at that. "Let's discuss your bad leg, then."

He turned back around in time to see the vivid flush climbing his father's cheeks. It had been a guess, but damned if it didn't hit the exact mark.

"How in the bloody hell did you find out?" Douglas demanded stiffly.

Sebastian shrugged. "You just told me."

"Like hell I did!"

"Suffice it to say, I'm good at adding things up. Too many mentions of a limp. Your reaction merely confirmed that you have some sort of medical problem you don't care to share with anyone. So what's wrong with your leg?"

Douglas clamped his mouth shut. The color was still high in his cheeks. He walked over to the reading chair by his window and sat down. No limp whatsoever on the way there, Sebastian observed with a frown. Had he guessed accurately or not?

"Damned if I know what the problem is,"

Douglas began, his tone still defensive. "It started quite a few years ago."

"What did?"

"I'm getting to that!" Douglas almost snarled, making Sebastian realize that embarrassment was causing his father's high color. "I was on my way to the stable for my morning ride, realized I'd forgotten my riding crop and turned about abruptly to fetch it. I heard the pop quite clearly, it was so bloody loud. Thought I'd snapped the bone in my knee. And it swelled up immediately, nearly twice its size. But oddly, it didn't feel like a broken bone. It was painful, but nothing I couldn't tolerate."

"What did Culden have to say about it?"

Brighter color infused his cheeks as his father admitted, "I never sent for him."

"Why not?"

"I was going to, but the groom who helped me back to my room that day mentioned that Culden was in the next county visiting his sister and wouldn't be back before evening. He offered to ride over, but with the pain lessened as soon as I elevated my leg, I figured it wasn't an emergency and could wait. And by that evening the swelling was already starting to recede."

"So you didn't actually break any bones?"

"No indeed, and it seemed to be getting

better by the hour, so the good doctor wasn't needed. A couple days later the swelling was completely gone and I was even able to walk on the leg again. By the end of the week, there was no discomfort left a'tall. I figured I merely tore some muscle and it mended itself. I gave it no further thought."

"But that wasn't the end of it?"

Douglas sighed. "No. Once or twice a year my knee simply gives out on me. Usually I can catch myself before I fall, but sometimes it just happens so abruptly that I go down hard. And it goes through the same bloody routine each time, the swelling, which only lasts a few days, some pain, enough to keep me from putting my full weight on it, then right as rain again, as if nothing happened."

"Your accident on the cliff?"

Douglas made a look of disgust. "My own fault, that one. I felt my saddle loosen up and realized the new groom hadn't known any better than to saddle a horse when it's bellowed. I should have noticed it m'self before I left the stable, but I didn't. I was in the process of dismounting to tighten the straps when my knee gave out."

"So every accident you've had has been the result of your knee buckling?"

"Most of them, yes."

"And this last accident?"

Douglas snorted. "No, that was my stallion acting like a silly mare when a field mouse shot across the road under his feet. Damned animal reared up then bolted off the road. The lower branch there caught me by surprise, or I would have been able to duck under it."

Sebastian shook his head. "Care to mention why you've kept all this to yourself?"

Douglas scowled. "I despise this weakness, but I'll live through it. I've learned to take precautions. And it's nobody else's business, so I'd appreciate it if you don't mention it to anyone, including Maggie."

Sebastian finally understood. His father viewed his infirmity as a personal weakness, so he was actually ashamed of it. Pride. It could manifest itself in the oddest ways.

"As you wish. I believe I can convince her to take my word on it, that her concerns were groundless. And since that concludes my business here . . ."

He turned to leave. He did pause briefly at the door, but his father said nothing to stop him. He had to force himself to remain silent, or he would have snarled out his own bitterness. He wasn't welcome here. He'd merely been tolerated.

Chapter 40

Margaret was eating a late breakfast when Sebastian entered the dining room. He didn't sit down to join her, just stood there at the entrance looking — not ominous, but certainly not friendly.

"I'm leaving," Sebastian said.

Margaret went very still. Something similar to panic seemed to be rising in her.

"Without finishing the job?"

"It's finished. The culprit has been found, it's just not what you were expecting."

"Explain."

His lips turned an ironic slant. "I spoke with my father again. He took me into his confidence merely to put the matter to rest. I had to assure him what we spoke of would go no farther. So you're simply going to have to trust me on this, Maggie. No one is trying to kill him."

She was relieved, and yet annoyed that he wasn't going to tell her why, which prompted the remark, "That's asking a bit much, don't you think?"

He raised both brows, actually seemed surprised. "You don't trust me?"

She did, of course, but she reminded him, "You say one thing and then do another. That isn't a strong basis for trust."

"What are you talking about?"

The blush was immediate. She was not going to mention that conversation where he'd agreed not to touch her again — then later that night barged into the bathroom and joined her in the tub.

But he guessed, and snorted. "There are times in a man's life when he throws all caution to the wind. When he's in the grip of lust is one of those times."

How crude. Lust, not love. She was such a fool to keep trying to switch the two around.

She put down the muffin she'd been eating and said coldly, "A gentleman would have phrased that much more delicately."

He gave a short bark of laughter. "A gentleman wouldn't have mentioned it a'tall. Give it a rest, Maggie. You know I don't fall into that category anymore."

She sighed and followed his advice to drop the subject. "If Douglas was willing to take you into his confidence, does that mean you've patched things up with him?"

"No."

He said that too abruptly, and his expression turned inscrutable again. She had a feeling that no amount of prying would get him to reveal his thoughts on the matter.

She asked him pointedly, "What about Juliette?"

"What about her?"

"Did you find out why she set the duel in motion?"

"No," he replied. "And frankly, I've concluded that her motive is never going to come to light, so there is no point in pursuing a dead end."

"You must be joking!"

"Maggie, the longer I stay here, the more certain I am I'll end up killing someone, and for no purpose. It won't bring Giles back. It won't erase the last eleven years."

"So Denton doesn't know either?" she pressed. "You asked him?"

"Yes, I asked, and no, he doesn't know why, or he simply won't speak of it. It's hard to tell which it is with him, since he is hiding something that causes him a great deal of guilt. By the by, do you know where he is?"

"London," she said tonelessly.

Margaret's sense of panic was growing

stronger. She was running out of reasons for Sebastian to stay, had only one last wild card that she could play, but she doubted it would work.

He appeared frustrated by her answer, had probably wanted to say good-bye to his brother. Would that be enough to keep him here a little longer?

"When did he leave?" he asked.

"This morning. Juliette left for London at dawn. Denton followed an hour or so later, whether to bring her back or finish the fight that sent her off, no one knows."

"Does she usually hie herself off to London when they fight? Or is she just making sure she doesn't run into me again before I leave?"

"She has been known to spend a week or two in London after they have a really loud fight, but since no one mentioned anything more than raised voices, you might have the right of it."

"Someone should let her know then that I'm gone."

So much for that delay. "I take that to mean you plan to leave immediately?"

"Indeed."

She chewed on her lip. For a wild card, it was rather pathetic, but that sense of panic prompted her to play it anyway. "I need to ask you . . . a favor."

"Maggie —"

"Hear me out," she cut in. "I know you probably feel you've done me enough favors, but I really wasn't expecting you to leave this soon, and it's going to put me in quite a pickle if you do."

He was already frowning. "Why?"

"The dowager duchess's party. If we don't both show up for it, she'll never forgive me."

"So?"

"So the quickest way to court social ruin is to get in her bad graces. Getting a divorce won't be nearly as ostracizing as earning Alberta's disfavor."

His scowl darkened. "Why do I have the feeling you aren't joking about this?"

She tsked. "Because I'm not. And it's just one more night in England, Sebastian. You can leave the morning after the party."

He made her wait for a few moments before he said, "Very well, but only if we both return to White Oaks immediately. You can send someone back to tell your maid to pack your bags."

"That's rather extreme, isn't it? It would take me only a few minutes to find Edna to tell her."

"Now, or we don't have a deal."

"What about your grandmother?" Margaret asked. "Aren't you going to say goodbye to her?"

A pained expression flitted across his face. "Where is she now, the conservatory?"

Margaret nodded.

"What is your rush?" she asked in exasperation as she stood up to leave the table.

"My father is going to be coming down those stairs any moment now. Whatever convalescing he still has to do, he refuses to do in his room. And I am not going to be here when he finds out the man you married is me."

"I see," she said tightly as she walked out of the dining room. And she did see. The man wasn't going to take any more chances on being forced to marry her for real.

Chapter 41

"You're looking rather perky," Margaret remarked when Florence joined her on the sofa in the parlor at White Oaks that afternoon for a cup of tea. "I would have thought you'd be harried with our abrupt return, at least for a day or two."

It wasn't unusual for the housekeeper and the lady of the house to be sharing tea in White Oaks. Margaret refused to abide by the strict class structure in her own home. Her servants were like family and that's how she treated them. And Florence always had been her closest confidante.

"And you're looking a bit dour," Florence rejoined. "Care to share why?"

"I asked first."

Florence chuckled. That particular answer was one they'd both used all through their childhood together.

"Very well," Florence said in a lowered tone, even glanced toward the door to make sure they were still alone. "I confess I missed John when he left."

"John Richards?"

"Yes. We'd just been getting better acquainted when he packed up and moved to Edgewood."

"You like him, I take it?"

Florence grinned. "You know I had begun to despair that I'd ever meet a fellow up to my standards."

"You're just too picky," Margaret teased.

"No, the men around here are either too old or too young for me."

"Rubbish. You're too picky."

Florence laughed. "Very well, I do have certain standards, and John meets them all. I haven't spoken to him yet since you returned, but now that he's back, I expect we'll be getting even better acquainted."

Margaret was torn. She wanted to take Florence into her confidence but realized if she did, her friend would end up being as miserable as she was. Then again, if she knew in advance, that would give her time to convince John to stay if she cared to try. Sebastian was determined to leave. That didn't mean his valet had to go with him. John just might prefer to settle down and start a family.

"There's something you should know,

Florence. I would have told you eventually, but it might be to your benefit to hear it now instead."

"Goodness, to go by your expression, I don't think I want to know."

"Very well —"

"Don't you dare not tell me now."

Margaret rolled her eyes. "You know why I went to Europe. I'm sure you didn't expect me to come home married to my quarry."

"No, that definitely bowled me over. I should tell you, there's been quite a bit of speculation on whether you would move back to Edgewood permanently now."

Margaret began to blush before she could get the first word out. "I didn't actually marry Sebastian."

"Eh?"

"Edna and Oliver know, and you'll have to keep it a secret as well. I had to hire him to get him to return to England. Even after I explained the situation, he still refused to come willingly."

"That doesn't sound like Sebastian Townshend."

"Probably because the man he used to be was buried along with Giles. His bitterness is, well, let's just say it's extreme, and now I understand why he feels that. Not many people know that he went to that duel expecting to die, and Giles, by all accounts, was certainly angry enough to kill him."

"Then how did the opposite occur?"

"It was an accident, a shot meant to be fired into the air that got redirected when Giles's shot nicked Sebastian's arm. Then on top of that anguish, his father disowned him. So you can see why he didn't want to come back here. He was convinced he'd be denied access to Edgewood, which would make it next to impossible for him to discover any plots that might be afoot."

"So he suggested you pretend to be wed just to gain access?" Florence asked incredulously.

"No, I did," Margaret said, her blush deepening. "And yes, I know that was an outlandish solution. I confess I didn't give it much thought at the time. And he did try to talk me out of it, but given his attitude, I merely wanted to counter any stumbling blocks he came up with. It wouldn't even have come to that, if we hadn't found out that Douglas is still so unforgiving that he considers Sebastian dead. Douglas's estrangement from Lord Wemyss is probably why he can't forgive Sebastian. The irony is, our pretend marriage wasn't necessary."

"Because of the earl's most recent accident?"

"Yes. And because Sebastian was able to talk to his father before Douglas was fully recovered. He caught him off guard, as it were."

Florence grinned. "He does have a certain effect on people. They want to answer his questions quickly just so he'll go away!"

"The intimidation you are referring to wouldn't have affected Douglas. Letting him think that Sebastian knew more than he did worked, though. He's assured me no one is trying to kill his father, which was my concern. Though the dratted men aren't going to share what is the problem, if there even is one aside from rotten luck. At any rate, Sebastian did what I asked of him and is now eager to return to the Continent."

"But what about your marriage? It might not be real, but everyone certainly thinks it is. Are you just going to announce that it was merely a ruse to an end?"

"That would have been an option if Sebastian hadn't insisted we give it a good show by sharing the same room at Edgewood."

"Maggie, you didn't!" Florence's scandalized expression made Margaret burn with embarrassment. "Good Lord, not that, too!"

"It certainly wasn't intentional, but I confess I've felt strangely attracted to him since I first clapped eyes on him. He's everything I can't abide in a man, and yet, with him it seems not to matter." Margaret leaned closer to add in a whisper, "Lust, he calls it."

"Nonsense, you aren't the least bit lusty," Florence said indignantly.

Margaret burst out laughing, which relieved some of her embarrassment. "I should hope not. But what's done is done. I can't even regret it since it was so — nice. There's no question, though, about owning up to the marriage's not being real. I simply can't. Everyone at Edgewood, aside from Douglas, knows we shared a room there just like a normal married couple. And Douglas will eventually know, too. I had originally intended to pretend a divorce in the same manner we pretended the marriage. I can let it be known why I married him, or not. I'll decide that at the time. Most of the ladies in the neighborhood consider it scandalous that I married him a'tall, so it might be a relief if I explain, so they can stop thinking I've lost my mind."

Florence sighed. "A divorce is so —"

"Yes, I know," Margaret cut in. "Quite the stigma. But I am wealthy and my son stands to inherit a title. The notoriety of being a divorced woman shouldn't affect that."

Florence humphed. "I don't know why you refuse to acknowledge the fact that you're a prime catch, Maggie. You don't need to bribe yourself a husband."

"I never refuted that. I'm just too set in my ways to put myself forward in the normal manner. Too impatient, too, to deal with a traditional courting."

"Nonsense. You've got the patience of a saint, or you wouldn't have waited this long to make a proper effort to find a husband. You should have just gone to London, enjoyed the social whirl, and let nature take its course. You would have had yourself a husband, a real one, in no time, and wouldn't now be facing the scandal of a divorce."

"I have the fortitude to weather that storm. But what about you? Are you going to let John leave with Sebastian without trying to convince him to stay?"

Florence paled with the realization, "He will be leaving, won't he? What bloody rotten luck that your marriage isn't a real one as we all thought."

Margaret found herself actually agreeing, though she wouldn't say so. If there weren't so many extenuating circumstances for why marriage to Sebastian was out of the question, she might follow her own advice. But Florence wasn't so restrained.

"You could ask him to stay," she reiterated.

"I can't be that bold. Our acquaintance hasn't progressed that far, though I've been hopeful and encouraged that it soon would. Why don't you ask Sebastian to stay? You know you want to."

The trouble with close friends was they could read right through you. Margaret sighed. "Because I already know his answer. The reason he wants to bolt back to Europe so quickly is that he fears Douglas will demand a real marriage if he finds out we just faked one."

"How the devil would he find out?"

"From Sebastian. He seems to think that Douglas will open the doors fully again in approval when he hears of the marriage, and that will so stick in Sebastian's craw that he'll confess the truth. So he intends to avoid Douglas at all costs. The man doesn't want to be married for real."

He was so desperate to be gone that he wasn't even going to investigate his brother's dilemma, whatever it was, even though if anyone could get to the bottom of that, Sebastian could. Considering that, she was surprised he'd agreed to stay for the party.

She supposed she should warn Sebastian that while it was very unlikely that Douglas would exert himself beyond leaving his room today, he *might* attend the dowager duchess's party, if only to make a brief appearance. No, she didn't think she would. It was time for fate to step in, and just maybe, it would favor her.

Chapter 42

Alberta Dorrien's mansion was the showcase of the neighborhood. It had taken several years to build, and the lady hadn't actually moved to the neighborhood until it was finished. Her first grand ball had been talked about for months, right up until she threw the second ball. Margaret had been too young to attend either but had certainly heard about them.

The dowager duchess had actually designed her property for entertaining. Not only was the ballroom immense, but also the parlor, the music room, the billiards room. There was even a large room strictly for gambling, filled with card tables. The only room that wasn't huge was the dining room, since sit-down dinners were reserved for only her close set of friends. She fed the masses at her large parties with buffets, and since she employed not one but four cooks, each one a master, no fault could be found with that arrangement.

Her invitations were sent far and wide and were eagerly sought, and she'd even prepared in advance for that by building actual guesthouses. Not of the traditional sort, they were like miniature mansions! And all of them were usually used for a ball.

The party tonight wasn't of the grand sort, it was merely a local gathering. Only Alberta could get away with throwing a party on such short notice and expect full attendance. But other engagements could be broken. No one declined the dowager duchess's invitations. They were treated like a royal summons!

Margaret still hadn't expected to see quite so many carriages lined up, waiting to unload their passengers. She had to allow, though, that the draw tonight was more likely Sebastian. The entire neighborhood would be eager to learn if he'd been reinstated or not. It would be interesting to see if anyone would dare to ask him.

She was rather pleased with him at the moment. She didn't think it would last, but at least he'd got into the spirit of the occasion and was dressed properly in formal togs. Not too formal, but definitely evening wear.

It was only the second time she'd seen

him wearing a cravat, or an underwaistcoat, for that matter. Pearl gray satin it was, very subdued with his black tailed coat and the white cravat. No bright colors for him. She had to agree that gaudy just wouldn't suit him. No haircut for the occasion, though, but she was so used to the clubbed-back queue he wore that he'd probably look odd to her without it.

No top hat, either. John had actually found one for him, but when presented with it at the door just as they were leaving, Sebastian had given his valet such a hard stare that John had put the hat on his own head and stomped off. That had relieved the tense moment when she'd come down the stairs and was met with Sebastian's brow raised appreciatively. It flustered her to no end when his glance turned admiring. She'd grown accustomed to dealing with his ominous looks, but when his golden eyes turned sensual, she forgot how to breathe.

Edna had done her proud, though, in her own attire and coiffure. Her evening gown was a deep burgundy wine color with white satin cord trimmings. The puffed shoulders weren't too bouffant and had the white cording interlaced with the dark velvet. Satin slippers in the same dark burgundy peeked out from under her full skirt.

Margaret couldn't deny that she was nervous about the party. Nor had she seen Sebastian since they returned to her house. Not once. So she'd been unable to discuss her worry with him. In fact, he made himself so scarce that she might have thought he'd changed his mind and left if she hadn't seen John about.

She supposed it was for the best. He'd be gone for good tomorrow. She had to get used to that. If she'd thought anything positive would have come from this last day they could have spent alone, well, she should have known better.

Knowing that tonight would be the last time she'd ever see him put quite a damper on her spirits. And ended her nervousness. Aware of him more than she cared to be on the drive to Alberta's, she did sense his own tension.

As their coach slowly moved forward in the line, she asked him, "You aren't going to disappear on me, are you?"

"Play the coward? You wound me."

She snorted. "You look wounded, 'deed you do. But this is going to be easy," she added, hoping to convince herself of that as well. "Just treat it like any normal party. Accept the well-wishes graciously, evade the questions. See? Nothing to it."

"I recognized the Wemyss coach a few in front of us," he said baldly.

"Oh, dear." Margaret frowned. "I can't imagine why Cecil would come — unless he didn't dare to ignore Alberta's summons either."

"Look on the bright side, Maggie. He's probably here to shoot me. Save you the trouble of a divorce."

She glared at him. "That isn't funny."

"It isn't beyond the realm of possibility, either," he replied.

"Nonsense. He took Giles's death hard, even somehow blamed Douglas for not preventing it, or they wouldn't be estranged. But he's gone on with his life. I heard he's currently courting some duchess he met in London."

"How nice for him," he said with disinterest.

She narrowed her eyes on him suspiciously. "You were just trying to distract me, weren't you?"

"You looked like you were the one about to bolt, yes."

She could wish he wasn't so astute. "It's your fault," she said defensively. "You were coerced, as it were, to be here tonight. Given that, it's a reasonable assumption that you'll make no effort to see the evening go smoothly."

"As I recall, these things can last all bloody night," he said. "But as long as we don't stay till the end, I'll muddle through this."

"Certainly," she assured him. "We can leave as soon as it's decent to do so."

"Then relax, Maggie. I'm not going to kill anyone tonight."

That was a slap and uncalled for. She hadn't thought he'd do any such thing. But before it occurred to her that he might merely have been teasing, he leaned forward, caught her hand, and pulled her across to his side of the coach and into his lap. There wasn't even time to gasp before he was kissing her.

It was the kiss she would remember most clearly because it was beyond sensual, beyond thrilling. If she wanted to be romantic, she would say he put his heart into it. The way he held her, firmly yet so gently. The way his hand cupped her cheek, so tenderly. He wasn't trying to incite her desire, and yet she couldn't get this close to him and not have it rise. But it was warm, it was sweet, and it drew her into participating rather than demanding that she do so.

All thoughts of the party in their honor

were gone. She could have stayed there all night in his arms, tasting the delicious languor of that kiss.

She was brought back to earth rather hard when he set her back on the seat across from him and said, "There, now you look married instead of like a sacrificial virgin. We've arrived. Get out of the coach, Maggie."

Chapter 43

Margaret had angry color still high on her cheeks after the dirty trick Sebastian had played on her in the coach, kissing her simply so she'd look like she'd just been kissed. For the role they were playing, not because he wanted to kiss her. But her cheeks got even hotter, with embarrassment, when the hush fell on the room as they entered the large parlor.

It had nothing to do with curiosity finally being appeased as Sebastian's neighbors got their first look at him after eleven years. There was some surprise, surely, but there was a lot more alarm and wariness in the expressions she could see. The men even glanced away a bit too quickly, as if they feared catching his gaze.

"Good God, they're terrified of you," Margaret gasped quietly. "You couldn't send The Raven away for just one night?"

Sebastian glanced down at her and

scoffed, "You exaggerate, m'dear. And why do you continue to think The Raven is a role I play?"

"You forget I've seen you with your grandmother. The old Sebastian is still there."

"I take pains to conceal from her who I've become. The Raven is a result, Maggie, not a contrivance. It's what the last eleven years have made me."

"Then take some more pains to conceal that man tonight, would you? Or is this how you planned to avoid any questions you don't care to answer? A splendid idea, appear so menacing no one will dare to approach you."

He actually grinned at her. "Maggie, you're starting to think like me. But as it happens, I had no particular plan for the evening. If anyone is so rude as to ask personal questions, he'll merely be met with the silence he deserves. Is this better?"

He smiled at her so widely she could count his teeth. "No," she said huffily. "It bloody well looks like you intend to bite me."

He burst out laughing. She was so disconcerted by his laughter, because it was genuine that she didn't notice Alberta approaching them until the lady spoke.

"Welcome home, Sebastian. Is your father feeling well enough to join us tonight?"

Maggie almost laughed now. That wasn't a personal question by any means, but it would certainly answer the one on everyone's mind — if father and son had reconciled.

And yet Sebastian managed to avoid a direct reply by saying, "I didn't think to ask."

Unfortunately, the duchess turned her gaze on Maggie with the same question in her expression, forcing Maggie to add, "Neither did I. But with Douglas back on his feet, we returned to White Oaks this morning. He is still convalescing, though, so I doubt he's feeling up to socializing just yet."

Alberta tsked. "Yes, I should have taken that into account at your suggestion and delayed this party for at least another week or two. But hindsight, while superior, is rarely useful in correcting an error. So let me be the first to congratulate you this evening. You've made quite the catch, Sebastian. We were beginning to wonder if our dear Maggie would ever find a chap to suit her. So many have tried, you know."

"No, I didn't know," Sebastian said with a raised brow at Maggie.

"Now, now, Sebastian, there's no reason

for jealousy to rear its ugly head," Alberta said. "Beautiful gel like her, it was to be expected. Had them camping on the steps of Edgewood while she was staying there. It quite amused Douglas, I'm sure."

Margaret was blushing by then and said defensively, "I was fresh out of the schoolroom and nowhere near thinking about marriage yet. It was a bloody nuisance, if you must know, having all those young bucks showing up, half of them I didn't even know!"

Alberta chuckled. "M'dear, that's when all you young gels get married."

"Douglas was kind enough not to point that out and let me decide for myself."

"Which was fortunate for me," Sebastian put in, coming to Maggie's rescue.

"Indeed!" Alberta was forced to agree. "Well, come along, then. I can't monopolize you when everyone here is eager to wish you well."

Margaret managed not to laugh, since she was sure everyone there would just as soon not speak to Sebastian, given their initial reaction to him. But she was surprised. His earlier laughter had eased most of the guests' wariness, and in the next hour, the well-wishing did sound genuine. Only Cecil and his fiancée hadn't spoken to them, and

Alberta had the good sense not to force that particular confrontation.

She left them soon after to mingle. "Thank God that's over with," Sebastian remarked.

Margaret shared his sentiments, though she allowed, "That went much better than I expected."

"I passed muster, did I?" he replied dryly.

She looked up at him and was struck again by how handsome he was.

"Indeed. One might actually think you were Sebastian Townshend, rather than The Raven."

He didn't actually roll his eyes at her, but she had the feeling he would have if the old Sebastian really were in attendance. But then abruptly, any amusement he'd been experiencing vanished.

He couldn't have looked more somber when he said, "I have one more duty I feel obliged to perform."

She went very still. He was staring at Cecil. She didn't have to ask what he meant. She ought to talk him out of it. It wouldn't be pleasant for either man. But that word "duty" kept her from trying.

"I'll fetch some punch," she said, but added hesitantly, "or would you like reinforcements?"

"I doubt your presence would ease the situation. Cecil always was one to speak his mind."

She nodded. "Then let us hope he can do so quietly."

Chapter 44

Sebastian recognized the woman with Cecil. The duchess of Felburg had aged very well and still bore a close resemblance to the picture he'd been shown, which had been taken more than twenty years ago.

He thought it rather foolish of her to let it be known she was a duchess in the country where she was seeking refuge from a vengeful duke. Even more foolish to plan to marry an Englishman when she already had a husband. Did Cecil know? No, of course not, or he wouldn't have asked the lady to marry him.

"Cecil?"

Giles's father turned and flushed angrily at the sight of Sebastian. "You dare speak to me? My presence here doesn't mean I condone yours. Get out of my sight!"

Sebastian had steeled himself for this. Cecil's reaction didn't surprise him.

But before he could reply, the woman

standing with Giles's father implored in a low voice, "Cecil, please, do not cause a scene. I am barely accepted here yet."

He patted his fiancée's hand, which was resting on his arm and gave her a reassuring smile. It was apparent now that he'd come to the party only for her sake.

"I will keep that in mind, m'dear," he told her. "Now, if you will give me a moment —"

"She should stay," Sebastian said. "I have news she will want to hear. But first — I'm sorry, Cecil. No one regrets Giles's death more than I do."

"Don't," the older man choked out. "I come home to find my son dead and already buried. And you —"

"It was an accident," Sebastian cut in. "You can't really think I meant to kill him? I went there to fire into the air. If he was angry enough to kill me, so be it. But his bullet nicked my arm, lowering it just as I fired. Good God, did no one ever tell you what happened there?"

"Does that bring him back?" Cecil demanded. "He was my only son!"

For such an emotional statement, Sebastian would have expected to see more than just anger in Cecil's eyes. But nothing else could have brought the pain back so strongly for him than those particular words. His own heart ripped open, "He was my best friend! How many times do I have to die because of that slut he married?"

"Please!" the duchess begged again.

She was right, they were drawing notice. And it had been a long time since Sebastian had lost control like that, to let his pain be so obvious. By sheer force of will, he put it back where it belonged, behind the iron shield that encased his emotions.

He wanted to walk away, but there was one thing left to say on the matter, to appease his own curiosity. "Why have you blamed my father?"

He didn't think Cecil would answer. His face was growing red with anger again.

But in a low, baleful tone Cecil said, "I went away to mourn. I couldn't bear being in the house where Giles was raised. I come home months later and find that French whore who caused your duel married to your brother. Douglas should have prevented that. He should have prevented the duel."

"What more could he have done than forbid it, which he did?" Sebastian replied. "I defied him. I went there to die myself, Cecil. I didn't expect to have to come home and tell him that a quirk of fate reversed the outcome."

"Douglas could have told me that, instead of telling me to get out and never come back! You have been misinformed. I didn't end our friendship, he did."

Sebastian was so surprised by that, he almost forgot he wanted to tell them something else. They had both turned to walk away, eager to end the confrontation. He almost stopped them but decided not to upset Cecil anymore. What he had to say to the duchess could be said in private.

It took him a few minutes to catch her eye and indicate that he wanted to talk with her. It took her a good ten minutes more to come up with an excuse to get away from Cecil. Margaret had rejoined him by then, but the duchess didn't approach him. She left the room instead. He made his own excuses, leaving the parlor as well, and noticed her entering the empty ballroom at the back of the house.

The large room was quite dark, as the candles in it weren't lit. The woman grasped his arm as soon as he entered.

"This will be brief, yes?" she asked. "Cecil has been upset enough this evening. I do not wish him to know we are speaking."

He could barely make out her silhouette, though his eyes were adjusting quickly.

"Does he know you already have a husband?"

"He knows I had a husband, yes. But that was many years ago."

"Well, the husband you had is currently looking for you. He wants a divorce — or your demise. Your guess is as good as mine which he would prefer."

"No!" she gasped. "This is impossible. Too many years have passed. He would have had to set our marriage aside. He would have needed an heir."

"Do I understand you correctly? You were going to marry Cecil on the mere assumption that your previous husband would have made you free to do so?"

"Why are you telling me this nonsense?" she demanded. "I assure you, his position would have demanded he marry again in order to sire an heir."

Sebastian shrugged, though it was doubtful she could see it in the dark. "Apparently he was in no hurry to do so. Now that he is, his bride-to-be wants absolute proof that his first marriage is ended. My guess is that she won't settle for any divorce that he could arrange. She wants to see for herself that you agree to it. She doesn't want you showing up later, thereby making any heirs she gives him illegitimate."

"I am truly still married?" she said in a small, incredulous voice.

"Not just that, madame. He is hiring people to find you and bring you back to Austria. He knows your path led to this country. It wasn't very wise of you to remain here, or to keep your name."

"I changed my name."

"You should have dropped the title, too."

She was silent for a moment, then said tiredly, "Vanity, yes, that was unwise. But I didn't stay here. I have been living most of these years abroad, always traveling. I am sick to death of traveling. I was enchanted with this country when I passed through it. I yearned often to come back here to settle. I finally gave in to that yearning."

"Bad timing, then, since this is where he'll be looking for you."

She started to cry. Sebastian couldn't help but feel sympathy for the fugitive duchess. "I would suggest you tell Cecil the problem. He will know who to see to arrange a quick divorce for you. Get those papers sent with all swiftness to your husband the duke. That should satisfy him."

"How did you come to know about this?"

"He tried to hire me to find you." The Raven grinned menacingly. "I didn't particularly like his way of asking."

Chapter 45

"Should I be jealous?" Margaret asked when Sebastian joined her in the parlor again.

"What the deuce for? Ah," he said, following her gaze.

She was watching the duchess of Felburg reenter the room just moments after he did. Not that she sounded the least bit jealous. There was merely curiosity in her tone.

"I needed to speak to the lady about some old unfinished business," he explained. "My good deed for the — century, as it were."

"The century, eh? Good deed opportunities show up so infrequently for you?"

"No."

Her lips twisted sourly. He felt an urge to hug her. Margaret wasn't very good at teasing. Lord love her, she tried, but she tended to leave herself wide open for broadsides that she didn't know how to parry. Of course, she probably fared better with others in the matter of teasing. She'd just never come up against someone with his odd sense of humor, or lack thereof.

He was going to miss her. It struck him poignantly that it was the first time he'd felt that way about anyone other than his own family or Giles. The bluestocking had grown on him. He'd gotten used to her hard-nosed candor, her incessant chatter, her forthright way of looking at things. She was quite the gem, Maggie was, so unexpected after their first meeting when she'd walked all over him with her indomitable determination to help someone she cared about.

He actually admired that in her and had from the start, though he'd been too annoyed with her to admit it. And good God, the attraction between them was killing him. He never should have agreed to delay his departure in order to attend this party with her. It had been pure hell staying away from Maggie for most of the day when he'd wanted to spend every last hour of his remaining time in England with her in his arms.

The simple fact was, he had nothing to offer Margaret. That he had even come to that realization amazed him, since it put her into a category that he'd never put any other woman — the desire to keep her. But Margaret needed stability, a man she could depend on, a man who would always be there for her — a man like he used to be.

"Oh my."

Sebastian followed Margaret's gaze to the door. He went very still. Douglas and Abigail had walked in, arm in arm. Margaret groaned. Abbie might not be on speaking terms with her son, but with Denton in London, the old girl would make an exception and enlist her son to escort her to a party in honor of her grandson's marriage.

Having done his duty, Douglas patted his mother's hand, and Abigail moved to the first group of acquaintances she recognized, while Douglas moved straight toward Sebastian and Margaret. Quite a few people stopped him along the way, determined to speak with him, either to offer congratulations on the new member of his family, or to ask after his health.

"Bloody hell," Sebastian swore.

"Buck up," Margaret said in her staunchest tone. "You can withstand this."

He glanced down at her and shook his head. "You don't understand, Maggie. We've committed the worst sort of manipulation. My father is tossing his convictions out the door — based on a lie we perpetrated. When I agreed to this farce, I expected only grudging compliance from him, and only for your sake. I had no idea how much he wants you to be part of his family, so much so that he'd actually forgive me. It's not just that I can't do that to *him*. I can't bloody well stomach his acceptance of me for a reason that isn't even real."

"You don't know yet that he's tossed out anything. For appearance's sake, of course he must play the role of the proud father, just as you've been playing the role of the redeemed son."

"Don't count on it."

"Then you should leave now, right now," Margaret urged. "I'll think of some —"

Too late. Douglas had reached them, and after hugging Margaret, he said, "I can't believe that neither of you mentioned your marriage to me when we last spoke. Did you think I couldn't withstand the shock while I was still recovering?"

He was smiling. Worse, his smile seemed to be genuine. There was warmth in his amber eyes. This was the man Sebastian remembered, the father he'd had — before the duel.

"We need to talk," Sebastian replied in a clipped, hard tone.

"Certainly," Douglas agreed.

"In private," Sebastian added.

Margaret sighed quite loudly at that. Douglas was now frowning but said, "Alberta's study is off of her library. I'll let her know we need to use it and I'll meet you there."

"I'll join you," Margaret began as soon as Douglas moved off to speak with the dowager duchess.

"No, you won't," Sebastian cut in. "Stay here."

He left her before she could summon up her determination and insist. The study was easy enough to find, a small utilitarian room for conducting business, lacking the frills one might expect a duchess to favor.

Douglas entered a few moments later, closed the door behind him. His expression was shuttered now.

He began, "I suppose this is overdue."

"No," Sebastian said, "not overdue, just necessary. Before you say anything you might regret, you need to know that Maggie and I aren't really married."

Douglas stiffened. "What nonsense is this? You haven't consummated the marriage yet? I happen to know you shared the same room —"

"I'm afraid you misunderstand," Sebastian interrupted. "Not married as in we

392

never got married to begin with. It was a ruse."

"This is nothing to joke about, Sebastian."

"I agree. I told you she hired me. I told you why. The pretense of a marriage was to assist me in my investigation. I couldn't very well do as she wanted if the door to Edgewood was still barred to me."

Douglas was quite red cheeked by now. "Good God, I can't believe that a son of mine —"

"I'm the dead son, remember?"

"What the devil are you talking about? You ruin that girl and for such a flimsy reason?"

"The reason was sound at the time. We didn't expect you to have another accident, or to become so seriously ill with a fever that could very well have killed you. If you had been fit and hale, you would have kicked me out of the house without the least bit of discussion — just as you did eleven years ago!"

Sebastian turned away. The shield on his emotions was cracking. He had to fight to repair it. He'd had excuses eleven years ago that never got said, that Giles's death had been an accident. He wasn't going to make excuses for this.

"She will announce a divorce not long after I'm gone," Sebastian said. "My desertion will gain her sympathy and understanding."

"You're leaving?"

Was that surprise in his father's tone? He glanced at Douglas again, but his expression hadn't changed. He was probably furious over the deception and bitterly disappointed that Margaret was not truly his daughter-in-law.

"Of course I'm leaving. I never wanted to come here in the first place."

"Then you will marry her first. Or will you stand there and try to tell me you never touched her?"

"No, I can't tell you that."

Even more angry color shot up into Douglas's cheeks. "Then by God you will marry her."

"For what? So you can claim her as a daughter-in-law until she institutes a real divorce?"

"Because it's the right thing to do," Douglas said, glaring at him.

Chapter 46

Margaret took part in several conversations of which she couldn't remember a single word. Sebastian hadn't returned yet from his private talk with Douglas. What was taking them so long?

She should have insisted on joining them. The marriage idea had been hers, after all. She would have explained it all to Douglas herself, after Sebastian was gone. She would have had to, when she announced the divorce. She wished she could do so now in order to alleviate some of the backlash Sebastian was no doubt receiving from his father.

She had a feeling Sebastian wouldn't mention that the pretense had been her idea. She even had a feeling why. He seemed to want Douglas's anger directed at him. It was what he had expected all along, so keeping it that way prevented him from finding out if they really could reconcile.

Perhaps Sebastian was so certain his father would never forgive him that he couldn't help but be defensive and resentful. Actually, it could be that he wouldn't forgive his father. Good God, she hadn't considered that. It would certainly explain why he had refused ever to return to England.

She was fretting herself sick on what was happening in the study. She didn't doubt she looked it, too, so she sought out Alberta to let her know they would be leaving as soon as Sebastian returned. The duchess claimed to understand and even commiserated with her.

"Happens to all you young gels," Alberta told her. "You let the nerves get the better of you. Why, I've had some of them faint, before and after the party I've given for them." And with a stern eye, Alberta demanded, "You aren't going to faint, are you?"

Margaret managed not to laugh. "I have an aversion to lying on floors, so I will most certainly restrain m'self. But I am feeling rather peaked, so I'm going to seek my own bed. I just wanted to thank you for the lovely party and to warn you that once Sebastian sees that I'm not feeling well, he's likely to drag me straight home. He's like that, you know."

"Is he?" Alberta chuckled. "Well, some men do overreact when they're concerned. Don't give it another thought, m'dear. I confess that even I was a tad nervous about tonight, but it went splendidly, if I do say so m'self. Well, I need to rephrase that," she added with a glower as she faced the door. "It was going splendidly."

Margaret didn't have to turn around to know what Alberta was talking about. She winced, hearing Juliette's raised voice behind her. When she'd spoken with Abigail about a half hour ago, she'd learned that Denton and his wife had planned to attend the party, but must have been delayed in their return from London.

Alberta tsked in high annoyance, admitting, "I've asked that gel to stay out of my house. Even if I wasn't obliged to invite the Townshends, I would have anyway because I adore Abigail. But Denton's wife is not welcome here. I told her so as politely as I could, and when that didn't work, I confess I was quite rude about it. Other hostesses in the area have experienced the same predicament with that gel. I swear her understanding of the English language is selective. She still comes and still disrupts."

Margaret was surprised to hear that Juliette had become a social pariah. No one wanted to shun the Townshends, but everyone seemed to disapprove of Juliette and her appalling behavior. Denton had probably been beseeched to control his wife, but Denton had no control over her. Juliette seemed to control him.

Seeing the duchess so indignant when she was renowned for maintaining a social demeanor that never got ruffled amused Margaret.

"At least she keeps the gossips busy for a while," Margaret said, trying to appear sympathetic.

"Which is quite the point. People should be talking about my parties, not the scandalous behavior of one of the guests, an uninvited guest, I might add. Now that you are a member of that family, I hope you can break through the language barrier and convince her to keep her outrageous antics at home where they belong."

"I'll see what I can do," Margaret promised.

"Good." Alberta huffed and with a scowl in Juliette's direction, marched off to find some consolation from her cronies.

Ordinarily, Margaret would join Juliette and try to calm her down, but Juliette hadn't spoken to her since she'd learned of Margaret's marriage. If the one glare she'd intercepted hadn't been enough to warn her that their so-called friendship was over because of it, Juliette's loud complaints across the room certainly did.

"The traitor marries him and gets honored. Why was I not honored when I married you, eh?"

Denton didn't appear to be embarrassed. He was too used to being the center of attention at parties because of his very vocal wife. But Abigail looked flustered. Juliette was loud enough that even Abigail, with her poor hearing, had caught every word.

So Juliette considered her a traitor? That was amusing, Margaret thought. Before Juliette could offer even more insults and disrupt the party further, she decided to leave the room and find out what was keeping Sebastian.

She wouldn't be surprised if he'd already left without her, especially if Douglas had demanded that he truly marry her.

She didn't quite make it out of the parlor before Juliette focused on her next target. "And him!" the Frenchwoman snarled contemptuously. "Disowned and yet —"

The remark ended abruptly. Margaret glanced back at Juliette and then stopped in surprise. Denton had actually put his hand over his wife's mouth to shut her up. Although he might be immune to the insults she leveled at him, he wasn't going to let her slander his brother. Bravo, Denton! Margaret wondered if Sebastian's return had given him courage. It was about time he took his wife in hand. And, apparently, she wasn't the only one who thought so.

Someone clapped. Loudly. Then someone else did. Within seconds, the entire room was applauding. Juliette looked furious and embarrassed. She broke away from Denton, snarling a French expletive that Margaret was quite glad she didn't understand and ran out the door.

Barely managing to get out of the way before Juliette knocked her over, Margaret backed into a hard body. She turned to apologize but didn't get the words out. It was her temporary husband standing there, and he looked like hell warmed over.

For a moment she thought he looked angry because he'd been there long enough to have heard Juliette. But, amazingly, his tone was bland as he asked her, "Did I miss something pertinent?"

"Just your brother keeping his wife from reviling you in public."

"Good for him," Sebastian said. "Shall we go?"

She frowned. His lack of interest puzzled

her. But his expression hadn't changed. He was furious about something, and if not Juliette . . .

She was afraid to find out what, so she merely said, "Yes. I've already told our hostess we're going home."

"We'll be stopping there," he said as he took her arm and escorted her outside.

She braced herself to encounter Juliette on the steps, but fortunately, Juliette hadn't waited for her coach to be brought up. She'd found it herself and it was racing down the road.

And then Margaret realized what Sebastian had just said. "What d'you mean, stopping there?"

"To pick up John and Timothy and any traveling companions you'd like to bring along."

"Bring along to where? Where the devil are we going that we need an entourage?"

"Where else but Scotland? They do still marry people up there on the spot, don't they?"

Margaret drew in her breath sharply. "We need to discuss this."

"There's nothing to discuss."

"The devil there isn't," she rejoined hotly. "One doesn't just hie off to Scotland in the middle of the night. At the very least, wait until morning when you'll see that this isn't necessary."

"No waiting," he said as he shoved her into the coach that had pulled up. "If I sleep on it, I won't be doing the 'right thing.'"

"But —"

"Not another bloody word, Maggie, or you will spend this entire trip in my lap."

She opened her mouth, but the menacing glint in his eyes arrested her and she quickly clamped it shut. This was The Raven she was dealing with now, and the dratted man was serious!

Chapter 47

"I've a bone to pick with you, sir," Margaret announced as she caught up with Douglas on the eastern trail leading to the cliffs.

He had resumed his morning rides. She had ridden over to Edgewood bright and early only to be told that she had just missed him. It was just one more frustration to add to the long list of them that had plagued her since the night of Alberta's party.

She still couldn't believe that Sebastian, at least the reasonable Sebastian, hadn't appeared once on that long trip to Scotland, that she'd had to suffer The Raven's company for the entire journey. Cold, mercenary, silent. That odious man would have done exactly what he'd said he would do if she had tried to argue with him. And glorious fool that she was, she didn't really want to argue with him, so she hadn't put it to the test.

She'd foolishly hoped that if they did get married, he'd stay with her in England and really be her husband. Those hopes had soared when he'd kissed her in the church after he'd signed the papers that bound her to him. It had been a hard, passionate kiss that had pushed aside all her doubts. She'd even thought he'd mumbled that he loved her when he'd hugged her before walking out of the church, leaving her there alone.

When she went outside, however, he was gone. John and Tim were gone, their horses were gone, and she'd burst into tears. She'd known, deep down, that was going to happen. Sebastian might have ridden in the coach with her, but he'd brought his horses along. Once he'd finished doing the "right thing," she was sure he'd ridden straight for the nearest dock to catch a ship back to Europe.

"I expected you sooner," Douglas said a bit hesitantly, since her face was florid with agitation.

"Did you? Well, where shall I start? First, there was that mad dash to Scotland where we didn't stop once to sleep, not once, just long enough to get baskets of food to take with us and answer nature's calls. Sleeping in a vehicle that is racing across the countryside is next to impossible, if you didn't know."

"Then he did marry you?"

The question disconcerted her. "You didn't think he would after you talked with him?"

"I wasn't sure," he admitted. "I bloody well haven't been sure about anything since his return. He's — changed. I got no sense of his feelings."

"It was like dealing with a stranger? Yes, I know. But that's who he is now. There's nothing left of the old Sebastian in him. That fellow died with Giles."

That was brutally blunt, even for her. But she was too annoyed at the moment to mince words. Douglas did appear stricken, though she might be reading him wrong, which wouldn't surprise her. Her judgment did seem to be utterly off the mark lately.

"Well, as I was saying," she continued, "I would have been back sooner, but I spent an entire day in bed recovering from that mad dash, and then the dratted wheel on my coach broke. That couldn't happen before I wasted a day in bed, no, it had to happen afterward to delay me further!"

Douglas was now looking embarrassed, confounding her until he said, "You don't have to make excuses for enjoying a brief honeymoon."

Margaret blinked. She might have laughed

hysterically if she weren't so frustrated with the Townshends, father and son.

"Did I neglect to mention he deserted me at the altar? I would have much preferred he do so before he married me, but no, he signed those papers first, then left me there without a by your leave. You do realize that what would have been a simple matter of just saying I got a divorce is now going to be a major inconvenience for me? I will have to go to London, hire a solicitor, appear before the courts and —"

"Then don't get a divorce."

"I beg your pardon? Why the deuce would I remain married to a man whom I will never see again?"

"Because I don't for a minute believe you'll never see him again. He was sufficiently enamored with you to ruin your reputation, was he not?"

She snorted at his own bluntness. "My reputation is just fine, thank you."

"It won't be if you institute a divorce."

"Nonsense. I happen to have the most valid, sympathetic reason possible. The man has deserted me. You are mistaken if you think he actually had tender feelings for me. Lust was all he felt for me."

She hadn't meant to be that frank.

"You cannot convince me that you succumbed to lust, Maggie. You love him, don't you?"

She sighed. "Not that it matters, but yes, I am that foolish."

"Did you tell him?"

"Certainly not! I admit I'm a fool, but not that foolish. He gave me no indication, ever, that he returned my feelings. A woman has to have some encouragement before she bares her heart. Now it's your turn to be truthful with me, Douglas. Did you hope this marriage would make Sebastian stay here in England?"

"That did occur to me, but only after you two had left the party that night. It certainly wasn't why I insisted he marry you."

"Then why?"

"Do you really need to ask? He's a Townshend. No son of mine will dishonor a lady of your quality and not correct the wrong he did you."

She stared incredulously at him. "Did you hear what you just said? A son of yours? Do you not realize that he no longer considers himself that? If your disowning him didn't fix that in his mind, he arrived here to find —"

"Maggie, listen to me," he interrupted rather quickly, as if he were afraid he might change his mind. "You're his wife now, at

407

least for the moment you are, and I've cut myself off from those I could have confided this to."

"What do you mean, cut yourself off?"

"Deliberately, mind you. I felt I didn't deserve to have a shoulder to cry on."

She frowned, not quite understanding, and then she did. "Good God, you regret disowning him, don't you?"

"Of course I do."

"Why didn't you tell him? Why didn't you tell your mother, for that matter, instead of living with her silence all these years?"

"Because I deserved her contempt, but even that wasn't enough punishment. I wouldn't allow myself the comfort she would have offered. Sebastian was gone. Nothing could have absolved me of being responsible for that."

"You've regretted it that long?"

"Oh, yes. And I wasn't even angry at him, I was angry for him, because I knew what he'd done would destroy him. But I let that anger get out of hand. Having a wicked hangover the morning of that dratted duel didn't help, because I'd gotten foxed the night before over the entire mess with Giles. But once the fumes of anger left me, and my head stopped pounding, I realized what I'd said. Even then, I didn't think he'd taken me literally. But when I went to find him to tell him I didn't mean it — he was already gone."

"You didn't send someone after him?"

"No, I went myself. I'd guessed the right direction he'd taken, but his ship had already sailed by the time I reached Dover. I got passage on the next ship available, but — obviously I never found him. I've sent others more capable than I over the years, but it was as if he disappeared from the face of the earth."

"Or changed his name, which he did. Now for God's sake, Douglas, why didn't you tell Sebastian all this while he was here?"

"Do you really need to ask, when you said it yourself? I wasn't going to bare my heart, either. Not once did he appear willing to hear what I had to say on the subject. If anything, he was as closed as a sealed tomb when he was with me. He isn't going to forgive me. Nor can I blame him, when I can't forgive myself."

Chapter 48

"You've been damned moody since we got back," Sebastian remarked as he listened to John slamming lids back on pots on the stove.

The kitchen was cold, despite all the cooking that had been done in it that day. What had been left to simmer on the stove for their dinner just didn't heat a room of that size. The fire crackling in the hearth was too far away from the table as well. They should have moved the table closer to it, but Sebastian couldn't seem to get up the gumption to do anything. Eight inquiries about jobs had been left with Maurice, the caretaker, but he hadn't bothered to read any of the notes.

"I take my cue from you," John replied as he came to the table with a bowl of thick stew.

"The hell you do," Sebastian shot back. "You usually just try to distract me out of my dark moods."

"Would it work this time?"

"No."

"There's your answer, and your dinner is getting cold. Or were you going to eat that bottle of brandy tonight?" John asked, eyeing the brandy in front of Sebastian.

"I'm thinking about it."

That reply cracked a grin out of John, but it was brief. Sebastian had never seen his friend like this before. Sebastian had moods, but John was the optimist who could be depended on to pull him up from the depths.

"Spit it out, John."

"The boy is unhappy. He really took to your grandmother and misses her."

"And that's what has had you making a nonstop racket for the last two days?"

John sighed. "I actually thought we would remain in England. Why, you might ask? Because you married Lady Margaret! You might not ever speak with your father again, but she is there and is reason enough to stay. If you had no intention of doing so, you shouldn't have married her."

"So," Sebastian said thoughtfully, "you've been slamming things around because you are annoyed with my decision? Or because, like Timothy, you find yourself missing someone we left behind?"

John flushed angrily. "Unlike some people, I don't deny I've met the woman I wouldn't mind spending the rest of my life with."

"You don't need to wait this out with me, John. Go on back and claim your lady."

"And leave you to drown in your mistakes?"

"I don't make mistakes."

"You're here, aren't you?"

Sebastian laughed at the rejoinder. When John was annoyed, he was quite amusing. But he supposed he shouldn't have left him in the dark.

"I'm giving Maggie a week to start divorce proceedings," he explained. "It's the gentlemanly thing to do. But if I find she hasn't done so, then she will have lost her chance to be rid of me."

"That implies you're going back to check?"

"Of course."

"Well, damn me, you couldn't have mentioned that sooner?" John complained.

Sebastian shrugged. "It wasn't an easy decision to make. Maggie deserves better than me. But for once I'm going to be selfish."

"That's if she hasn't started the proceedings. What if she has?"

"Then fate will have decided the matter."

John rolled his eyes. "Why leave it to chance? She doesn't think she'll ever see you again. She has no reason to delay a divorce."

Sebastian's lips thinned out. He'd decided only that morning to keep Margaret — if she didn't immediately get her divorce. He really hadn't thought much beyond giving her a few more days to see to it. But chivalry didn't suit him at all. Why indeed leave it to fate?

"If she's divorced me, perhaps I'll get down on bended knee and actually ask for her hand. How long do you think she'll laugh?"

John scowled at him. "Why do you do this? Why do you feel that the life you've taken on is contemptible? You've helped a lot of people who were desperate and would otherwise be flat out of luck if not for you."

"And done a lot of meaningless jobs that merely served the greed or vengeance of the ones hiring me."

"So there were a few bad jobs mixed in with the good. The good ones still count. What made you think Lady Margaret would turn you down if you offered her your life rather than the one she's accustomed to?"

"I said I'm going back," Sebastian said defensively.

"But you were joking about asking her to marry you, the real you, the man you are now, not the one you used to be. What makes you think she wouldn't have you?"

"What makes you think she would? Every interaction I've had with her was forced on her, including making that marriage real. She had a host of reasons why she didn't want to marry me and would have trotted them all out had I let her."

"Perhaps because you forgot to tell her that you wanted to marry her? Or am I reading this wrong? Did you tell her how you feel about her?"

Sebastian downed the remaining brandy in his glass. "You've made some good points, John. I'll give it more thought."

"By the by," John added curiously, "what did Denton have to say?"

"When?"

"In his letter."

"What letter?"

John rolled his eyes. "I should have known you were too deep in thought earlier to hear me tell you I put his letter in your room. It arrived this morning."

Curious, Sebastian went to fetch the letter but was disappointed when he read it.

He returned to the kitchen to tell John in disgust, "Cryptic as usual. I don't know what his problem is these days, that he has to skirt every issue."

"Why did he write to you, then?"

Sebastian snorted. "To tell me that if I want answers, I might find them with Juliette's brother. Why the deuce doesn't Denton just give me the answers?"

"Perhaps he doesn't know what they are," John offered.

That thought gave Sebastian pause. He reread the letter:

Seb,

I didn't think you'd leave this quickly. I needed time to readjust my thinking. Juliette had me convinced for the longest time that you were the culprit. It quite removed the halo I'd placed over your head.

I should have told you this sooner, that yes, Juliette has been responsible for father's accidents. Although he suspects nothing and swears they were just accidents, and she hasn't stated clearly that she's caused them, she's implied it, and has promised worse will happen if I divorce her. But before that, there were other things she held over my head.

God, even now I don't have the guts to tell you. But her brother, Pierre Poussin, might know. She had him tossed in prison on some charge she fabricated, because he was going to stop her. At least, she throws it in my face that she got rid of him for me. Maybe he doesn't even exist. Maybe everything she says is just lies. God, I just don't know.

"Actually, he says as much," Sebastian remarked, handing the letter to John. "That he doesn't know. Although it sounds like Juliette has him convinced that she is causing my father's accidents, which I'm not sure is the case a'tall. She's using them as a means to control Denton, though."

John looked up from the letter. "Ah, Juliette's brother in prison . . . her remark the gardener overheard at Edgewood makes more sense now."

"That she got rid of her brother for him, and got rid of me for him? For him? Hmm, I just may have to beat my brother senseless and rearrange his guts for him, since he seems to have lost them."

John chuckled, but only for a moment. "It does sound like Lord Denton is or was involved in more than we imagined. Though it also sounds like he wants it out in the open, or he wouldn't be suggesting that you find Juliette's brother in order to get some answers. Does he say which prison?"

Sebastian shook his head. "He probably doesn't know that either."

"Well, this all began in Paris where they met Juliette, so we can perhaps assume it is one near there. You are going to pay him a visit?"

Sebastian frowned. "You know, if you think about it, Juliette's name comes up too often in relation to strange events — the duel, Maggie's sister's abrupt departure from White Oaks, my father's accidents. This is one hell of a convoluted scheme, whatever it is, much bigger than we could have guessed."

"Cause and effect?" John suggested thoughtfully. "What might have started as a single plot could have spiraled into many more."

"Could it be that simple?"

John chuckled. "Probably not, but —"

The caretaker opened the door to announce in high annoyance, "A visitor, monsieur. I tell him to come tomorrow at a better hour, but no, he will not go away. He says he knows you, but he will not give his name."

"Where is he?" Sebastian asked.

Maurice thumbed his hand behind him. "Out front. It is amazing how many people will honor those outer steps as if a door still stood there blocking their way. Is that stew I smell?"

"Help yourself to a bowl, Maurice. I'll see to our visitor."

"Want me to go?" John asked. "Half of them say they know you just to gain access to you."

"Which will make it easier for me to send him on his way. Is there light out there, Maurice, or should I take some with me?"

"My lantern. I leave it on the steps."

Sebastian nodded and left the kitchen. He hadn't needed to be concerned with light. It was a clear night. Moonlight bathed the debris in the ruined old great hall he had to pass through. And the glow of Maurice's lantern was a beacon that outlined the broken stone arch that was all that was left of what used to be the entrance to the keep.

The chap stood on the steps there, his back to the arch, staring out at the moonlit countryside as he waited. He wore a tiered greatcoat for warmth, a thick scarf about his neck, and a hat pulled down low.

And then, apparently hearing Sebastian's footsteps behind him, he turned. And

Sebastian did recognize him. He just didn't believe what he was seeing.

"I'm real," he assured Sebastian. "Flesh and bone."

"And blood? Let's just make sure you aren't vapor, shall we?" Sebastian said as he slammed his fist into Giles's face.

Chapter 49

Sebastian reached for the bottle of brandy as he took his seat again at the kitchen table. He ignored the glass now, drinking straight from the bottle. He didn't want to think. He didn't want to know. He was so close to losing all semblance of humanity that the slightest thing could tip the scale.

John was staring curiously at the body Sebastian had carted in over his shoulder and dumped on the floor. "Should I wake him?" John asked.

"If you want to see me commit murder, go ahead."

John glanced at Sebastian in surprise. "Good Lord, what did the fellow do?"

"Turn him over."

John did and then stepped back with a gasp. "Oh, I say, he looks just like, well, that is, the likeness is uncanny, isn't it? Didn't know Lord Wemyss senior had another son tucked away. A bastard?"

"No."

"But the resemblance is remarkable!"

"Because it's not a resemblance."

"But —" John didn't finish because he came to the only conclusion left. He shook his head firmly. "I don't believe in ghosts."

"Neither do I."

"But you killed him!"

"Yes, and I'm going to kill him again as soon as he wakes up."

"I'll help you," John said with some ire of his own. "When I think of all the repercussions due to his death, and for him not to be dead, well, it quite boggles my mind. By the by, what'd you do to him?"

"He was always a great shot, but he never could take a punch," Sebastian said in disgust. "A bloody feather could knock him over."

"That isn't quite true," Giles said as he sat up and fingered his jaw. "I can withstand punches well enough, just not from you. And you're going to let me explain before you kill me, right?"

"Probably not. An explanation eleven years ago would have been welcome. Now there is nothing that can justify —"

"They were going to kill him!" Giles cut in. "When he showed up in Paris, he was already running for his life."

"Who?"

"My father. God, Seb, I had no idea of what he'd done to us with his damn gambling. He paupered us! There was nothing left."

"Bloody hell," Sebastian snarled. "Start from the beginning!"

Giles nodded and rose clumsily to his feet. The years hadn't treated him well. His brown hair was dulled, riddled with gray. His face was nearly like leather parchment, lined and deeply tanned. There was little semblance of the aristocrat left in him.

"May I sit down?" Giles asked, indicating the extra chairs at the table.

"You'd be pushing it to get that close to me."

"Quite right," Giles agreed and began to pace. "So where shall I start?"

"That's been established."

"Very well. We were in Paris, Denton and I, rounding up the last week of our tour. He hadn't enjoyed the trip, spent most of it foxed. Having reached his majority, the fact that he was a second son was making him miserable."

"If you're going to tell me that my brother was behind this —"

"No," Giles said quickly.

"Then stick to the facts, which is all I'm willing to hear."

"We were having dinner at our hotel. The Poussins, brother and sister, were eating at the next table and struck up a conversation with us. We were asked to join them. Nothing out of the ordinary."

"What were they doing there?"

"Merely having dinner. They lived in the city nearby, often ate at that hotel. The brother, Pierre, didn't stay long but didn't insist his sister leave with him, either, which made me suspect that while they were portraying themselves as French aristocrats, and certainly dressed the part, they really weren't. But anyway, as soon as her brother left, Juliette started flirting outrageously with Denton. He was too deep in his cups to really notice, but they ended up going up to his room together."

"Why didn't you stop them?"

"Whatever for? I concluded by then that she was a high-class whore who would cost him a few pounds instead of a few coppers. He'd been having such a lousy time on the trip, I thought he might enjoy the diversion. She was beautiful. She spent the night with him."

"And yet ends up married to you? You might want to explain that quickly before my fist finds your face again."

"I never married her. But do you want this out of order, or shall I continue?"

Sebastian gritted his teeth. "Go on."

"The next day my father showed up. He was waiting in my room when I returned to dress for dinner. I was delighted to see him until I got a good look at him. He was distraught. Good Lord, I could almost smell his fear. I was alarmed, of course. I'd never seen him like that before."

"Gambling away one's inheritance will do that to people," Sebastian concluded from Giles's earlier remark.

"I wish it had only been that, but it wasn't. He'd not only lost his inheritance, and mine for that matter, but he'd continued to gamble in order to recoup his losses!"

"With what?"

"Borrowed money, of course. He'd been borrowing from your father for years, apparently. The debt got so high he'd even been obliged to turn over the deed to our home to Douglas. But even someone as generous as your father had to draw the line somewhere and refused to give him any more money. My father resented that. I could hear it in his tone when he was explaining all this to me."

" 'Douglas had everything,' my father said. 'A better title, a wonderful mother who doted on him, more money than he'd ever need.' My father didn't understand why Douglas had to cut him off."

"You said Cecil was running for his life?"

Giles sighed. "He ended up borrowing money from the wrong sort of people in London, the sort that won't tolerate out-standing debts. They'd given him a date to pay up or pay with his life. He couldn't meet the deadline."

"And you had no prior warning of any of this?"

"None, but I didn't really see my father often in those last couple of years. And he did rage at me once for spending too much money, which was a shock. But I didn't take him seriously. He was foxed at the time. You see, he was trying, desperately, to continue our lives as if nothing had changed. Good Lord, he even let me take the tour, when there was no money to pay for it. Your father paid for it, by the way, and without being asked. He might have refused to support my father's gambling anymore, but they were still friends — at least he thought they were."

"What are you implying?"

"I think my father's resentment against

Douglas had turned to hatred by then. How else could he come up with such an outlandish scheme to use against Douglas in order to get himself out of debt?"

"Your supposed death?" Sebastian guessed. "How the devil was that going to get him out of debt?"

"Guilt. He was certain that Douglas would be so overcome with it that he would cancel their debt and even make further recompense. And he was right. Your father did exactly that."

"And disowned me," Sebastian snarled as he stood up.

Giles put up a restraining hand. "Wait, that was never part of it. I didn't even know that had happened until years later. It was certainly never mentioned as a possible outcome. And I was in shock the day my father confessed all this and told me the solution he'd come up with. You don't think I wanted to participate in my own death, do you?"

"You don't want to know what I think right now," Sebastian said, but he resumed his seat. "Continue."

"My father really was running for his life. He didn't come to Paris with his plan already thought-out. He'd arrived a few days earlier and apparently had a run-in with

Juliette. She'd tried some scam on him for money, which didn't work. He'd laughed in her face because he had no money. But then he saw her having dinner with Denton and me and how she was flirting with Denton. He figured she was setting Denton up for a scam as well, and that's when the plan came to him, to use her to manipulate you and me into a duel."

"So he'd already talked to Juliette before he came to see you?" Sebastian asked.

"Yes."

"And how did he get her to go along with his 'plan'?"

"He threatened to have her tossed in jail if she didn't comply. But later, when I learned she married Denton, I realized your brother was the real reason she got involved."

"Let's leave my brother out of this for the moment," Sebastian said. "So the duel and the reason for it — my having slept with your 'wife' — all of it was planned ahead of time?"

"Yes. And you fell right into that. If you hadn't touched her — you know, I actually had hoped you wouldn't. I was so sick at heart. You were my best friend! I was to make you think you killed me and then disappear for the rest of my life. I didn't mind disappearing so much. My father was going to send me money after he got his accounts settled. And I wasn't really ready to marry Eleanor yet, so although I knew I would lose her because of it, I wasn't heartbroken over that."

"She was."

"Yes, I know, and so was I later, but I'm getting ahead of myself. The morning of the duel, I had a leather pouch of blood I was supposed to break, to make my death look real. That was Juliette's idea. She supplied it. I wasn't going to fire at you at all. But you!" Giles burst out. "Standing there obviously not going to shoot at me, either. That was ruining the plan."

"You fired at me," Sebastian reminded him.

"I had to, but you know I'm an excellent shot. I only nicked your arm to lower it so you'd at least be pointing your damned pistol at me. But bloody hell, you actually did shoot me!"

Giles tore open his shirt to show Sebastian the scar.

Sebastian wasn't impressed. "Not severe enough," he said.

Giles stared at him incredulously for a moment, then said calmly, "Actually, it did nearly kill me. She didn't get me a doctor. And my father wasn't there, because he was hiding in France until it was all over. Juliette couldn't have cared less if I died at that point. She'd played her part as the grieving widow. She merely had Anton get me to the coast and put me on a ship back to France."

"Bloody hell, that's where I remember him from. He was your second at the duel, wasn't he?"

"Yes, he was one of her lackeys."

"So my being disowned was a minor consequence to you?" Sebastian said, and there was nothing calm about his tone now.

Giles cringed and replied quickly, "Nothing that occurred back then was minor to me, but you haven't heard the last of it yet. I don't remember much of that trip back to France. I was dumped on the docks, since the captain didn't want me dying on his ship. An old woman found me, promised to fix me up if I married her and worked her farm. I'll be deuced if I know how she pulled it off, but I did end up married to her, and she did patch me up."

Sebastian had heard enough. He stood up and started to approach Giles. Giles read him correctly and started backing away.

"One," Sebastian said in a cold, hard voice, "you had ample opportunity to tell me what was going on before anyone could harm your father."

"So you could do what? You didn't have the blunt to pay off my father's debts, I certainly didn't, and those men really were going to kill him if they found him before he had their money."

"So instead of letting my father know that his foolishness had progressed to that point — and don't for a minute think that my father wouldn't have gotten him out of that mess if he'd known — he had to perpetrate this cruel deception instead? You should have told me, Giles!"

"You don't know how much I agonized over that, how many times I convinced myself that something could have been done. But he was convinced that your father wouldn't bail him out again."

"But it was all right if my life was ruined?"

"I didn't know about your being disowned, not until several years later. My father never mentioned it. I did keep in touch with him, you know. When I confronted him about it, he swore he hadn't expected that either. And you weren't ruined. I saw you a few years later, here in France. I was tempted to hail you, but since you appeared well and quite prosperous, I slithered off. That did end my worst agony for a while. You were always the question mark that weighed on my conscience until that day."

"Appearances are deceiving, Giles."

"Nonsense. I had no doubt that you would fare well, I just needed confirmation. You were always resourceful. There was nothing you couldn't do if you set your mind to it. I idolized you. I wanted so much to be like you, but I just couldn't cut it."

"Two," Sebastian said, "you not only ruined my life, you ruined my father's."

"The hell you say!" Giles gasped. "I have checked on our families. My father did stop gambling. With the money your father gave him to assuage his guilt, he managed to invest a little, has learned from his mistakes. But everyone at home is hale and hardy —"

"Good God, are you really that much of a fool? Did you find out in your 'checking' that my father has been estranged from his own mother since the duel? Did you find out he's also been estranged from your father? They haven't spoken in all these years! And although Juliette did end up married to my brother, she's made his life miserable."

Giles had paled. "God, no, I didn't know any of that."

"Then you're as much a failure as an investigator as you are as a friend!" Even John blanched over that slur, but Sebastian wasn't finished. "What have you done all these years other than hide?"

"I've been raising my son," Giles said quietly.

That gave Sebastian pause. "You had a son with that old woman you married?" he asked incredulously.

"No. I married Eleanor."

Chapter 50

"Did you have to knock him out again?" John complained. "His tale was just getting good."

Sebastian didn't reply.

"Should I wake him?" John asked.

"Go ahead, but if his jaw isn't broken this time, I'll just have to try again."

John winced and left Giles where he was on the floor. "I know what you're thinking," John said after a moment. "He's been happy all these years, married to the woman he loved, enjoying a son, while you've merely been amassing a fortune —"

"Do not trivialize the harm he's done!" Sebastian cut in with a snarl. "I'm not the only one who was affected by what he and his father did."

"He gave up the life he knew to save his father's life," John pointed out. "Some people might consider that noble."

"Noble?" Sebastian snorted. "He pursued

no other avenue of recourse. He went along with Cecil's ridiculous plan, and the results were mind-boggling. And all the while he assumes everything is just fine, that no one else lost a bloody thing, all because of his sacrifice. By God, what sacrifice did he really make? He's gone on with his life and even found peace and joy in it."

Giles groaned, sat up, locked his gaze on Sebastian across the room. "Did you have to hit me again?"

"The other option was to cut your throat," Sebastian said simply.

"Quite right," Giles said with a wince. "But you know, if I had known of all these repercussions —"

"You would have done what? Shown up to prove you weren't dead? I've news for you, friend. That wouldn't have bridged the gap between my father and me. Your courage should have come before that duel, before you let your father tear so many lives apart."

"God, Sebastian, I'm sorry. But the only alternative I saw at the time was to let my father die. I couldn't do that. I'm not proud of my part in this, and I'm ashamed that my father's weakness has hurt so many people. He's safe now, but you know I'll never forgive him for what he set in motion. I really don't care if I ever see him again."

"Just finish your story while I'm still willing to listen to it."

Giles sighed. "There isn't much more to tell. The old woman died three years later, leaving me her farm. I was accustomed to the life of a farmer by then, even enjoyed it, if you must know. But I had begun to regret losing Eleanor, realized too late just how much I did love her. She was never far from my thoughts. I finally contacted Eleanor. I simply couldn't help myself. She ran off to be with me. We were married in Scotland."

"So that note from her cousin about her death was a lie?"

Giles turned away, said with a catch in his throat, "No — that was true. She wanted to stay in Scotland. She liked it there, didn't take to the idea of being a farmer's wife. So we stayed with her cousin, but Harriet lived so bloody far from any towns! Eleanor died in childbirth, before I could get back with a doctor. I came back to the farm here with my son, have been here ever since. Ironically, the farm isn't too far south from here. I was selling my crop in a town nearby when I first heard of The Raven quite a few years ago."

"Is that why you're here? To hire The Raven?"

"Actually, if I'd known sooner that you were The Raven, I would have come to you sooner. And yes, I did think of hiring you, when I first heard about you. I was actually saving up for it. Didn't think I could meet your price, though."

"To do what?"

"To find you for me. I've wanted to make a clean breast of it for a long time now. Then when I saw you a few days ago in Le Havre and had it pointed out that you were him, well, that bowled me over, 'deed it did. And there you have it, all of it."

"And eleven years too late."

"But this will reinstate you with your father, won't it?"

"I think it's too late for that. The rift between me and my father is too deep now. But before I find out for sure, I need the inconsistencies cleared up first."

"Such as?"

"Such as why Denton married your father's accomplice and why she's been making his life miserable ever since."

"What are you suggesting?"

"Nothing, but I bloody well don't like loose ends. And I'll never get the answers from her. I've already tried that, just to hear lies."

"I'll leave in the morning," John offered,

"to find out what prison her brother is in. He appears to be our last —"

"Pierre Poussin is in prison?" Giles cut in.

Sebastian nodded. "According to Denton, Juliette arranged that. We'll all leave in the morning."

"We?" Giles asked.

"You don't think I'm letting you out of my sight until this is over, do you? My last option still remains with you."

"Which is?"

"Why, your death, of course. Having already paid the price for killing you, there isn't much incentive for me not to kill you a second time, is there?"

"Bloody hell," Giles mumbled. "I can think of one. Your namesake. My son."

Sebastian threw the now empty brandy glass at Giles's head. "You named your son after me?! Why?"

"For the obvious reason. You may not like the way this has played out any more than I, but I still consider you my best —"

"Don't say it, don't think it. If we are going to get through tomorrow without any bloodshed, don't ever mention it again."

Chapter 51

The prison looked like a medieval fortress in the middle of nowhere with a village grown up around it. As they rode closer, it merely looked like a dreary square stone edifice with no ornamentation, just two stories high. But high walls surrounded it, and guards stood at the only gate, barring entrance.

Finding out that Pierre Poussin had been sent here had been easy. Getting in to visit him proved to be more difficult. Not because visitors were allowed in only at certain times, but because Pierre was ill.

"You are welcome to wait," the guard told them in a friendly manner. "There are rooms at the tavern. They will welcome the business. But, truthfully, the doctor does not expect Poussin to last the week."

"What bloody rotten luck," John said as they nursed ales at a table in the tavern that night. And then he asked Sebastian, "Will you employ stealth or brute force?"

"Eh?" Giles injected. "Did I miss something? Are we going to wait this out or not?"

"Not," Sebastian said. "I'm not going to let the man die without talking to him first."

"I see I did miss something," Giles said. "If he doesn't recover, how the deuce do you expect to get around that?"

"By getting him out of there, of course."

"Oh, of course!" Giles exclaimed sarcastically. "Why didn't I think of that? Perhaps because that implies —" Giles paused, abashed as he realized, "Oh, I see, stealth or force. You're used to this sort of thing, are you?"

Sebastian didn't reply. While Giles had been behaving as if the last eleven years had been erased from their memories, Sebastian had erased nothing. So he spoke to his ex-friend as little as possible. Every time he tried to get beyond his own anger, to consider all the other circumstances, he couldn't get past one glaring point. Giles had suffered not at all for what he'd allowed to happen, while everyone else involved had suffered too much. Deep down he might be glad Giles was alive, but that emotion was behind his shell, remaining there unexamined.

John spoke up when it was apparent Sebastian wouldn't. "We've done this a few times before, yes. Though those targets were able to assist in their own extraction." And to Sebastian, "You've considered that? That you might have to carry Poussin out?"

"Yes. I noticed the mortuary at the end of the village, though. I'd say they need a few new employees."

"Ahh, quite right. That will do it."

"Do what?" Giles wanted to know but was ignored.

"We'll wait until after the changing of the guard at midnight," Sebastian continued. "That will give us the 'notification' that a body needs extracting, delivered by one of the guards on his way home, and the new watch won't have heard yet that Pierre died."

John nodded. "Much cleaner than bashing in heads on the way in."

Giles sat back with a glower. "And what will I be doing while you two do whatever it is you're talking about?"

"John is sitting this one out," Sebastian replied. "You'll be coming with me. There is risk involved. If we're caught, John will know what to do, whereas you'd just sit out here crying in your cups."

Giles flushed. "You really have a low opinion of me now, don't you?"

"You noticed?"

Several hours later, Sebastian and Giles drove the mortuary wagon they'd confiscated up to the prison gate. As expected, the two guards there complained that the collection could wait until morning. The late night guards were lazy. Most of them slept through that post and didn't like being disturbed. Surprisingly, Giles put on quite a performance of whining and insisting he'd lose his new job if he didn't come back with the body he'd been sent for.

Sebastian would have just started bashing heads together, but as it happened, having one of the guards escort them to the infirmary saved them the time and effort of having to search for it, and got them past one other guard along the way. Unfortunately, there were four prisoners sleeping in the room where the sick were kept. No guards or medical staff there at that time of night, but their helpful escort was determined to find the body for them and started checking each occupied bed.

Locating Pierre, the fellow exclaimed, "He is not dead! What — ?"

Giles probably thought he was being helpful again by grabbing a tin water pitcher next to Pierre's bed and denting it on the guard's head. All he managed from that feat was to get them all sloshed with water, and the guard turned in his direction with an angry snarl. Sebastian didn't appreciate the damp clothes at this time of year, but it did turn out to be helpful inasmuch as the fellow drew his pistol and pointed it at Giles, leaving his back to Sebastian. So it was an easy matter to move up behind him, wrest the pistol from him, and bash his head properly with it.

Fortunately, none of the other prisoners woke up during the commotion. The guard was dumped in the nearest empty bed to sleep off some of the headache he would have, and they quickly got Pierre onto the stretcher they'd brought in.

"What if he wakes up on the way out?" Giles questioned. "I doubt the remaining guards will think he's had a miraculous return from the dead if he starts making noises."

"If you didn't feel it when you lifted him," Sebastian replied, "he's burning up. If he wakes up, it will be miraculous."

"Oh, I say, you don't think what's killing him is contagious, do you?"

"He would have been isolated if it was," Sebastian said simply. "And I'll take the feet end of the stretcher. If I need to drop it to deal with anything threatening, make sure he doesn't slide off."

Back in the hallway, the guard at the end of the passageway was diligent. He'd locked the door again after they came through it.

"Where is Jean?" he demanded, referring to the chap they were leaving behind.

Sebastian said with a shrug, "Seeing all those empty beds in there was too much temptation for him. He decided to take a little nap."

He didn't expect that to be a sufficient excuse, and it wasn't. "Wait here," the guard said and started to head toward the infirmary.

The feet end of the stretcher dropped. Sebastian's foot tripped the man as he passed. He hit the floor, rolled, reaching for his pistol as he did. A hard right knocked his head against the floor. It took one more punch to put him out for the duration.

"How are your knuckles holding up?" Giles asked.

"There's still some skin left on them for you," Sebastian replied nonchalantly as he retrieved the key to open the passageway again.

"What luck!"

Sebastian almost smiled.

Outside, their lack of escort prompted the remaining guard to meet them halfway to the gate. Sebastian didn't give him a chance to ask where his friend was. The stretcher dropped again.

"This was too easy," Giles remarked as they put Pierre in the wagon they'd left out-side the gate.

"It wasn't a normal prison."

"There are different kinds?"

"According to John, who got a look at the records in Paris, no killers ever get sent here, which was why there weren't that many guards, even in the daytime. No high risk, fewer guards needed, and a much more relaxed routine."

"You could have mentioned that sooner," Giles mumbled and got the wagon moving back to the mortuary, where John was waiting for them with a coach.

"Why? So you could treat this as a lark without risk? There was still risk, and it's not over yet. We still have to vacate this area before one of those guards wakes up. And hope Pierre survives the trip."

"We're a long way from that ruins you call home," Giles mentioned. "As it happens, I believe my farm is only a few hours from here. I could be wrong. I've never traveled this far east on the coast. Didn't know this place was here. But I have been to Paris be-fore and we did take the same road south to get here that I use to get home."

"So?"

"So my son's tutor is a retired doctor," Giles said. "Or were you planning on nursing a dying man back to health yourself?"

"Lead the way. I just want answers from him. He's welcome to die after I have them."

Chapter 52

"What about the pink tulle?" Edna asked as she rifled through Margaret's wardrobe for a dress to replace her riding habit.

"I'd prefer something dark. I suppose my mourning clothes are packed away?"

"Of course they are," Edna replied. "You aren't in mourning."

"Odd, it certainly feels as if I am," Margaret remarked with a sigh.

"I take it your morning ride didn't cheer you up?" Edna guessed.

"Was it supposed to?"

"Well, it used to." Edna huffed, then, "What about this beige batiste with the — ?"

Margaret gave her maid a few moments to finish the description, then glanced behind her to see why she hadn't, and caught sight of Edna scurrying out the door — around Sebastian. She went very still. She was struck with an unseemly giddiness over his presence, such joy, when she'd thought she'd never see him again, at least not in England, and certainly not this soon, a mere two weeks after he'd left.

She'd already concluded that she would see him again, though. Even if she had to spend years tracking him down, she was going to find him just to tell him — well, she hadn't got that far ahead in her resolve yet.

Which was too bad, since there he stood, and she wasn't sure what to say to him, bowled over as she was, other than to wonder aloud, "Did you leave something behind that you need to retrieve?"

"Yes."

How bloody disappointing! But she didn't have time to feel it. As soon as he said it, he began crossing the room toward her in a determined manner, and she simply didn't know what to think until he reached her and immediately pulled her into his arms and began kissing her like a starving man.

Well! That wasn't disappointing a'tall! In fact, it satisfied the urge that she'd had to fly into his arms. She'd been starving, too, apparently, for the sight of him, the taste of him.

She'd been standing next to her bed while changing her clothes, which made it too easy for Sebastian to drag her onto it with him. His knee thrust between her legs, her chemisette was yanked down. He buried his face between her breasts, breathing deeply.

"God, I've missed the smell of you, the taste —"

"You aren't going to embarrass me with lusty words, are you?" she hurriedly interrupted.

He leaned up and actually grinned at her. "Would it embarrass you?"

She didn't have the heart to tell him yes when he was grinning like that. "Possibly not."

"That's what I thought. But I'll compromise," he said and licked a path to her ear. "Did you start getting that divorce yet?"

The shivers his tongue was causing prevented her from thinking clearly, or she would have been highly disturbed by that subject. She did manage to get out, "not yet."

"Then what would you think about not getting one, Maggie?" She was shocked speechless. He added, "That was as close as I'm getting to asking for your hand."

He seemed to have gone very still himself, waiting for her response, while she was having trouble dealing with that much happiness dropped on her all at once.

"What would you think about closing the door?" she finally got out.

He glanced over his shoulder to see he'd left it open. She added, "That's as close as I'm getting to saying yes."

His gaze dropped back to hers. It was there, what she'd seen only once before in his eyes when he looked at her. Tenderness, and so much of it, her breath caught in her chest.

"Are you going to tell me you love me?" she asked.

"I'm thinking about it."

She gasped, sputtered. He laughed and kissed her really deeply, then shot off the bed to slam the door shut. He tore out of his coat and shirt on the way back.

"While I had no doubt —" he began.

"Course you didn't."

"I'm bloody well glad that you love me, Maggie."

"Don't need to hear me say it, eh?"

"No, no more than you do, though if you feel like saying it, I won't try to stop you."

She laughed. "Course I do, you dratted man."

He rejoined her on the bed, gathered her close. His kiss was exquisitely gentle but quickly turned remarkably passionate, kindling the fire between them. Amazing how easily he could do that.

"God, Maggie, I never thought I would ever feel this kind of happiness again. I do love you, m'dear, more than I thought possible to love anyone."

She could make him even happier, she realized, and said, "I should mention —"

"It can wait," he replied, stripping them quickly of the rest of their clothing between his kisses. "We've an appointment at Edgewood, but that can wait, too. Everything will have to wait — on this."

He entered her as he said it, catching her gasp of pleasure with his mouth. That "appointment" at Edgewood might have stirred an inkling of curiosity in her, but he was quite right. That and everything else could wait.

Chapter 53

Margaret had never been so rushed in all her life. Not during the lovemaking. Oh, no, that had been sublimely paced, well, actually, the extent of her passion had dictated a rather swift conclusion that caused her a few blushes afterward. Nothing could have slowed that down, however, when they were both so hungry for each other.

But while she'd wanted to lie there and savor what had just occurred, Sebastian mumbled something under his breath and to her. "There wasn't time for this. I rode ahead, but we're still going to be late. Hurry."

She tried, she really did, but not knowing what the urgency was about, she couldn't muster the haste he wanted. "If you could just sum up in a single statement what —"

"No, you'd have a hundred questions when there's no time for any. Besides, you'll have all those answers shortly, so hurry!"

He was putting on his clothes nearly as fast as he'd removed them. He ended up helping her with hers, getting her back into the sapphire riding habit since it was closest at hand on the foot of her bed. But one button wasn't aligned and she had no stockings on under her boots when he was dragging her out the door!

He'd already told someone to bring her horse back from the stable. Now that was disappointing. She'd thought she'd at least have an opportunity to get something out of him during the coach ride, but galloping across the fields allowed for no conversation of any sort.

By the time Edgewood was in sight, she was lagging behind. A coach was seen moving up the drive. Sebastian still didn't stop until he was at the front door. He did wait for her there, though, and helped her dismount.

"We're in time, after all," he told her. "Surprising after that delay you caused us."

"Me!" she sputtered. "I didn't pounce on you, you dratted man."

"But you wanted to."

"Beside the point," she said with a snort.

He smiled and caressed her cheek. "I promise, the next time we're in your bed, you won't be leaving it for hours, possibly days."

Margaret blushed furiously because that coach had stopped behind them and John and Timothy could have heard what Sebastian had just said as they alighted from it. They gave no indication, though, as they both greeted her warmly. And she was then distracted by the others who stepped down from the coach after them, three men, two of them somewhat official looking, wearing caps similar to those she had seen on French gendarmes.

Someone else was still in the coach, a mere shadow, but Henry had already opened the front door and was saying, "Welcome back, sir. The family is having luncheon."

"All of them?" Sebastian asked.

"For a change, yes."

"Splendid. No need to announce us."

Sebastian took Margaret's arm and escorted her straight to the dining room. The others followed. Without a word, he pulled out a chair for her, sat her down, then took the chair next to her.

Timothy went straight to Abigail and gave her a hug. The old girl beamed. Margaret understood now why Abigail had still been moping, even though she'd finally made up with Douglas after he'd confessed to her what he'd told Margaret. She'd grown quite fond of Timothy while he'd been there.

John had moved to stand by the door to the kitchen. One of the other men moved to the French doors that faced the back lawn. The other two waited by the hall door. It quickly became apparent that all exits were being blocked, it just wasn't apparent why.

Douglas stood up and demanded, "What's going on?"

"A housecleaning," Sebastian replied. "Long overdue."

"I'll need a better answer than that."

"Certainly, and you'll have it. But let's get rid of the rubbish first." And he nodded toward Juliette.

Margaret only glanced at the Frenchwoman now and saw that she'd turned a sickly white as she stared at one of the men by the door. Another had come up behind her chair and was reading from a long list of charges before he placed her under arrest and escorted her from the room. She went without a word. No hysterics, no shouted expletives, none of the dramatics she was known for. For once, Juliette was completely cowed, and it was due to the man she'd been staring at the entire time.

"By the by, Denton," Sebastian said and tossed a piece of paper at his brother. "That's a divorce decree that only needs your signature. Courtesy of one of the men your wife used to blackmail, in his gratitude for being exonerated of the crime he'd thought he'd committed. That's assuming you still want a divorce?"

Denton appeared wary of accepting. "I do, I just — how is this possible, without an appearance before the courts?"

"The same way she had her own brother imprisoned without a trial. One of her victims was a high French official. But I did say this was going to be a housecleaning. Pierre, would you like to begin?"

"Certainly," Pierre Poussin said and introduced himself. "I should first explain about my sister. She had made a career of dramatics that supported her very well but did not involve the theater. She was blackmailing at least a half dozen prominent citizens in Paris. None of them had actually done anything wrong, she had merely set up dramatic little scenes and enacted them flawlessly to make them think they had. She had several cohorts who assisted her in this. Her favorite scheme was to have one of her accomplices pick a fight with her target until the target would either push or punch him away. He would fall, break a sack of blood to make it more dramatic, and then she would pronounce him dead and accuse the target of killing him. Of course she would offer to clean up the mess. Then a month or so later she would go to him for money."

"You were part of this?" Douglas asked.

"No, I never condoned what she did. But she considered me her greatest audience. Everything she did, she had to brag about to me. I was sick of the extent of her fraudulence. She would never listen to me about how wrong it was, what she was doing. She would only laugh. She really thought it was amusing that people could be so gullible. So I had already reached the conclusion that she must be stopped. I had even been following her for weeks, to acquire the names of the men she was blackmailing. I was going to have them all gathered in one place to have her denounced. But then she comes to me and she is changed. I could not discern what it was about her that was different until she mentioned him."

He nodded toward Denton, who flushed furiously as every eye in the room fell on him. "For God's sake, I barely remember meeting her! I was foxed to the gills. She claimed —"

"We know," Sebastian cut in. "Let Pierre finish."

"She was struck with love from the moment she met him," Pierre continued. "It was like a fire in her. It was hard to believe it was possible, and yet I could not doubt it. For her, a woman without a heart, without morals, to suddenly be in love — my first thought was pity for the object of her devotion. I warned her that a man of his social stature would never agree to marry her. She said that she was going to England anyway, that she'd been shown a way to trick Lord Townshend into marriage and even end up with a lofty title. My mistake was trying to talk her out of it, and when that failed, telling her I would have to stop her. Not three hours later I was arrested and taken straight to prison, where I have remained ever since."

"She actually sent her own brother to prison?" Douglas asked incredulously.

"A stay in prison she would see as a satisfactory arrangement to keep me from becoming an obstacle to her goals," Pierre said. "She would not see it as my suffering."

"You make excuses for her?"

"No, she just never saw things beyond her own agendas."

"You poor man," Abigail sympathized.

"No, madame, it was not a bad place to be. The official, in his guilt, made sure of that. I was detained, but it was not like a real prison. We were a community of friends, like a big family. But a cut on my foot became infected and I became very ill."

Sebastian said, "He probably would have been dead in another day or so if we didn't get him out of there."

Pierre coughed. Abigail demanded, "But how did you know to 'get him out of there'?"

"Denton sent us there."

"You mean I finally did something right?" Denton said in self-disgust.

"What was this about Juliette's being shown a way to trick Denton?" Douglas asked.

Pierre nodded toward Denton again. "People who knew him were aware that he bore some resentment toward his brother. My sister was shown how she could use that information to blackmail him into marriage if she couldn't get him to marry her by normal means."

"My God." Denton blanched. "That's exactly what she did, and I'd been too drunk that night to remember, so I couldn't even call her a liar."

Sebastian raised a brow. "You actually thought you'd made such an infamous bargain?"

"No! It's not something I would have

agreed to, or ever suggested, no matter the circumstances. But it was so involved, what she did, to marry Giles just so she could seduce you to cause a duel between you two. Who would believe she did all that without a promise of some gain? And she did threaten to tell everyone that it was all my idea. You don't know how much I've agonized over that, that maybe I did say something that she misconstrued, or —"

"Stop blaming yourself, Denton. She was made promises, but you didn't make them."

"But it's still all my fault," Denton said. "She did it all for love of me. And the irony is, she's hated me now for years. It's the only reason she's stayed here this long, to make my life miserable."

"That would not be the only reason," Pierre said. "She and I grew up in the slums of Paris. This house," he waved a hand to indicate the grandeur around him, "and the social stature that comes with it, she has always craved. She would never have left here willingly, for any reason. But indeed, it was all in her own mind, this grand love she imagined the two of you would have. If you never returned her love, she would blame you for destroying her dreams and want revenge for that, to make you miserable, as you say."

Denton groaned. "What kind of twisted love is that, to get people killed — ?"

Sebastian cut in. "She has committed crimes that will put her away for a long time, but she's never caused anyone's death."

"Giles died," Denton said, "and if you don't see how she was directly responsible —"

"I believe this is my cue," Giles said in the doorway.

Chapter 54

When the incredulous reactions settled down, the questions began to fly. Sebastian listened with only half an ear as Giles repeated his story and Pierre filled in a few loose ends, mainly that Cecil hadn't just shown Juliette how she could trick Denton into marriage. He'd also promised her there would be a nice title involved eventually. He'd been that sure that Douglas would disown Sebastian because of the duel. And it was that promise that had won him Juliette's cooperation, part of the plan he hadn't shared with his son.

Giles made no excuses for his father, just told his audience exactly what he'd told Sebastian. He had done one last thing for Cecil, though. He'd sent him word to warn him that he was coming home to put an end to both his and Sebastian's long exile. Not surprisingly, Cecil had left England himself rather than face the condemnation of his peers for what he had set in motion. Sebastian was annoyed at how Giles's mere presence was miraculously ending long estrangements.

"Douglas and Abigail had already made up," Margaret said beside him.

Was she reading his mind now? She'd been holding his hand under the table, or rather, he'd been holding hers. He just wanted to get out of there with her. He'd done what he came there to do. Watching Giles be so easily forgiven and welcomed home was turning his stomach.

"I convinced your father to stop punishing himself," Margaret continued, as if he knew what she was talking about.

"Excuse me?"

"That's what he's been doing all these years, you know. He deliberately cut himself off from the two people who would have consoled him. Well, it doesn't sound as if Cecil would have consoled him a'tall, but —" And then she gasped, because she'd been listening to Giles with half an ear, too. "A son! I have a nephew?"

She started to cry in joy. Sebastian rolled his eyes but dragged her chair closer so he could put an arm around her. She wasn't the only one crying. So was Abigail. And Douglas hadn't stopped smiling. Bloody hell, he had to get out of there before some of that good cheer turned in his direction.

He stood up to leave and told Margaret, "Let's go."

She looked up at him in confusion. "You're joking, right?"

"Not even close."

"But — oh, dear," she guessed. "You haven't forgiven Giles yet, have you?"

"Was I supposed to?"

"Well — yes." She yanked him back down to his seat. "You don't blame your brother for being tricked. How is Giles any different, when what he did he did out of love and loyalty for his father?"

"Denton's only fault was having a pretty face that Juliette fell in love with. He's suffered just as much as I have all these years and saw no way out of it. While Giles hasn't suffered at all and could have come home at any time to put an end to all this."

She frowned. "This isn't about Giles, is it?"

"Don't press it, Maggie."

"Of course I will," she retorted. "I'm your wife now and I will not tolerate your being unhappy."

He stared at her and then he burst out laughing. God love her, she was serious. And priceless. He didn't deserve her, but she was his lifeline to happiness and he was going to hold tight to it.

He stood up again, lifted her up, and kissed her. "We can discuss this at home."

"But this is your home."

"Not anymore. And shh, it's all right, Maggie, really. Nothing else matters now that I have you."

She tenderly cupped his cheek. "You're going to make me cry, saying things like that."

"As long as you do it with a smile, I suppose I can tolerate a few tears," he replied dryly.

"Is something wrong?" Douglas asked behind them.

Sebastian stiffened. "No. Maggie and I were just leaving."

"Why?"

Sebastian closed his eyes. Just a few more seconds, and he wouldn't have had to deal with this.

"Because this," he waved a hand toward Giles, "changes nothing."

"I agree," Douglas surprised him by saying. "I was already displeased with Cecil back then for his weakness and lack of restraint. He was gambling with money he didn't have anymore. He'd already lost everything. I took the deed to his home with the hope that it would make him step back and realize what he was doing and stop it. Of course I would have helped him one more time, if he'd come to me and told me his life was in danger. But Giles was right. I sensed he'd begun to resent me, resent that I had so much more than he did. I'm not surprised he'd rather trick me into canceling his debt than simply ask for my help again. But I never dreamed that he could perpetrate something this destructive. I had ended our friendship when he came here after Giles's supposed death to force even more guilt on me, as if I wasn't already carrying enough. I never did quite understand how he had the gall to do that, but you've cleared up the mystery. You don't take any credit for that?"

"For what? Bringing Giles back from the dead? He could have done that. For getting the shackle off of Denton's neck? He could have done that."

"But neither of them would have. It took you to end this nightmare."

"So I'm the hero? Funny, it doesn't feel that way, Father. Still feels like I'm the dead son."

He said it lightly, but the pain was still there and rising fast to choke him. He gripped Margaret's hand and walked away with her. She was trying to stop him, but nothing could. He had to get out of there. . . .

"Sebastian!"

That tone again that had always worked, and it still did. He stopped, but he didn't turn around.

"You never gave me an opportunity to say this," Douglas continued. "You still aren't, but I'm not letting you walk out of here again without hearing it."

"Don't," Sebastian whispered.

Douglas didn't hear him. "What was said that day, my rage, was for your pain. Your pain. I never meant it. Cecil had been wrong in that, when he promised Juliette that the husband she wanted would end up being my only heir. He thought he knew me so well that that would be my reaction, and while it did happen, it wasn't for the reason he assumed. I would have corrected that before the day was done, if I could have found you. But you'd left immediately."

Sebastian dropped his head back, stared at the ceiling. Grasp the lie and — no, it would grow like a canker between them and never let go. There was no resolution to this. Giles had returned from the dead. Sebastian hadn't.

He said nothing. The room had grown quiet waiting for his reply, but anything he said would rip him apart.

"I told you he wouldn't believe me, Maggie," Douglas said.

"Yes, you did," she replied, then poked Sebastian in the ribs. "Are you listening, you dratted man? Your father told me this last week, when Giles was still dead."

"Cor!" Timothy exclaimed from across the room. "He's your father? But he's not the man I spoke to in the stable, who said his son was dead."

Sebastian turned incredulously to the boy to catch his furious blush. John came up behind Timothy and gently yanked a lock of his hair.

"No more reconnaissance for you, my lad," John said.

"It was just one mistake!" Timothy complained.

"But a whopper."

"Have you figured it out yet?" Margaret asked sternly beside Sebastian.

"That I let assumptions cripple me and never did anything about it?"

"Sort of what happened to Giles, eh?"

"Leave that blighter out of this."

She sighed. "One step at a time, I suppose. But if you don't hug your father and forgive him right now, I may have to divorce you after all."

"You lost that chance, m'dear."

"Don't lose yours."

He glanced at his father. Douglas was expressionless now, guarded, afraid to say anything else that might tip the scale the wrong way. God, he'd done that to him with the blasted shell he'd erected for his emotions, the shell that had just been cracked.

"I've missed you," he said simply.

Douglas's expression crumbled. He put his arms around Sebastian and hugged him hard. "Welcome home, son."

Such simple words, and years of pain were washed away. The moisture gathered, uncontrollable, and then he caught sight of his ex-friend over his father's shoulder, smiling happily at him.

"Giles, I'm going to kill you again," he said, though without heat.

Giles grinned cheekily. "How many times have you said that now? You know you're glad to have me back."

Denton came up and hugged Sebastian as well. "It's good to have you back. And I'll help you kill the blighter."

Sebastian chuckled. "It's over. Get on with your life. Find a nice girl to marry this time — and no, you can't have Maggie. I'm keeping her."

Margaret beamed at them, bursting with

pride for her part in bringing this family back together. Why, if she hadn't thought Douglas's life was in danger and listened to Abigail's urgings, she never would have tried to hire the notorious Raven — and ended up finding love instead.

"So you're really home?" she asked her husband a while later.

She had dragged him up to the balcony his mother had so enjoyed, stood there with him at her back, his arms around her as they watched winter waves breaking on the coast. It was chilly, but he offered enough heat for them both.

"I was home the moment you told me you loved me, Maggie. My home is wherever you are."

She turned around to hug him. "I'm glad my sister found some happiness with Giles, however briefly. I just wish she had trusted me enough to tell me."

"He probably infected her with his fears that you might tell someone."

She looked up at him. "Not everyone can be like you."

He raised a brow. "Like me?"

"Spitting in the eye of death."

He snorted. "It's easy to be courageous when you don't have anything to live for.

Now that I do, I'm going to be a veritable coward."

She chuckled. "Rubbish. But you have forgiven Giles, right? He's the father of my nephew. I expect to see a lot of him, often."

He sighed. "I'll tolerate him, but only because he named his son after me."

"Did he? And what shall we name our son?"

"Are you — ?"

"No, but I want to be."

"Good God, Maggie," he said and surprised her by picking her up in his arms. "You shouldn't say things like that right before dinner, not if you want to eat anytime soon."

She laughed as he carried her off to her old bedroom, which had been his old bedroom. Rather appropriate that it was now theirs.

About the Author

Johanna Lindsey has been hailed as one of the most popular authors of romantic fiction, with more than 58 million copies of her novels sold. World renowned for her novels of "first-rate romance" (*New York Daily News*), Lindsey is the author of forty-one previous national bestselling novels, many of which reached the #1 spot on the *New York Times* bestseller list. Lindsey lives in Hawaii with her family.